Angus MacDonald OBE has lived all his life in the Scottish Highlands. He served in the local regiment, the Queen's Own Highlanders, before embarking on a career in business. He runs the Moidart Trust, a charitable organisation that helps West Highland people and projects. He owns The Highland Bookshop in Fort William and The Highland Cinema, also in the town. He is the author of three other books: *Ardnish, Ardnish Was Home* and *We Fought for Ardnish.*

Praise for *Ardnish*

'If ever there was a story ready-made for the big screen, Ardnish is it'
National Trust magazine

'A heart-felt, ingeniously plotted and wonderfully resonant novel . . . a deeply moving reminder of the global reach of the Gaels and the impact they've had on world history'
William Dalrymple

'Opens a window on two worlds . . . evoking both of them vividly in well-crafter, deceptively simple prose'
The Herald

Praise for *Ardnish Was Home*

'A genuine portrait of a time gone forever . . . a very good read'
Rosamunde Pilcher

'A fast-paced narrative with deeply likeable characters . . . far more than yet another wartime love story . . . impossible to put down'
Scottish Field, Book of the month

'Extraordinary. I closed the book with the strong feeling of the importance of kinship, the need to nurture one another, and the power of love. It will enter your soul'
Scots Magazine

Praise for *We Fought for Ardnish*

'An intense and bittersweet love story . . . the descriptions of travel from Scotland to Canada and the Italian front combine to make this a compelling and engaging story'
Scottish Field

'An excellent reflection of love of one's home and heritage. A page turner'
Oban Times

'A haunting salute to a past way of life and a testament to the timeless values of loyalty, faith and family'
National Post

THE SECRET OF ARDNISH

A NOVEL

ANGUS MACDONALD

BIRLINN

First published in 2022 by
Birlinn Ltd
West Newington House
10 Newington Road
Edinburgh
EH9 1QS

www.birlinn.co.uk

ISBN 978 1 78027 752 3

British Library Cataloguing-in-Publication Data
A catalogue record for this book is available on request from the British Library

Typeset by Hewer Text UK Ltd, Edinburgh
Printed and bound by Clays Ltd, Elcograf S.p.A.

Author's Note

The Secret of Ardnish is dedicated to Peter Sandeman, owner of the Ardnish peninsula. Peter has a deep love for the area and an extraordinary knowledge of the land and settlements. I have greatly appreciated how supportive he and his family have been of my books.

This book is set in 2016 and, more than the previous three in the series, celebrates the close relationship that the Scottish Highlands has with Canada. Many of those who emigrated from the Arisaig area of Lochaber went to settle in Arisaig, Nova Scotia, and folk from Brae Roy went to Inverness County, Cape Breton, taking their courteous ways, music and Gaelic language with them. Even today, hundreds of years later, a strong link and affection remain between those in the Western Highlands of Scotland and the eastern seaboard of Canada.

Angus MacDonald

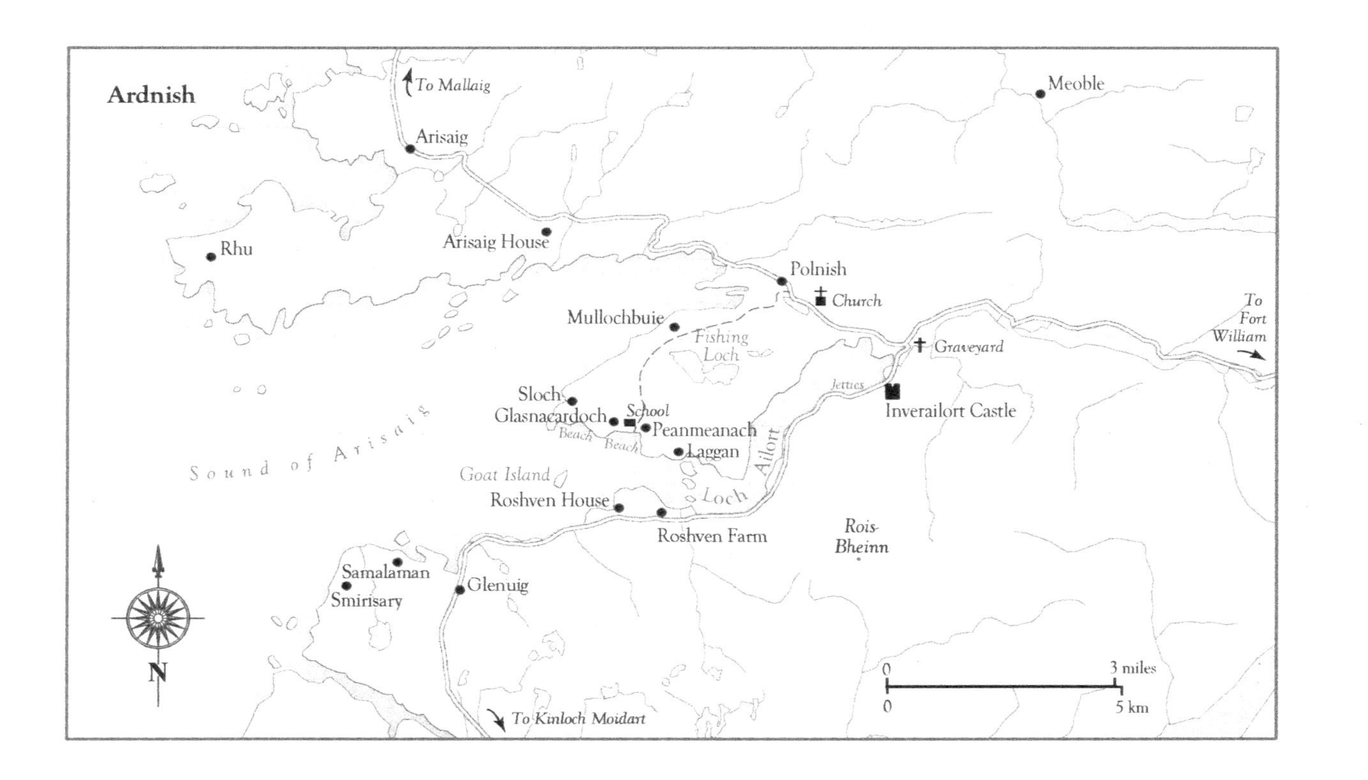
Ardnish
To Mallaig
Meoble
Arisaig
Arisaig House
Rhu
Polnish
Church
To Fort William
Mullochbuie
Fishing Loch
Graveyard
Jetties
Inverailort Castle
Sloch
School
Glasnacardoch
Peanmeanach
Beach
Beach
Laggan
Ailort
Sound of Arisaig
Goat Island
Loch
Roshven House
Roshven Farm
Rois-Bheinn
Samalaman
Smirisary
Glenuig
N
0
3 miles
0
5 km
To Kinloch Moidart

Chapter 1

You know how it is: when you have such high expectations, they are bound to be dashed. After a restless night's sleep on the plane, I landed in Glasgow in low cloud and steady drizzle. I was all set to get the bus into the city and then straight onto the train north, but luckily the man I spoke to at the travel desk kept me right. There was a landslip on the line at Crianlarich, he told me, so my best option was to take the Number 915 bus straight from the terminal.

As I jammed myself into the narrow seat and rested my head against the coach window, I found myself remembering an evening many years ago at home. It was after dinner, and Grandfather, whisky in hand and a roadmap of Scotland on the table in front of him, was at his most expansive.

'When you finally go to Ardnish,' he'd said to me and my sister Nathalie, 'you'll be taking one of the most beautiful train journeys in the world. There's the steady clank-clank-clank as the train creeps north, past the old Caledonian Forest above Loch Lomond, then there are views of miles of hill and peatbogs as you go across Rannoch Moor, which is the largest uninhabited area in Britain. There will be red deer trotting alongside the tracks and glorious sunlit mountain peaks reflected in the lochs. That train is how generations of our family have arrived in, and left, Lochaber, and it's how your grandmother arrived from Cape Breton to nurse me when I came home to Ardnish, injured, in 1945. It is truly God's country.'

I recalled the emotion in his voice as I peered out of the steamed-up window, trying to take in my surroundings. We had been driving along a trash-strewn industrial corridor and were now on the A82 beside Loch Lomond, a route evidently not fit for use as the coach driver frequently slammed on his brakes to avoid hitting other vehicles and had to slow to a snail's pace to inch past other vehicles.

Arriving at last in Fort William, we were all dumped out unceremoniously at the back of a supermarket. Dragging our luggage behind us, in fog and lashing rain we trailed along the back of an ugly 1960s railway station and then under a smelly walkway and into the town. Drenched and dejected, I headed into the Alexandra Hotel where I had booked a room for the night.

As I slumped onto my bed I thought it was no wonder my people had left. Today was April Fools' Day – well, I was the fool for coming over here. 'Pull yourself together, An Gillie,' I said firmly, before deciding to venture downstairs.

With as broad a smile as I could muster, I attempted to engage with the girl behind the bar. 'Hi. I'm Canadian, and I've come over to see where my family were from,' I said.

Her reply came in faltering English. 'I am from Poland. I just got here, too.'

'May I have a beer, a local one?' I asked.

She poured me a Heineken.

She didn't seem keen to talk, so I took my pint to a quiet corner of the bar and considered my situation. Right that minute, I wished I was back home in Cape Breton. The town was grey, the skies were grey, my journey had been lousy, and

I was off to stay with an eighty-year-old man I barely knew. Then heading off camping for two weeks. Probably in the rain. What the hell was I doing? Summer was coming, back home, and I could be dating Lexie Cameron. I looked morosely into my glass and swirled the beer around.

My train to Arisaig was leaving at 4 p.m. the next day, so I would have plenty of time to look around the place and visit the West Highland Museum, as instructed to by Grandfather. It was only 7 p.m. Cape Breton time, but here it was midnight and I was the last in the bar. I drained my pint and trudged upstairs.

But, of course, I couldn't sleep. My mind kept drifting back to the moment when everything had changed, back home, in February, only ten weeks before.

Chapter 2

As the days passed Grandfather faded, then revived, then faded again. Cousins came by to hold his hand and pay their respects, while Nathalie and I fielded endless phone calls of condolence from all over: Scotland, Boston, Ontario.

Some days, his spirits would lift and he'd talk. But he knew he was dying. He spoke of how he was looking forward to being reunited with his wife again and hugging his son. Other days, he just lay there, with the Fox radio station blaring a little too loud.

Dr McAllister came by every other day to supervise the palliative care. He wanted Grandfather to go into hospital but never managed to persuade him that it was a good idea. Grandfather was adamant that he would die in his own bed and his body be laid out in the sitting room. It was an old tradition from Scotland, Grandfather's homeland, but it was unfamiliar these days in Cape Breton and it shocked the young doctor.

Luckily, Father Calum, an old family friend, came over and caught the tail end of a heated discussion. 'Being laid out at home is completely legal,' he told the doctor. 'Donald Angus Gillies will have his final wishes respected, and that's that.' He then reassured Grandfather that he would have a word with the funeral home and make all the arrangements.

The previous night, it had appeared that Grandfather was weakening considerably, so I phoned Aunt Maggie in Hamilton. She'd been expecting the call and promised to get the first flight. 'There's a storm coming,' I warned her.

'No matter,' she replied. 'I'm coming to be with Dad.'

Next day, I woke to a snowstorm so severe that it had been given a name: Storm Elena. Gale-force winds drove the snow in blizzards, forcing it under doors and through double-glazed windows.

'Good morning, Grandfather,' I called through the door as I always did when I went downstairs to let the dog out and make Grandfather his usual strong, tarry cup of tea. There was no answer.

When I returned, I knocked on the door and said good morning again. There was no response. My heart lurched as I looked into his room, then hurried over to his bedside. He was lying motionless, eyes shut. I really thought he was dead. The teacup fell from my hand and clattered on the bedside table, which roused him.

He opened his eyes and looked into mine. 'Morning, An Gillie,' he said, his voice a hoarse whisper. 'I need you to do something.'

'Anything,' I replied.

'Behind my workbench, against the wall, is a brass plate. Would you fetch it for me?'

I nodded and left, running down the stairs to my sister's room. 'Nathalie, Iain Bec! Wake up! I think Grandfather will pass soon.'

'Oh God!' Nathalie wailed. 'I can hardly move!'

She was heavily pregnant with her first child and was already a week past her due date.

'I'll help her,' Iain Bec reassured me. 'You get back to him, Peter Angus.'

I rang the doctor and Father Calum, then frantically rummaged around the garage until I found what I decided must be the brass plate. It was a package about sixty centimetres square, wrapped in brown paper and tied with string.

Nathalie, Ian Bec and I huddled around the bed. 'Aunt Maggie's on her way, Grandfather, she'll be here very soon. Oh, and is this what you wanted me to get?' I showed him the package.

He nodded. 'Undo the paper,' he said, struggling to sit up.

Iain Bec heaved him into a sitting position as I did as I was told. Sure enough, the package contained an inscribed brass plaque.

We all marvelled at the object; its lettering was so beautifully worked. Nathalie read out the inscription: '*A Dhia, dèan tròcair air Do chlann.* Will God have mercy on your children. *The Gillies family of Ardnish, pipers, farmers and soldiers, lived here from Before Christ to 1951.*'

'Did you make this?' I asked.

'I did,' Grandfather whispered. 'To put on the grave at Innis na Cuilce.'

'At Ardnish?' Nathalie asked, her eyes filling with tears.

He nodded, and I felt a surge of shame. 'I'm so sorry,' I mumbled. 'I should've gone over with you that time you asked me . . . I was such an idiot . . .'

His eyes closed.

'Grandfather?' Nathalie whispered. 'Grandfather . . . we love you . . .'

I gripped his hand tighter as his breathing grew shallow. Father Calum, who had slipped into the room a few moments before, began to read the last rites.

I wasn't sure when exactly he died. He just slipped away.

Chapter 3

Aunt Maggie arrived while Father Calum was still there. Nathalie had called her while she was driving over the causeway to say that her father had died and not to drive too fast in the snow. She admitted she'd pulled in to the side of the road for a good cry but was feeling more settled now. She was full of questions. She'd even written a to-do list on the plane.

Shortly afterwards, the undertakers came, and there was a discussion about what Grandfather should wear. In the end, he was dressed in his best suit, with a photograph of his wife and the holly bagpipe chanter his grandfather had carved for him as a boy laid alongside him in the coffin, his hands holding his rosary. They covered a trestle table with a white cloth, set the open coffin on it for the visitations, and promised to be back tomorrow, provided the snow ploughs had been out.

We shivered in the house as the heating failed to cope with the freezing temperatures. Word of Grandfather's passing spread quickly, and a stream of people began braving the storm to come and pay their respects. I anticipated a late night or two ahead. There would be many glasses raised to his memory and stories told around the coffin, and I knew I would be called to play a few of his favourite tunes on my fiddle.

As I went around the room refilling cups, I heard Nathalie cry out from the kitchen. I ran through to find her slumped on the floor, grimacing in pain, being supported by Aunt Maggie.

'The baby,' Nathalie gasped. 'No – not now!'

'Out with the old and in with the new,' remarked Aunt Maggie, rather irreverently. 'Peter Angus, will you make yourself useful and run and fetch Nicky, please.'

I stood rooted to the spot in shock.

'Be off with you,' Aunt Maggie cried, 'before the snow gets any deeper and she'll not get through.'

I walked as quickly as I could through the deep snow. Nicky, the midwife, was an old school friend of Nathalie's and fortunately lived just down the street. She rushed back with me immediately, by which time Nathalie and Aunt Maggie had made their way upstairs to the bedroom.

As the afternoon wore on, I tried to block out the distressing sounds of Nathalie's labour by chatting to the visitors, who kept pouring in to pay their respects and peer into Grandfather's casket. The phone rang constantly. Despite the blizzard, there must have been thirty people who dropped by, and I was run ragged fetching tea and gratefully accepting scones and buns for the wake.

Glenora Distillery had sent around half a dozen bottles, not because Grandfather was one of their best customers – although he was – but because he had been a director when the company got going thirty years ago.

It was early evening when a frustrated Aunt Maggie finally cracked, she stormed downstairs, shushed people out of the house and took the phone off the hook. She then taped a hastily scrawled notice on the front door: NO VISITORS.

'Nathalie is having her baby,' she declared. 'That is the most important thing. She needs peace.'

However, Aunt Maggie's notice didn't stop the formidable Morag Sinclair, a neighbour who had plagued us all her life, from barging in and announcing that Donald Angus would have wanted her here and wasn't she one of the best friends of the family? A cousin, no less. Morag always flaunted her Scottishness, and this evening she was bedecked in tartan with an oversized silver brooch, her long, wiry red hair piled up in a messy bun.

She strode right past me into the sitting room, despite my protestations, and was soon helping herself to a handful of sandwiches from the mountain of food left by well-wishers. Casting barely a glance at the open coffin, she began chattering on as I fidgeted uncomfortably, listening to Natalie's exhausted moans from upstairs. Grandfather would have listened to her patiently and rolled his eyes at us, on the sly, as she regaled him with stories, peppered with Gaelic words designed to let him know that she had more of a Highland heritage than himself.

But Aunt Maggie had no such tolerance. Coming back downstairs, she caught sight of our visitor and absolutely went for the woman. 'Who do you think you are? Could you not read the sign? For God's sake, Morag,' she yelled, 'go home and come back another day!' Then, turning her back, she poured more boiling water into the ceramic bowl and rushed upstairs again.

Morag, who had decades of experience in overstaying her welcome, got the message, and as I helped her on with her coat and she furiously adjusted her tartan bonnet with a sprig of heather in it, she whispered loudly that it was clear that this house would never offer the same Highland hospitality as it used to, now that my grandfather had passed away. She was directing her fury at me, and I knew she'd hold it against me.

Later, sitting in the kitchen by myself, a plate piled high with homemade shortbread and cake in front of me, a beer in my hand, I was idly scrolling through Facebook and Instagram when Iain Bec came in, beaming.

'It's a girl!' he announced. 'And all seems to be fine for both of them.'

'Nice one.' I smiled, shaking his hand. 'Congrats.'

He opened the fridge, took out a beer, and slumped in a chair beside me. He let out a deep sigh, as if the tension and worry of the previous hours had caught up with him all at once. 'Thank God Nicky lives so close,' he murmured. 'There's no way an ambulance would have got through the snow. It must be a foot deep out there.'

'Didn't stop Morag getting through,' I said, and we both laughed.

It was about midnight when we clinked our last beer bottles together. 'To the girl,' Iain Bec declared before rising unsteadily to find a blanket to sleep under on the kitchen chair. 'No way am I going to lie in the same room as the coffin,' he said nervously, 'and Nathalie wants me out of the way. Aunt Maggie's going to stay with them. Night, Peter Angus.'

The last duty for me, as ever, was to take my grandfather's old collie, Seamus, for a walk. He struggled through the snowdrifts in front of the house, but luckily the plough had just cleared the road, so it was easier going there. Snow was still falling, and I was white from head to foot after only five minutes. Poor Seamus, he'd stayed in the sitting room all afternoon and not eaten his food. He knew his master had gone. I let him back into the room and went over to shut the casket lid. It didn't seem right to leave it open. I looked at Grandfather; his complexion was pale and waxy now. Those ruddy cheeks may have lost their colour but his hair still had traces of red. At the sight of his gnarled fingers entwined in his St Mary MacKillop beads, my eyes filled with tears. He and I had been so close. I needed to pray. Shutting my eyes, I started out loud: 'Our Father, who art in Heaven . . .'

The old man had been traditional, that's for sure. He had always wanted to be laid out in the house. It had been good to have Father Calum there to persuade the undertakers.

I thought of my parents, long gone. Grandfather had been my father, really. I wanted to lean forward to kiss him, but when I put my hand on his, it felt like cold ham straight from the fridge. I shuddered and decided against it, closing the casket lid gently and climbing upstairs to bed.

On the landing I heard the baby in the bedroom next door letting out a plaintive cry, my sister murmuring words of endearment. I knocked on the door and went in.

Nathalie looked up, an enormous smile on her face, the baby at her breast. 'Sit down, Peter Angus,' she said, patting the mattress beside her. 'I'm so sad Grandfather never met her, but isn't she gorgeous?'

'She is,' I replied shyly, not really knowing what to say or where to look. 'I'm glad Aunt Maggie's here to help you out, Nat.'

She nodded. 'It must be a tough time for her, too, though, with the funeral to organise. It'll be a big one, I think.'

'If the weather behaves,' I replied.

We sat in silence for a while as the baby dozed in Nathalie's arms. 'It's the end of an era, with him gone,' she murmured.

'And the beginning of another,' I said as I rose. 'Night, night, you two.'

Chapter 4

The next few days were a whirlwind. Aunt Maggie took charge as always, with Iain Bec and I being given tasks ranging from shovelling snow off the sidewalk to meeting the printers to talk about the order of service. The undertaker and midwife often passed each other in the doorway, and there was a constant coming and going of Nathalie's girlfriends wanting to see the baby and Grandfather's friends shuffling in with their walking sticks and whispering quietly in the sitting room.

A family friend, Donald MacEachen from Mabou, was sitting by the casket, nursing a dram, when he asked me a question that made me recoil in surprise.

'What will you do now, Peter Angus?'

I must have looked puzzled.

He rephrased the question. 'Well, now your grandfather has passed away and Nathalie has a family. What are you, twenty-six?'

'Eh, nearly twenty-eight,' I stammered.

'Is that so? Well, you must have plans for your future . . .'

'Er, I don't know. I haven't really thought about it,' I replied truthfully.

It seemed to me that from then on everyone had the same question and it began to annoy me intensely. Why was it anyone's business? After all, I was quite content living here.

Cape Breton was my home, I had friends, a social life of sorts and a job. What did people expect me to do?

The funeral was to be the next Saturday at Stella Maris down the road, the church where my family had worshipped for half a century and where Grandfather had mown the lawn, painted the windows and fixed the roof since he had arrived from Scotland. Despite his great age, a big turnout was expected. In his day he'd been a man of many parts: a well-respected carpenter, a member of the Gaelic choir, an instructor of the Cape Breton University Pipe Band and a lobster fisherman. The phone was red-hot all week, with family and friends driving from Ontario and Boston, and some even flying in from Arisaig. Aunt Maggie spoke fluent French, unlike my sister or myself, so she took charge of telling our Lacroix cousins from Chéticamp what the plans were. Every discussion about travel included an opinion about the weather: had the storm passed through, would the airport be open and so on, and I felt as if I was repeating the same conversation dozens upon dozens of times.

Aunt Maggie gave me the job of logistics manager. I was to take a rented minibus down to the airport and deliver people to their accommodation at the Hebridean Motel in Port Hood. Luckily, being February, there was no shortage of rooms available. The Legion Hall was booked for afterwards and a whole team of ladies from the church had spent the week baking. I was also given the task of arranging a sightseeing tour for the Scottish visitors; several were cousins and all were elderly. Aunt Maggie knew them all, having been over in Scotland several times, and she gave me a rundown of who each of them were.

I was relieved to have my aunt masterminding the arrangements. I had no idea where to begin and the sheer number of jobs to be done was overwhelming. Nathalie was engrossed in caring for her newborn, so, apart from discussing the order of service and who was going to do the eulogies, she wasn't able to offer much help.

I was up early on the Friday. It was a beautiful day for our Scottish guests. The snow, which lay two feet deep along the roadside, gleamed and glittered. I walked Seamus and made a pot of coffee. I needed to call my boss and let her know I'd be back in on Monday. She'd given me two weeks off to look after Grandfather during his final days. I wasn't looking forward to returning to work.

I was sketching a headstone on my notepad when Nathalie looked over my shoulder.

'Morning, brother,' she said, tousling my hair. 'Hey, that's pretty good – unusual, too. What are they called again?'

'It's a Celtic cross. For Grandfather, perhaps?'

'Lovely idea. Sleep okay? Hope Mairi didn't wake you?' She looked at me with a sweet smile.

'Mairi?' I exclaimed in surprise. 'That's wonderful. Grandfather would've been so pleased. When did you decide to call her that?'

'I think I've always wanted to have a daughter and name her after Mum. Do you remember my doll when I was little? She was Mairi, too.'

She poured herself a coffee and we chatted easily back and forth for half an hour, a precious time before the phone started ringing or the baby needed feeding. My sister and I had always been the greatest of friends. She was three years older than me and in many ways had been a combination of a mother and a sister to me. After all, it had just been Grandfather and the two of us here since I was ten.

'Oh, Ian Kennedy wants to meet us here on Monday,' Nathalie said.

'The lawyer? Why?'

'It's to do with Grandfather's will. He wants you, me and Aunt Maggie here. Shall I tell him ten?'

'I suppose so,' I replied, thinking about my need to get back to work. It hadn't really occurred to me that there would be a will. Grandfather didn't have anything to speak of, apart from his old Ford and our house. There had never been any spare money around. He never went on holiday apart from to Scotland a couple of times, the last time twenty years ago, I guessed, with a pang of guilt.

At nine on the dot I rang work.

'Good morning, Canadian Equitable,' said the cheery receptionist.

'Morning, Maureen. How are you?'

'Oh, y'know, bored as usual. When are you back?'

'Couple of days and I'll be in to rescue you. Listen, is Yvonne in yet?'

'I'll put you through, but I'm warning you, she's in a foul mood. All the stuff you normally do has been building up on her desk. She's had to do some work for a change.'

I told Yvonne that Grandfather had died, the funeral was tomorrow and I'd be back in on Tuesday. She offered her condolences and we left it like that.

I hung up with a sigh. I'd been eight years with the company, reviewing insurance policies, verifying claims and dealing with unhappy people who'd had a flood, a fire or were seeking a payout for their dead spouse.

Grandfather had known the previous owner of the company and had got me a summer job there. I ended up staying on, always waiting for something else to turn up. The work was monotonous, but I couldn't see any alternative elsewhere. As a teenager I'd dreamt of being a musician, but that ambition was soon quashed by the demands of my nine-to-five office life. Part of the problem was that the role had been given to me as a favour to my grandfather; it wasn't as if I'd earned or fought to get it. I hadn't even had an interview.

At lunchtime I was at the airport, shaking hands with distant Gillies cousins, two Ferguson ladies and a couple of MacDonald brothers. Not one of them was younger than sixty and a couple were well into their eighties. There was tremendous chatter in the van. All of a sudden we were back in 1951, the year my grandfather and his French-Canadian wife, Sophie, had left the farm at Ardnish. One of the Gillies men explained that farming over there had been too difficult, wartime rationing was still on, and my grandmother got terribly lonely across at Laggan, alone in the house a lot of the time.

'They were right to leave,' one of the women volunteered, and everyone seemed to agree.

They were all keen to tell me how they were connected, how we were cousins or how our families had lived next door to each other for generations.

I told everyone that my sister had had a baby only a few hours after Grandfather had died. 'He would have been overjoyed to have met the baby,' I said, rather surprising myself as I said this.

The Ferguson women were especially delighted to learn that Nathalie had called her daughter Mairi. One of them told me that their aunt, Mairi Ferguson, was from Ardnish. She, too, had been a great friend of my family from way back and, what's more, she herself was a Mairi.

I took the long route back in the twilight, via Pictou, our Arisaig and Antigonish, pointing out the migration ship, *The Hector*, and St Francis Xavier University. The Scots planned to spend the Monday after the funeral following the Ceilidh Trail in this same van and had employed a man as their driver.

Aunt Maggie had planned an excursion on the Sunday. I would pick them all up at John Gillies's apartments and take them to the old St Margaret of Scotland Church, up River Denys Mountain above Judique if, and it was a big if, the steep track was clear of snow. Father Calum had agreed to celebrate an extra Mass for them, at eight in the morning. With jetlag, they'd be wide awake by seven, they all agreed. Everyone had family who had emigrated here and they were keen to see the place where they would have worshipped.

I'd never met a more appreciative group of people. Despite the solemnity of the occasion, they seemed so pleased to be here. They'd already met many people from the county before, who'd been over exploring Lochaber, keen to find where their kinfolk hailed from. The group in the van had one thing in common: their families were all from Ardnish, the much-loved remote peninsula that had been part of my family folklore. At its peak there had been 198 people living there, and I knew my grandparents had been the last to leave, sixty-three years ago this coming November.

'Have you been over yourself, Peter Angus?' asked one of the Ferguson women.

I felt uncomfortable now. 'I haven't,' I admitted, 'but I already feel that I have. Grandfather brought us up on stories of the place. There's a map in his den that he drew himself, and he used to talk Nathalie and me through each of the hamlets, telling us who lived where and a story or two about each of them. I'll definitely go to see it for myself one day.'

'I think I remember Donald Angus writing to say he was coming over several years ago with yourself, then it turned out you couldn't make it and he cancelled his trip,' one of the woman remarked from the back of the van. 'Perhaps I'm wrong about that?'

My eyes welled up. 'No, you're right,' I admitted quietly, awash with guilt. 'I can't remember what was on, though.'

'Och, I'm sure you're a very busy young man,' she said kindly.

It transpired that several of them had been with Grandfather when he had been over there the time before, just after the accident.

'We were all quite elderly even then,' Mairi smiled. 'I remember we rented a boat in Arisaig from the marina with a couple of men to help us in and out. We motored around the Rhu peninsula, past Loch nan Uamh, looked at Sloch through binoculars and landed twice, once at Peanmeanach and then again at Laggan. It was a beautiful day in June. Your grandfather just sat with his back against the walls of the bothy, his parents' old house, and wept like a baby for a good fifteen minutes. He almost had to be dragged away from the place.'

'He was always very emotional,' I agreed.

The Scots all encouraged me to come over to Scotland and proffered invitations to put me up when I did. As we drove, heading towards the Canso Causeway, one of them, Archie Gillies, began talking to another in Gaelic. '*S dòcha nach tigeadh, thug mo sheanair teist orm mar bhalach laghach ach seachranach, agus nach eil na h-òigridh a' suathadh ris an eachdraidh aca?*'

I winced and blushed furiously. They no doubt thought I couldn't understand them, speaking the old language. But I knew he was saying that I probably wouldn't come over, that my grandfather had described me as a nice boy but feckless, and the young weren't interested in their history anyway, were they?

I couldn't pretend not to have understood them so I fibbed. I told them, in Gaelic, that I'd been ill, and that was why I couldn't make it the last time, and that maybe I'd come over this spring. I kept looking in the rear-view mirror as I spoke, to see their reaction.

It was their turn to become flustered.

'I'm sorry, Peter Angus. I didn't know you'd have the Gaelic,' said Archie Gillies. 'That was rude of me.'

'Please, don't worry at all,' I laughed. 'My grandparents spoke it around the house all our lives and it's taught in the school here, by my sister, actually. Nathalie and I often speak to each other in Gaelic – we always have. It's something we share.'

It was pitch-black by this time. The road was well gritted but there remained deep snow banks on each side of the road. Only the odd vehicle was out and about.

'We're all tired, aren't we?' said Mairi, before deftly changing the subject. 'What's that big building over there, Peter Angus?

'That's the Stora paper mill, one of the biggest employers around, and this is the Canso Causeway,' I replied. 'It was finished in 1955 by Premier Angus L. Macdonald. The island was losing people fast and it was felt that the causeway would help. In the old days, people would come and go from the island by ferry, as would the coal and steel. And do you see over there?' I gestured to the lights of the town on my right. 'That's Port Hawkesbury. I work there ... as a clerk for an insurance agency.'

'Do you like it?' asked Big John, one of the two MacDonald brothers.

'Is it a long commute?' enquired another.

I suddenly regretted talking again as we were about to pass the spot where the accident had happened. 'May I tell you all about it on Sunday?' I said, rather too abruptly. I must have sounded petulant, but even now, years on, I found it difficult. I crossed myself as I drove past the Tim Hortons junction, hoping the passengers wouldn't notice. I certainly didn't want to talk about the deaths.

Suddenly I was beat. How come these old people had so much energy? Their body clock was four hours ahead. I just didn't want to engage with them anymore. Fortunately, the last half-hour before home was silent. Tomorrow was the funeral and it would be a hectic couple of days. My heart sank at the prospect. The house would be full tonight with visitors, and my aunt would be in full hospitality mode. Nathalie and Iain Bec were taking the baby to stay for two nights with a friend down the road. I was envious and wished I could join them. I hated the thought of enforced cheerfulness, and could already hear mourners saying in my head, *Oh, I remember when your grandfather and I were fishing . . . or piping . . . or . . . whatever.* I longed for peace and quiet.

I sat there, deep in thought, the occasional headlights coming towards me, until suddenly, the reality of Grandfather's death hit me. I'd been by his side for two weeks, day and night, as he lay dying and a lifetime before that. We were best friends despite the sixty years between us. I shared with him the trials of my daily grind at work, we talked endlessly about our shared love of piping, and I'd listen as he'd sit with a glass of whisky in his hand and regale me with fantastic stories of his time spent training the French resistance. He'd met my grandmother then. It was astonishing stuff, from a different world. She'd parachuted onto a glacier to assassinate a German colonel. I remember him talking of the time he was gathering a thousand sheep in a blizzard on the Ardnish hills when he broke his leg in a peat hag and had to crawl home.

And, of course, there were tales about my father which I couldn't get enough of. I brushed away tears. As I did, I caught the eye of one of the women in the mirror. She seemed to know what I'd been thinking and gave me a reassuring smile.

Aunt Maggie always told my grandfather that he spoilt me and that he should push me more. She once said, cruelly, that I was using the excuse of the family tragedy to take the easy option for everything. As a teenager, to my shame now, I'd often wanted to play computer games in my room or watch television rather than spend time with him. He'd be impatient and demand that Nathalie and I sit down and eat at the table so we could talk, and I could still recall the feelings of teenage rebellion that used to overwhelm me. At the word 'Ardnish', my sister and I would roll our eyes at each other as the old man went on and on about the old country. Grandfather had wanted to take me back to his birthplace, but I'd refused point-blank, telling him it would be boring. He never did go back, and now he was gone.

Chapter 5

Iain Bec, Nathalie and Mairi, Aunt Maggie and I sat in the front pew with Seamus the dog lying at my feet, his face looking up at the coffin. The order of service listed Grandfather's favourite hymns, a reading by me and, unusually, three eulogies. On the front cover was a photograph of Grandfather, Nathalie, myself and the dog, taken a decade ago. And on the back, one of him holding my dad, a baby.

I looked around the church. People were chatting and smiling, and I felt a bit indignant at the buzz of conversation: didn't they know there was a funeral on? The organist was playing 'Highland Cathedral' – pop music, as Grandfather would have described it while enjoying it nonetheless.

There must have been four hundred in the church. I knew that very old people rarely had many mourners at their funerals, so the turnout was remarkable.

As I prepared to go up to give my reading, Nathalie must have sensed my nervousness. She leant across and whispered, 'Stand tall, take a deep breath, speak slowly, and remember he'd be proud of you.'

It was a reading from *The Book of Wisdom*. I'd read it and re-read it over the last few days and found that once I'd begun, I barely needed to glance at the card. It ended with: 'They who trust in Him will understand the truth, those who are faithful will live with Him in love; For grace and mercy await those He has chosen.'

After I sat down, John MacDonald, one of the passengers in the van, was first up to deliver his eulogy. My aunt had described him as a great friend from Grandfather's childhood and army days. He was unknown to most of the congregation and must have been well into his eighties if he was a day. He wore a kilt, which was unusual to see over here, and stood ramrod straight, all six foot three of him. His voice was clear and powerful, beginning in Gaelic and then moving to English. I listened as he began to describe a great man, descended from generations of enormously respected Highland gentlemen, a legend who, it became clear, I had hardly known.

I listened, rapt, as my grandfather's life story was recounted. Donald Angus had served in the famous Highland regiment the Lovat Scouts and had soon been singled out and transferred to the Special Operations Executive where he had come up through the ranks, being commissioned as a captain. The SOE had been founded by Winston Churchill himself, and after training, both men and women were sent across the English Channel with the remit to 'set Europe ablaze'. Grandfather had been an explosives expert, and along with his team in the French resistance had cut major routes through the Alps. I could hardly believe my ears as MacDonald read from the citation for the Military Cross that had been presented to Grandfather after the war, which declared him to be 'perhaps the man who did more than anyone to stop the invasion of Switzerland'.

My sister and I exchanged increasingly astonished glances as the Scotsman went on. Stories of eluding German patrols, setting explosive charges under railway bridges while the sentries above were so close you could hear them breathe, ash from their cigarettes flicking down on him as he set the detonator on the bridge supports, giving only minutes to escape with an ammunition train due over shortly.

MacDonald finished by telling the congregation that Grandfather won the Highland Society of London Gold Medal at the Northern Meeting when he was just nineteen years old. I felt my jaw drop. We'd talked about piping in general, but that medal was *the* premier accolade in the bagpiping world. He must have been a celebrity. How come I'd had no idea?

Next up was a Lacroix cousin, Philippe, now living in Quebec, whom we hardly knew. He was my grandmother's nephew, a doctor from Chéticamp originally.

'Perhaps Donald Angus was one half of the most romantic love story that this island has ever known,' he began, in a strong French accent. 'For a start, both Donald Angus and his wife would claim that the other had saved their life before they got married . . .' His voice alone bewitched us all, it was so deep and expressive. Soon, everyone had their hankies out and I noticed women reaching for their husbands' hands as we heard how my grandmother, a Cape Bretoner, one of few women in the SOE, had been given a mission in France which more than likely would end in torture or death. Grandfather had spent a year trying to track her down and eventually found her, and she in turn had travelled three thousand miles to be with him when he was seriously injured later in the war. Philippe noted that they hardly spent a day apart from each other in their entire married life and that every single night, Donald Angus would kneel beside their bed and thank God for allowing his wife to be with him.

The last to say a few words was Grandfather's best friend, old Tommy Anderson. Tommy had been in and out of our house since I could remember; the two of them watched the hockey, got heated about politics and went fishing together. Until the last couple of years, they would inevitably be found in the Red Shoe on a Sunday having lunch together. We all heard of Grandfather's generosity, his profound Christianity and his kindness. How he would 'forget' to bill people in the area when he fixed their roof or whatever. Tommy spoke about Grandmother and our parents and how they had all died together at such a young age, leaving Donald Angus to rear the little children, Nathalie and myself. Nathalie was sobbing now, and I passed across the tissues that Aunt Maggie had thoughtfully given me, despite needing them myself.

I agreed with his every word: no one could have done a better job of bringing us up. Although sixty years older than his charges, he would play with us, help with homework, and read us stories in bed. It was his passion that had encouraged my bagpiping and fiddling and fostered Nathalie's renowned excellence in teaching Gaelic. In short, he had been father, mother, grandmother and grandfather all in one.

Father Calum said a few poignant words, along the lines of Grandfather being one of the most understated and decent men he'd ever met, and then looked around at all of us, saying: 'Did anyone here in church know even half of what you have heard about Donald Angus Gillies before today?'

I don't know who started it off, but suddenly everyone was clapping. It was so unexpected and spontaneous that people exchanged delighted smiles, happy to be sharing their love and respect for such a gentleman. My heart sang; I was so proud to be part of him.

The rest of the service passed in a blur. Nathalie finally stopped crying and we sang his favourite hymn, 'All Things Bright And Beautiful', as we filed out.

My arms were sore and my face ached from smiling as everyone wanted to shake my hand and tell me what I already knew: what a great man he was and how they would miss him. We stood around the grave in the cold for half an hour as prayers were said and, finally, he was lowered into his final resting place beside his wife, my father and my mother.

The pipe major of Grandfather's old band struggled to play 'The Dark Isle' with his frozen fingers as we sprinkled a handful of dirt on the coffin. Suddenly Seamus started to howl; he knew his master had gone. I had controlled myself until then, but now the emotion all came out. A deep, guttural sobbing rose from the depths of my chest. It was surreal as I heard myself, as if I were observing someone else. Aunt Maggie was immediately across beside me, and it was her support that stopped me collapsing. Nathalie came to my side, too, and the three of us clung to each other in a triangle of grief, our dog alongside, as the few who had braved the cold and not gone into the church hall drifted away.

After a while, we composed ourselves and started to walk towards the hall together, but Aunt Maggie suddenly grew agitated and rushed off across the road. There, a man wearing a fedora hat was standing by a battered old truck.

'What's she up to?' I asked my sister.

'Christ, I think it's Tom Holland!' Nathalie replied.

The killer. I felt I was going to be sick, doubling over as if I'd been kicked in the stomach, suddenly pathetically weak.

'How dare he come here! How dare he!' Nathalie cried.

I don't know what came over me. All of a sudden, I was sprinting over the road, and just as Aunt Maggie was about to confront him, I threw myself at him, fists flailing. We tumbled into the snow.

'You bastard!' I shouted, driving my fist into his face again and again.

He made no effort to defend himself; he just lay there as I pummelled him. I could hear Aunt Maggie and Nathalie shouting at me, then they grabbed my arms and pulled me off.

'Leave him, Peter Angus – he's not worth it!' screamed my sister. 'Come on, let's go.'

I staggered to my feet and looked down at him in disgust.

His nose was bleeding badly. 'Sorry,' he mumbled. 'I'm so sorry . . .'

Aunt Maggie linked arms with both of us and led us away. 'Come on. Leave him be. We have work to do playing host,' she said determinedly.

Nathalie was staring intently across at me. 'My God, what happened there? You turned into a madman.'

We heard Holland's truck starting up and pulling away, but we didn't look back.

By the time we got to the hall, it was getting dark and the older generation were anxious to get home. The church worthies were clearing cups and plates away and the buffet table was almost bare. As we entered, Aunt Maggie began rushing around apologising for being so late and asking the visiting Scots, Tommy and some others back to the house for a bowl of chilli. My heart sank. I so wanted a moment's peace.

Back at the house, about a dozen of us crowded into the sitting room.

'There's more snow forecast tonight,' Aunt Maggie warned, 'but there's still a chance we'll get up to St Margaret's tomorrow. Peter Watson, the farmer, has agreed to take a tractor and snow-plough the track up River Denys Mountain tonight. So, fingers crossed.'

Nathalie slipped off to be with the baby, and Iain Bec and I passed around the food, poured tea and even persuaded the sceptical Highlanders to try Cape Breton whisky.

I came across Big John in Grandfather's den, peering at the beautiful hand-drawn map on the wall; before long, more folk came into the room and pushed forward for a closer look, all full of admiration.

'It's easy to see where your artistic ability comes from, young Peter Angus,' said Tommy.

'I've never seen such a thing,' Big John exclaimed. 'We've all heard about it, of course. Isn't it amazing to think that Ardnish history is being preserved like this, thousands of miles across the Atlantic?'

'Wouldn't the Land, Sea and Islands Centre in Arisaig love to have this,' one of the Scots remarked. 'It's a historically important work of art.'

'Grandfather drew it when he came back from a visit when I was a boy,' I said. 'It took him months. He worked on it every evening. I remember a sheet of hardboard in the sitting room all pinned out and him bent over it, drawing away. He called it the "centenary map" because it was drawn in 2000. He was the last person to have lived there, so he felt he knew it best. I guess he didn't want people to forget its history.'

As I spoke, I began to think that perhaps he really compiled it to take his mind away from the accident, but I didn't mention that. It would be on everyone's mind but would remain a taboo subject unless I brought it up.

'And how amazing to have all the families marked on it so we can see who was the last to live in each house,' Big John added. 'Look, the MacEachens at Mullochbuie, and the Bochan at Sloch. Peter Angus, you see the horseshoe of houses following the curve of the beach here at Peanmeanach? You'll be astonished by its beauty when you see it.'

As he said this, it triggered a thought. A pencil sketch of each township in the wide margin that remained around the poster would be a great addition. People looking at it in the future would get a much better feel for the place.

As the guests drifted back to the sitting room John and I continued our talk. 'Have a look here, Peter Angus – that's where my uncle, Johnny Bochan, lived and my grandparents before him. MacDougall the famous piper was in that croft in the corner. You'll know where your family lived, I'm sure,' he added tentatively, allowing me to nod. 'All the folk with me over here are Ardnish families,' he repeated proudly.

He was off now, pointing out landmarks such as the two schools, the church known as Our Lady of the Braes, the path in and the big field. 'There' – he prodded the map with his bent, arthritic finger – 'is a graveyard in the corner here, all grown over with bracken.' I'd heard it all a dozen times before, but I didn't mind hearing it again from him. Big John had the same pleasant Highland lilt to his voice as my grandfather, and if I closed my eyes, I could almost imagine it was himself speaking.

'I mind your grandfather telling me about Kirsty MacDonell and the coat. You'll know that story, of course, Peter Angus?'

I stared blankly at him.

'Well, I'll tell you it. Kirsty and her brother John lived together in a very remote cottage in the glen between Glenfinnan and Meoble called Kinlochbeoraid. It was a good two-hour walk to any other house. John was the postman, and three days a week he would walk over the pass to Glenfinnan, collect the post, walk back past Kinlochbeoraid, along Loch Beoraid itself to Meoble, then along Loch Morar to the people at the east end, at Oban and Kinlochmorar, where he would stay the night before walking back the next day. A huge distance, and a nightmare in the winter.

'One early summer's day, the two of them needed to go to Glenfinnan, John to collect the post, and his sister to take the train to "the Garrison", as they called it, to meet your grandmother, go to the shop and bank. Kirsty had misjudged the temperature in the cool morning and had left wearing her big, heavy winter coat. Halfway up the steep incline above their house she asked her brother if he would carry her coat. "I will not," he replied. "I told you not to bring it."

'She asked him again later and got the same response. She was furious. Anyway, later that day, when she was in the post office, she bought some brown paper and string, wrapped the coat up and posted it back to herself, for her brother to carry home.'

We laughed.

'Wasn't she the wily one?' I said.

'The two of them died just two days apart from each other, and their coffins lay side by side in the Glenfinnan church. I've never seen that any other time. It was about 1959, I think.'

A thought occurred to me. 'Did you know Donald Angus's father and grandfather, John?' I asked. 'Donald Peter and Donald John?'

He shook his head. 'No, but I knew your great-grandmother. She was a remarkable person. It was Louise who held the Ardnish community together for its last twenty years. She was born in Wales, but after the war she moved to a council house in Arisaig, sharing with her neighbour Mairi Ferguson. Louise died in 1951, and it was straight after that that your grandparents emigrated over here . . . My mother would look in on them every day. Everyone looked after the old folk in those days.'

There was a lull in the conversation, both of us peering at the map. I could envisage Grandfather beside me; like Big John he would be swirling his dram around in the glass. Perhaps the passion they felt for the place was contagious after all.

'Grandfather always told Nathalie and me that there's a knoll above Peanmeanach that has the most amazing view in the world,' I said. 'His best memories were when he and his mother would climb up onto the hillock and sit and watch the sun go down over the Small Isles. It would curve above Eigg and finally drop down behind the Rum Cuillins. I'll never forget the look on his face when he talked about it. He said the sea glistened like molten silver and the sky would be a bright orange, with the hills of An Stac and Roshven glowing in the sun for half an hour after dusk had arrived at sea level.'

'Aye, that's right. May or June is the best time – after the lambing is finished and before the midges become a nuisance.'

I felt a catch in my throat. 'I'd definitely like to see it someday.' I surprised myself with my words, and with the fact that I really meant it.

Big John gripped my arm and looked at me intently. 'You really must visit, son. You would be made welcome.'

We returned to the sitting room to find one of the Ferguson ladies shooing everyone out. 'Come on, everyone, bed. It's three in the morning Arisaig time and we're back here in only a few hours for Mass.'

Chapter 6

I woke the next morning to the sound of clattering and, pulling on my clothes, went down to see what was going on. Seamus was chasing his steel bowl around the kitchen trying to find a last morsel and Nathalie was making coffee, showing impressive one-handed skills with wee Mairi draped over her shoulder, sound asleep.

'Morning, darling brother,' she chirped. 'Come here and give us a hug. Late night? Awful weather outside. Yesterday went okay, don't you think? I still can't get over how nice it was of all those folk to come over from Scotland. Oh my God, what fantastic speeches – what a tribute!'

She'd always been perky in the morning, our Nathalie.

I finally got a word in. 'I had a good chat with Big John last night. We were looking at the centenary map. He loved it – they all did. We talked about me going over.'

'Do you want to?' Nathalie asked.

'I think so . . . maybe . . . sometime,' I replied. 'But when? I get so few days off work and there's so much to do around the house . . .'

Aunt Maggie came rushing downstairs. 'They'll be here in a minute. Will someone pour me a coffee? Now, where are my boots and hat?'

We said our goodbyes to Nathalie, who'd decided the trip to

the church would be too much for her and the baby, and headed out to the van. Aunt Maggie and I climbed in, and I hauled Seamus into the footwell to a rousing chorus of good mornings from those wrapped up like Eskimos in the back. We set off with Aunt Maggie explaining that Mass had to be held early as Father Calum had his normal schedule of services to carry out.

It was sixteen years since I'd been up to St Margaret's of Scotland, the same day my sister and grandfather last visited. I wasn't going to talk about it with the Scots; I'd only cry and make a fool of myself.

It was still pitch-black when we arrived. Father Calum had come ahead of us. He had three young girls with him who I recognised – they'd come to sing – and he'd lit a couple of gas heaters to take the chill off the old building. The Miramichi MacDonalds were there, too. They were great friends of the priest and knew my family from way back.

While the priest put on his cassock he told us the history of the church. 'It was built in 1851,' he began. 'The thirty families who settled and farmed up here were from Arisaig, Eigg and South Uist, and they would have celebrated Mass in Gaelic of course. If you look outside when it gets light, you'll see that the graves have exactly the same names as those of you in the congregation.'

'Everyone in my part of Scotland has heard of this church,' Mrs Ferguson said. 'It resonates with us the way Cillie Choirill in Roybridge resonates with the Cape Breton people. You know, Father, the people of Lochaber will never forget how the people of Cape Breton raised the money to rebuild Cillie Choirill in the 1930s – your John MacMaster especially. And we all know how little money there was here.'

Father Calum began the Mass. As he spoke, my mind went back to when I was ten. Grandfather, Nathalie and myself had come up here on a bitter winter's day, squashed together in the front of his pickup. It was the day after the accident. My sister and I were a bit young to fully comprehend what had happened and the cataclysmic effect the deaths of my parents and grandmother would have on our lives. Nathalie was cradling our dog, Seamus's mother, burying her face in her neck as she wept. Inside the church, Grandfather had led us in prayer and lit three candles on the altar. I remember now how brave and strong he'd been despite losing his adored wife and son. He was an example to us then and had been ever since.

The girls stood up and sang 'Westering Home', their beautiful voices in perfect harmony. The priest's gentle voice alternated between English and Gaelic, and the crucifix flickered in the candlelight. I wondered, not for the first time, if I ought to have chosen to train for the priesthood.

I decided to walk Seamus down the hill and let the others head off sightseeing. I'd see them tomorrow for breakfast. Tommy Anderson had taken them under his wing and arranged a visit to An Drochaid, the museum in Mabou, then lunch at the Red Shoe followed by a tour of Glenora Distillery. I was touched to learn that everywhere was opening up specially for them, even in the depths of winter.

Chapter 7

It was Monday morning. Aunt Maggie and a couple of her friends had laid on a farewell breakfast for the Scots in the Interpretive Centre in Judique, and a few cousins and friends of the family came along who had visited Lochaber on family reunions and the like. Aunt Maggie gave a nice speech and Big John replied in kind. There was lots of kissing, heartfelt farewells and warm invitations to come and stay.

Big John approached me. Staring hard into my eyes, he grasped my hand and wouldn't let go. 'Peter Angus,' he said softly, 'you are the last male descendant of the famous Gillies family of Ardnish, and your grandfather was the last to live there. Your family has a great history in our part of the world; it is your heritage. You need to come over. You know that, don't you?'

'I do. I will come,' I said. 'I really will.' I looked him right in the eye. I meant it, too. Some day.

After they all departed for the airport, we rushed home to meet Ian Kennedy for the reading of the will.

An hour later saw me reeling from the sitting room up to my bedroom, trying to grasp the information which the lawyer had imparted from Grandfather's will. Aunt Maggie was to get the small portfolio of stocks that had been left to him by Grandmother, which had presumably come originally from her father, the Chéticamp doctor. Nathalie had been left the house with all its contents, and I was bequeathed $5,000. I looked at the letter with my name on it and the word 'Personal' on the front of the envelope, written in Grandfather's familiar scrawl. I was shocked and hurt. I'd always thought Grandfather and I had been incredibly close. Nathalie and Aunt Maggie had been full of apologies, as if they had made the decision.

I lay on my bed and opened the letter. It was formal, typewritten, but signed by my grandfather. He must have dictated it to Ian Kennedy, because I knew he couldn't use a keyboard.

18 MacIsaac Street,
Inverness,
Cape Breton

Mo ghràidh Peter Angus,
I am gone, hopefully to join my darling wife and your parents. I am glad – how I've missed them. Since they died you have been as a son to me and my best friend, too. Who would have imagined I would have been a father again in my eighties? My biggest regret in going, of course, is no longer being with you and your sister and sharing your lives. I wouldn't have missed the last fifteen years for all the world.

The will has been read, and I know you will be disappointed. Don't be.

I have left you $5,000. My wish is for you to use this money to pay for a trip to Scotland. Stay for as long as you possibly can: a month or two, maybe three? Immerse yourself in Lochaber, spend a lot of time on Ardnish. I believe it will have the same impact on you as it did me.

I feel you are at a turning point in your life. You grow less shy by the day, you are good at your job, if yet unappreciated, and you have music as a much-loved hobby. Your faith is deep, thank God for that. Living with Nathalie, Iain and, please God, their baby, on your poor wages is unsatisfactory for a young Gillies man.

You need to take control of your future, Peter Angus. Set a distinct goal and head for that. It is many years since your parents died and you need to move on. Perhaps Nathalie and I have mothered you too much, not pushed you out into the big wide world. But your sister and Cape Breton will always be there for you.

You are from a distinguished family. Stand tall, be confident, expect respect.

At the end of your trip to Ardnish, go to see MacPhee & Partners in Fort William, ask to see Katie MacPhee there, and tell her who you are.

Athair gràdhach
Donald Angus Gillies

I was full of confusion. Where was his pride in me? I read and re-read the letter. He thought I was drifting, that my life was going nowhere. His letter seemed designed to jolt me into some kind of action, starting with a trip to Scotland.

The hurt began to give way to anger. How dare he tell me I was making nothing of myself, that I was some kind of loser! That's pretty much what he had written, reading between the lines.

I was enraged at the injustice. Why should Nathalie and Iain Bec get the house? It was worth a lot of money. She was a teacher, he worked for a utility company – the pair of them had the best-paid jobs on the island. It wasn't fair!

I must have lain there for hours, brooding, and it was mid-afternoon when there was a knock on the door.

Aunt Maggie put a sandwich on my bedside table. 'Can we have a chat?'

My heart sank. When my aunt said *we*, it meant *she* wanted to talk and *I* had to listen. It had always been the way. I was fond of her but pleased that she lived two thousand kilometres away in Hamilton and would leave us in peace once Grandfather's affairs had been settled.

'Ian Kennedy posted me a copy of the letter,' she said. 'My father had asked him to. Do you want to talk about it?'

'Not really,' I replied brusquely.

There was a pause, me resenting her interference and her keen to have her say.

'Nathalie has a family now, Peter Angus. At some stage you need to move out, make your own way in life.'

I sat bolt upright in my bed. 'For God's sake! Grandfather is barely cold and I'm being evicted. Is this Nathalie's decision?'

'No, of course not. You know she would never ask you to go, but it's the right thing to do. That's why Grandfather left her the house.'

I slumped back on the bed. 'I'll think about it,' I said eventually. Then I fell into a morose silence. If I didn't speak, maybe she would leave me alone.

But Aunt Maggie wasn't leaving until she was good and ready. 'You really should take this chance to go to Ardnish,' she said. 'It would do you the world of good to get away, see a different life, travel. Those Scots who came to the funeral, they'd look after you, point you in the right direction. You might even find a bit of romance!'

I smarted at this remark. I'd told my aunt a couple of years back, after we'd all had a few drinks at a ceilidh up at Glencoe

Mills, that I was on the lookout for the right girl and she had, annoyingly, asked me about the girls in my life ever since.

Little did she know that I had, in fact, dated a couple of girls: one from Stanley, a romance which petered out pretty quickly due to the distance between us, and later, the gorgeous Jenny who I'd been crazy about. She'd broken things off with me, then went off and got married before I had a chance to make amends. I have to admit that I wasn't exactly a catch for either of them.

'I can't go,' I replied. 'I've no holidays left. Well, only three days. My boss is already upset that I've taken more than two weeks as compassionate leave. And I've got to write some new music for Celtic Colours and that's likely to take months, and what about Seamus?' Lame excuses tumbled from my mouth as I reeled off the burdens upon my time.

'Seamus will be fine, you know that – your sister loves him too,' Aunt Maggie pointed out.

There was a pause, before my aunt stood up to go.

'Do you know why Grandfather told me to go and see the lawyer in Fort William?' I asked.

She sat down again and looked across at me, her brow furrowed. 'No, I don't. There's no way he would have ownership of any property at Ardnish because the whole family were tenants of Arisaig Estate. I confess that sentence had me wondering.'

I looked at her, and felt my shoulders relax. 'I'd better take the dog for a walk along the shore before it gets dark,' I said.

Seamus and I walked for miles along the old railway line. I winced in regret as I thought how sore and stiff he would be tomorrow. But I wanted to be out of the house. Aunt Maggie and Nathalie would be talking about me. My mind was racing. It seemed that everyone was pushing me off the island.

When I was seventeen, I had gained good grades and all the talk had been about my going to St Francis Xavier to study Music, Theology, Celtic Studies – anything I wanted, really. But I dug my heels in. I wasn't leaving home. At the same time, a job came up in Halifax, working in a music studio. I'd have loved the job but I somehow persuaded myself that the time wasn't right to leave the island. Since then, I'd carved out the semblance of a career at Canadian Equitable. I'd started as an office junior, working nine hours a day, with ten days' holiday a year and a salary that was less than an employee's at the Tim Hortons coffee chain, as Nathalie never stopped reminding me.

I did sometimes wonder about myself. There was an ex of Nathalie's from school who wasn't especially bright but he was already a director at the Royal Bank of Canada. Each summer he'd come back home in his fancy Jeep Wrangler and flaunt his success. He skied in Whistler and had a Caribbean holiday in the winter too, Nathalie said.

Maybe I was happy as things were because I was an orphan? I seemed content to stay in my safe family cocoon. My life suited me fine: I lived with the people I most wanted to be with, I paid no rent and I had enough money to run Grandfather's old car. Plus, I got a couple of hundred bucks each month playing at gigs around the place.

Dinner that evening was painful. Everyone was avoiding discussing the letter. I was certain that Aunt Maggie would tell my sister about it, and the look in Nathalie's eyes confirmed my fears. We talked about how lucky it was that there had been a break in the weather and we had managed to get the Scots up to St Margaret's. We discussed who had come to the funeral and who hadn't, and the people who came that we didn't know.

'Aunt Maggie, why do you think Tom Holland came to the funeral? How could he?' Nathalie asked. 'He's only been out of jail for a few months. I read about his release in the *Oran*.'

'Well,' she replied, 'people do strange things sometimes. When I asked him what the hell he was playing at, he said saying something about paying his respects and how he wanted to apologise for what he'd put us through. But then Peter Angus came flying over and launched himself.'

They both turned towards me.

'He deserved it,' I said quietly. 'And I'd do it again.'

'Well, you certainly surprised him,' Aunt Maggie said.

'Us too,' put in Nathalie.

Luckily, Nathalie's phone rang and I was spared any further conversation. I didn't want to talk about Tom Holland. I knew that dwelling on thoughts of his reappearance would rekindle the terrible nightmares I used to get. I rubbed my bruised knuckles, aching from the blows I'd rained down on him. I couldn't work out if the beating I'd given him made me feel any better or not.

Chapter 8

Back into the work routine, and I was standing outside the Coal Miners Café at 7.30 a.m. A bitter wind was hurtling up the Central Avenue and my friend Alan was late. We took it in turns, week about, to drive the hour-long journey. I dreaded my turn when the weather was bad: if Grandfather's car broke down, I didn't have the money to repair it.

I waved at John Mackenzie, off to work at Cabot Links, and chatted to Angie Cameron, who was coming into the café. These old-timers got together every morning for a coffee. They'd been lobster fishermen together and were inseparable.

Alan finally pulled up, apologising for his child keeping him up all night. 'What a funeral,' he said. 'If I have half that number at mine I'll be over the moon. He was a legend, your grandfather. And those tributes from Tommy and the other two – you must be so proud.'

I sat quietly and listened to his chatter as we flashed past Mabou, Port Hood, Judique, in the half-light

Alan dropped me off at the main entrance to my office. I was pleased to see my friend Maureen on reception. She'd worked here far longer than me, and we'd been firm friends from my very first day. Smart and efficient, she always made me laugh, and I couldn't imagine working there without her.

'Great to have you back, Peter Angus. Fancy lunch today?' she asked. 'I've got something to show you.' She waved a piece of paper in front of me, just out of reach. 'You'll be furious.'

I leant forward to grab it but she whisked it back. 'Lunch, or I'll burn it.' She grinned.

'Okay.' I shrugged my shoulders and headed to my desk. Passing the open door to Yvonne's office, I raised my hand in greeting. She looked up and waved back distractedly, but I kept walking. I felt annoyed. Why didn't she come out to greet me, offer her condolences and ask how things were at home?

On reaching my desk in the corner, I was horrified to find a mound of paperwork a foot high. I'd never seen a mess like it. I'd thought hotshot Julie had been covering for me in my absence. Even more annoyed, I sat down and logged in to my computer, only to discover over three hundred unanswered emails in my inbox.

I buried my head in my hands. Yvonne had assured me that Julie would cover my workload, with support from her, and it looked as though nothing had been done. The clients would be furious.

There was nothing for it but to make a start. Sighing heavily, I began to tackle the backlog.

After a couple of hours, Yvonne came over to see me. 'Welcome back, Peter Angus,' she said.

I opened my mouth to complain but Yvonne wouldn't stop talking. 'Tough times for you. How's Maggie doing?' Yvonne knew my aunt as they'd been at school together.

'She's at the house, helping with Nathalie's new baby. She did a great job with the funeral. It all went like clockwork, thanks to her. I think she'll be heading home to Hamilton pretty soon.'

'She still married to Sean?'

I nodded. 'No kids. I guess she must be pretty near retirement.'

'Send her my best.' Yvonne smiled sweetly and left me to it. I rolled my eyes. Aunt Maggie didn't have fond memories of Yvonne, and Yvonne had once told me that my aunt was too bossy. It was true, but I certainly didn't want to hear that from Yvonne. We adored bossy Aunt Maggie.

'Yvonne?' I called out. 'Where's Julie?'

'Taken the week off,' she called back.

I was livid, but not surprised. Julie seemed to take far more holidays than anyone else round here. I don't know how she got away with it.

The morning passed quickly as I slogged through the unanswered claims and queries and was glad to head to the staff-room at one o'clock, where Maureen was unpacking two meal deals for us.

'I can't believe Julie!' I raged through mouthfuls of sandwich. 'How can one person be so useless and get away with it? It takes her twice as long as anyone else to get any work done and she's never here. "Working from home", off sick or on holiday . . . what is it with her?'

'She's smart,' Maureen replied simply. 'Articulate. She talks a good game so everyone thinks she's super-competent.'

I snorted. 'Anyway, what's with the mystery piece of paper?'

'I'm not sure I should give it to you now,' she replied. 'You won't like it. I mean, you *really* won't like it.'

'Go on,' I said wearily. 'It's not like my day could get any worse.'

'I'm not sure about that.' Maureen handed me the letter, stamped CONFIDENTIAL in red capitals.

I read it in disbelief, before looking up at Maureen. 'She . . . she earns more than *twice* what I do?'

'Yup.'

'But this is shit!' I cried. 'How can Julie be worth two of me? She does next to nothing!'

'Beats me,' Maureen said, squeezing my hand. 'Look, everyone knows you're the one who keeps this place running. I'm really sorry.'

'I mean, I know Julie's got a degree and all that, but that's not the point! Have you seen the state of my desk? Nothing but work she was meant to take care of . . .'

'Can't argue with that.'

'How can Yvonne shaft me like that?' I was seething. 'I've given eight years of my life to her and to this place. I'm good, and Julie waltzes in like five seconds ago and gets twice the pay? I've never even asked for a raise, I've never taken my full vacation entitlement—'

'Well, more fool you,' Maureen cut in gently.

'I'm hardly ever late for work,' I continued, ignoring her, 'I don't make a fuss, and this is how Yvonne repays me? I'm going to give her a piece of my mind.'

I shot to my feet but Maureen grabbed my arm and made me sit down again. 'Don't, Peter Angus, please. First up, Yvonne will know I showed you the letter and I'll get fired, and second, you need to calm down. Do you hear me?'

Head down, I made my way back to my desk. I wondered what my grandfather would have advised if he'd known. I knew for certain that he wouldn't sit back and let everything carry on as before. And he'd have been right. Things had to change.

Chapter 9

'I mean, it's just so unfair! There's Julie with her fancy degree, lured over here with the promise of a fat salary then completely flunking it when she gets here!'

Aunt Maggie and Nathalie listened in patient silence as I ranted at them over dinner.

'She can't manage even the simplest tasks, she's always "working from home", especially when Yvonne's away, and she's taken more sick leave in four months than I have in eight years!' I swigged back my beer and slumped back in my chair. 'Everyone comes to me when they've got a problem. *Me* – not Julie! I mean, okay, okay, maybe I'm not assertive enough . . .' I was running out of steam.

Nathalie put down her knife and fork and stared at me. 'Just leave.'

'What?' I said, frowning.

'You heard. Ask for a sabbatical, tell them you've been with Equitable your whole working life and now you want a break. Let Julie mess it up without you there to clean up behind her, then you can come back in as Yvonne's heir apparent and collect a fat pay cheque.'

'Hmm. You think?'

'Totally. You've got the money now and you've got a British passport. Go to Scotland. You could get a summer job there.'

Aunt Maggie piped up. 'It's not your problem, Peter Angus, it's Yvonne's. Imagine! She'll be squirming when you confront her about the pay difference. But tidy yourself up, polish your shoes, wear a tie and jacket. Move out of that corner you've been hiding away in all these years. Stand straight, speak up and make sure Yvonne sees exactly how good you are at your job. She probably knows anyway, but you need to be right in her face, make her think of you as . . . senior management material.'

I was pretty sure my aunt didn't really believe I was management material; she had always treated me as if I was a teenager to boss about. But her words rang true.

'You're right,' I said. 'I'll give it three or four weeks, take your advice, then write a letter to Yvonne, follow it up with a formal meeting. I know I'm worth a lot more than I'm getting. And maybe I will take some time out, go somewhere. I've never been to the East Coast. I'd love to go to Vancouver.'

'I haven't seen you so animated for years,' my sister said. 'What will you do if Yvonne says no?'

'I'll resign . . . but she won't, she needs me,' I replied confidently.

I was considerably cheered up by the whole plan and we stayed up late with the conversation in full flow. Just before we turned in, Aunt Maggie, who, even from halfway across Canada, had been such an integral part of our lives since our parents had died, announced that she would be flying home at the weekend. She had a job and a husband to get back to. She volunteered to rent a car and take old Seamus home with her, but we refused. Nathalie and I knew Seamus wasn't long for this world and we wanted him to end his days in his own home.

That night, I sat on my bed and wrote down a list of how I wanted to change. I drove myself into work and did two hours more than anyone else. I moved to the desk nearest Yvonne's and dressed as smartly as the area manager who came in from Halifax. I began, at last, to feel a sense of purpose.

One morning, we were having a discussion about a big opportunity we had to pitch for. It was the insurance for the local Cabot Links Resort and the opportunity had come in from our Toronto head office. Seizing my chance, I volunteered to put the proposal together and visit the general manager, claiming I knew him personally. I didn't let on that I only knew him because I played the fiddle and bagpipes at functions they had there. Neither Yvonne nor Julie was free to attend that day, so they let me do it.

My proposal consisted of two contracts: one for when they were open, and the second for when the club was closed for the winter, which knocked twenty per cent off their premium. The manager, a keen musician, recognised me, so we had something of a rapport before I got started. Both he and his finance manager seemed impressed with my knowledge of their issues.

Anyway, we won the contract. Yvonne sent an email round the office congratulating me and gave me a $500 bonus then and there. My spirits soared: I was becoming a different man.

Chapter 10

Yvonne looked up from the letter on her desk and looked me straight in the eye.

'Okay. Thanks for coming to me about a sabbatical, Peter Angus. Your proposal is well thought out and completely in line with our vision for the wellbeing of our employees. But it's something of a problem at the current time. I know the employee handbook says sabbaticals will be considered for long-serving staff but I really don't want you to take the time off.'

She was talking more quickly than usual, a little nervously, and a buzz of adrenaline coursed through me.

'I have high hopes for you, Peter Angus. I want you to sit the CIP management programme – we'll pay, of course – and that would mean promotion and a bit more money.' Her demeanour suggested that I was to treat this news as a very big deal. 'I think I can get twenty-five per cent from head office.'

I was ready to play my ace card and couldn't wait to see how she'd react. 'So, how do you see my work and prospects against, say, Julie's?' I asked.

'Julie?' she repeated. 'Well . . . Julie's still finding her feet, but she's highly qualified. You're a great help to her, Peter Angus.'

'So, would you say I was as important to the business as she is?'

'Yes, yes, of course you're important to us here.' Yvonne nodded enthusiastically. 'You're a valued employee. Didn't I just make that clear?'

'Yes, I guess so. But this is very important to me. You know my personal circumstances, and I feel I would really benefit from time away. A sabbatical in no way undermines my loyalty to the company.'

She sighed and threw up her hands. 'Okay. You can take a month off, unpaid, and we'll firm up your career plan when you come back.'

'Thanks, Yvonne. I appreciate it.' I paused. 'Just one more thing.'

'Yes?'

'I know how much Julie is paid.'

Yvonne's face coloured. 'And how did you get that information?'

'Does it matter?' I replied.

'Are you planning to make a claim for a salary at Julie's level?' she asked.

'I'm better than her,' I said firmly. 'I believe I deserve the same terms.'

'Better?' Yvonne echoed. 'Peter Angus, is that what you heard when I said you were an important part of the organisation? You *are* important, but Julie's role is different from yours—'

'Actually, no, it isn't,' I protested. 'We do the same job, but I do five times her workload and you know it.'

'For now, perhaps,' Yvonne replied, shaking her head. 'Julie's only been here for four months. She's got to serve time in all departments, move around, gain experience—'

'That's not fair,' I cut in.

'Julie has a degree in Commerce from Carleton in Ottawa and a Master's in Business Analytics from Dalhousie. Her value to the organisation goes beyond her ability to process claims. Now, I'm happy to discuss the management programme after your sabbatical. It's a big step up from clerk to manager, but I think you have it in you. You've done exceptionally well these last few weeks, so let's leave it at that.'

She stood up. The meeting was over.

Chapter 11

'Nice try,' Nathalie said as she sat by the window feeding the baby later that day.

I could tell her mind was on other things. 'What is it?' I asked.

She turned to me with a huge grin on her face. 'Iain Bec's just emailed. He's back tomorrow from that Alberta job. He's been working fifteen-hour days but he's made thousands. He's delighted. And so am I – wee Mairi's growing like a mushroom. Look at her! Iain Bec will be amazed.'

'That's great,' I replied, smiling weakly.

'We'll be a family again.' Nathalie beamed, raining kisses on her daughter's tiny head.

'Yeah.' I turned and went up to my room.

That night, around midnight, I was creeping along the corridor to the bathroom when I heard Nathalie talking to Iain Bec on the phone downstairs. I was sure I heard my name so stopped to listen.

'I can't wait to see you,' Nathalie was saying. 'But I do wish An Gillie wasn't around.' I froze. 'It'd be nice for us to have the house to ourselves with Mairi.'

This was a message from my sister – something I hadn't heard before. Basically, she was saying it was her house now, and she wanted me out of it.

I couldn't sleep for hours, I was so angry and resentful. But then, gradually, I tried to consider it from Nathalie's point of view. I guessed she was quite right to want me away. She had every right to a life of her own, with her husband and child. Me slumped in front of the fire in the evening with a beer, waiting for her to cook dinner, wasn't how anyone would want things.

When my parents died, life stopped for me. I turned inward. I didn't want to play with my old friends; it was easier to watch TV or play on the computer. I was really into music for a while, but now my aspirations to be a musician had evaporated. At school, people excused me because I'd been orphaned, and then I began to use the excuse myself, made myself a victim. 'Oh, I couldn't finish the essay, Miss. I was too upset last night.'

What I really wanted now was respect. I wanted people to know that I was someone they could rely on. Grandfather had people's respect throughout his life; he really did. I wanted some for myself – from Nathalie, Aunt Maggie, Yvonne, Julie – I just didn't know how to go about it.

As the night dragged on, Ardnish kept coming back to my thoughts: the old family home, my heritage. Memories of my grandparents and parents. They were all gone now. My life was my own to live: I could do whatever I wanted.

Vancouver could wait. I was ready to go to Scotland now. To Ardnish, to take the plaque and visit the island graveyard, and to see the peninsula where my family had lived and died for a thousand years. But most of all I was ready to leave home, to go on an expedition. I really was up for a change in my life.

The next morning, a Saturday, I came down to breakfast. Nathalie was up, baby at her breast.

'Morning, darling sister,' I said. 'Get some sleep?'

She gave me one of her looks. 'What do *you* think?'

'Good point.' I grinned. 'Listen, I'm going to phone Aunt Maggie and I'd like you to listen in, if you don't mind.'

Nathalie nodded and sat beside me at the table as I put the call on speakerphone. I began by telling Aunt Maggie, word for word, how the conversation with Yvonne had gone: how she had agreed to the sabbatical and offered a modest pay increase as if it was a huge deal and how she had reacted badly when I'd mentioned Julie's salary. Predictably, she got straight to the point.

'Bad luck, Peter Angus. I can't say you handled that too wisely. What were you thinking when you mentioned Julie's salary! Still, you have your sabbatical now – well done – so what's the plan?'

'I've agreed with Yvonne that I can work until Easter and then head off. Big John and I talked a lot at the funeral, and he offered to do everything he could to help. I'm planning to go to the MEC in Halifax to get some camping kit, then I'll fly to Glasgow, get the train up to Fort William and rent a kayak for two weeks. I want to kayak around Ardnish.'

I could hear my aunt sighing. Beside me, Nathalie looked puzzled.

'But what do you really want to achieve?' Aunt Maggie said quietly. 'What do you want out of it, this time away? Just getting away from the office? What's the *plan*, Peter Angus?'

I could feel tears pricking the back of my eyes. 'I'm going to put Grandfather's plaque on our family grave. I should have done it years ago – with him. And I'd like to make some sketches to add to the centenary map when I come back. Grandfather used to say I should do more with my art. I think he'd approve.'

'I know he would,' Aunt Maggie said. 'Well done. I'm proud of you, Peter Angus.'

I ended the call, rose to my feet and began the washing up.

'I think you've just made a great decision for yourself,' Nathalie said. 'Amazing.'

'I know.' I grinned. 'Listen, Iain Bec is coming in on the Halifax shuttle at one o'clock, right? Well, it would suit me to go over to Halifax and start looking for gear for my trip today. I can stay with Dave MacIsaac – he's got a gig on tonight at the Lower Deck. I'll take my fiddle and join in. Then I can get the first shuttle on Monday morning back to Port and be at work by nine. Give you guys a chance for some quality time.' I nudged her.

Nathalie enfolded me in a hug. 'Thanks,' she said. 'It'll be really nice to have my man to myself for a change.'

'Straight after that, I'm thinking about renting a room in Hawkesbury,' I continued. 'There's one available, close to work. I'll have long hours to put in over the next month. I want to leave with Yvonne thinking I'm the best.'

'You don't need to do that, you know,' she replied. 'This is your home, too. And I'd miss you.'

'Course you will, you're only human,' I winked. I could tell she was trying to be kind. 'But my mind's made up. I'll pick my stuff up on Monday night.'

She nodded. 'Fair enough. But I'm throwing a party before you fly to Scotland. All your friends. No arguments.'

I went through Grandfather's stuff early that evening, after Nathalie said to take what I wanted. There was nothing of value to anyone except us. I loaded a box with maps and books to take to town to read. I left behind the photographs of my ancestors at the old post office at Peanmeanach, Grandfather all set for school aged five, with bare feet, and dozens of other pictures. I knew them off by heart. From beneath his bed I pulled out the musty-smelling old leather suitcase that had always been there. I hadn't looked inside it since I was a boy. I found an army jacket and his black Lovat Scout Tam o'Shanter. It fitted my head perfectly, so I did a fashion parade for my sister.

There was the Military Cross in its box that had been spoken about at the funeral; how modest he had been in not telling us about it. There was a dog whistle on a cord, and a copy of a 1950 St Mary's Arisaig funeral service sheet for Louise Gillies, his mother. A treasure trove of history. I could feel excitement building – my trip was being brought alive through these items.

I took photographs on my phone of the centenary map, to print out at work. Over the next month, I resolved to read everything I could of the peninsula. No one would know more than me, I decided.

It was late when the urge came to dig out the family's greatest heirloom: the famous Gillies bagpipes. I hoisted them onto my shoulder, coaxed the hide bag to life and tuned the drones. These old bamboo drone reeds were temperamental. I'd only intended to play a tune or two, but once I started, I couldn't stop. At first, I played 'The Dark Isle' and 'Flowers of the Forest', two incredibly mournful tunes, in my grandfather's honour. Then, barely conscious of the shift, I was on to a couple of marches, 'The March of the Cameron Men' and 'Cabar Féidh', and then some Strathspeys.

Nathalie came in, her ears stuffed with toilet paper to muffle the noise in the small room. She gave me the thumbs up to indicate that Mairi was sleeping through it, then sat and listened, rocking her body. Her feet started to twitch when I upped the tempo and moved on to some jigs, and finally, when I began to play 'Itchy Fingers' she was up doing her step dancing. Our own wee ceilidh was in full swing.

It must have been midnight when I could play no more. My lungs ached with the exertion, my lips were numb and my sister and I were dripping with sweat. We threw ourselves into each other's arms and waltzed around the room. I think we were both remembering our youth, when it would be Grandfather playing these exact same tunes and us dancing like mad.

It was later, lying in bed, when I realised that this really was my last night at 'home'. I was off – fleeing the nest at the ripe old age of twenty-seven.

Dave lived in a seedy apartment above a subway in the worst part of Halifax. He shared it with Estelle, his latest in a long line of girlfriends.

He welcomed me in and said how sorry he was to hear about my grandfather. 'And how's Nathalie? Gorgeous as ever?'

I remembered the crush Dave had had on my sister when we were younger. 'She's good, thanks. She and Iain Bec had a baby daughter last month.'

'Cool. You okay crashing here?' He gestured towards a stained, sunken couch, the only item of furniture in the room apart from numerous musical instruments and a games console.

'Perfect,' I assured him, resigning myself to two nights of absolutely no sleep whatsoever. 'I've brought a sleeping bag.'

Dave's gig was in a nightclub called the Lower Deck. He played in a Celtic rock band, Macashaw, who were much like The Proclaimers, and he invited me to join them. Our first tune, as always 'Maureen Was A Goer', kicked off at ten o'clock that night, and it was one in the morning before we left, a handful of bucks in our pockets, shattered but buzzing. Then it was off to Durty Nelly's bar and the Halifax Alehouse for a few refreshing ales before staggering back to his place at four.

This was Dave's life, and I had aspired to it for years, but gazing around the grimy apartment, full of unwashed clothes and dirty dishes, I realised it wasn't for me. Grandfather's advice to me about making music a hobby was sound. It was such a hard way to make a living and didn't work with a family life. Macashaw were very popular in Nova Scotia, but living hand to mouth and driving home in a filthy van for four hours after a gig to save money on accommodation no longer appealed.

All my thoughts were on Ardnish – my trip of a lifetime.

Chapter 12

The next month passed in a whirl. I rented the room in Hawkesbury I'd told Nathalie about; it was only a block from work and dirt-cheap.

I put in ten-hour days at work, followed by two hours of online research in the evenings, learning almost off by heart the history of Ardnish, written by the owner of the peninsula on the Moidart History Group website. I also documented the censuses of 1851 and 1891, which listed the names, ages and occupations of all who lived in which community. My thirst for knowledge about the area quickly became an obsession; every hamlet seemed to have a link to my ancestors, and every loch and glen evoked a recalled story from my grandparents. What made me methodical at work was helping me to focus and develop this history. I hoped my trip would give it colour and pull it all together.

I wrote a piece listing all the stories that Grandfather had told me, five pages in all. Had I been paying attention as a teenager, there would have been a lot more.

For example, the time when Donald John, aged only eleven, illegally shot a deer for the family to live off, probably saving them from starvation. Or the time when the army swarmed all over Peanmeanach in the middle of the night, on a training mission, and old Mairi Ferguson woke up thinking the Germans were invading. I knew all about my great-great-grandmother Morag's legendary ability with sheepdogs. With each anecdote remembered I felt closer and closer to my roots.

I found information about a 1746 naval battle at Loch nan Uamh. Two French frigates were delivering soldiers, arms and gold to Prince Charles Edward Stuart, not knowing that he had been defeated at Culloden only a few weeks before. The French were cornered in the loch on the north of Ardnish by three Royal Navy ships. The French escaped, but left dozens dead and a rumour about abandoned gold.

Big John MacDonald and I exchanged emails almost every day. He provided me with weather reports, advice on websites to visit and more information about which families had gone where. Many were near here in Mabou, or Arisaig and Antigonish on the other side of the Strait. Big John appreciated my passion for detail. I think he was looking forward to my visit as much as I was. I printed out a file, all condensed into the tiniest font size possible, as I was pretty sure there would be no phone reception for the whole visit.

I had never kayaked, but I planned to get a lesson in Scotland and I figured I'd be close to land the whole time. I googled what gear I'd need and then ignored it. My budget was limited so I opted for the basics.

In late March, I saw that the $5,000 had been transferred into my account from the lawyer. That same night, I booked my flight to Scotland for a week's time. It was my birthday on the Saturday.

Nathalie and Iain Bec gave me a tremendous welcome when I got back to Inverness to prepare for my departure. Iain Bec wanted me to help clean up his father's lobster boat for the season ahead the next day. Nathalie had asked a few people around on the Saturday night but refused to say who. It was all to be a surprise.

We had the boat finished by three, but my brother-in-law kept finding other chores for me, and it was after six before we finally got away.

There must have been seventy or more at Glencoe Mills when we arrived. My sister and her friends had been cooking up a storm and decorating the place all afternoon, Natalie MacMaster and other musicians were there, and the place was packed already. I could hear the pounding tempo of the step dance and feel the vibrations through the ground, even as we got out of the car.

It turned out that Dave from Macashaw had done most of the planning. He and my sister had decided that my birthday, my trip and leaving home were as good a reason as any for a party. Well, you'd think I was emigrating to Scotland for good rather than just taking an extended holiday and celebrating an insignificant birthday! Maureen from work was there along with a couple of the others from the office, cousins from all over showed up – the Gillies from Port Hood, Jamie and Louise MacIsaac from Judique – and there were numerous school friends and musicians from up and down the shore. My head was spinning as everyone came up to hug and kiss me. Lexie Cameron, who had been the unattainable beauty at school, even came up and asked me for a dance. I couldn't believe my luck.

Before Grandfather died, I would only come to life on stage with my fiddle or bagpipes. Otherwise, I'd be shifting from foot to foot rather shyly in a corner. Tonight, I felt like Mr Popular. Grandfather's legacy to me had been transformative. Nathalie made a speech, all about how I was setting off to discover the roots of our legendary family and how jealous she was that I was going without her, and I, for the first time ever, climbed up on stage and made an emotional speech. I was doing what almost everyone else in that hall had done or hoped to do: going back to the West Highlands to see the pile of stones where our families had lived before being evicted or starved off the land.

I was like a dog straining on its leash, ready to be off.

Chapter 13

I woke with a start to the phone ringing.

'Good morning, Mr Gillies. Sorry to disturb you but check-out is at eleven, I'm afraid.'

I blinked. 'Sorry,' I muttered, 'slept in. I'll be right down.'

God, where was I? It took me a few seconds, but as I stumbled around pulling my clothes on, I gradually remembered: the long, uncomfortable flight, the dreary bus trip.

Ah yes, I was in the Alexandra Hotel in Fort William.

Sun was streaming through the window, and I smiled. I felt well rested and keen to get going. Suddenly, all seemed well with the world.

Finding a decent coffee in Fort William proved a challenge, but it gave me time to explore the High Street. A good-looking place, but off-season and quiet. Some young men appeared round a corner, with what looked like hockey sticks over their shoulders. Shinty players, I reckoned. I checked out Nevisport for kayaking gear, then, taking advice from the tourist office, went up the hill to Three Wise Monkeys and entertained myself for a couple of hours on their climbing walls.

By the time I retrieved my backpack and headed off for the train that afternoon, I knew my way around.

My mind was whirling as the train moved off, and I was immediately glad that I had done such thorough research. The landscape was beautiful. The train conductor, speaking with a soft Highland lilt, announced points of interest along the line: 'Old Inverlochy Castle', 'Caledonian Canal', 'Locheilside' and other sights.

As she called out 'Glenfinnan', everyone on the train moved to the left to look along the famous Harry Potter viaduct, followed by the impressive monument commemorating Bonnie Prince Charlie's arrival in 1745, a few hundred metres away down on the shore. I also knew – and doubted that any of my fellow travellers did – that William Macdonald of Macdonald Tobacco, once Canada's richest man, had originated from here and had been instrumental in making McGill University in Montreal world-class. Then, I was thrilled to see Loch Eilt coming up on my right, complete with all its little islands that were rumoured to contain the gold of the '45.

I had an Ordnance Survey map on the table in front of me with all the placenames circled. I couldn't wait to see for myself where my ancestors had walked and what those hamlets they had known looked like now. On my left lay the Essan Bothy, named after the huge waterfall that tumbled down above it, and I immediately recalled a story my grandfather had told me. Once, after the Second World War, the old steam train was running ahead of schedule. The driver was a great friend of the shepherd who lived there and he thought he'd just stop for a minute and drop in with a present of half a sack of coal that no one would miss, have a quick dram and ask the shepherd about the ending of an old fiddle tune he couldn't quite get, before being on his way with no one the wiser. Leaving the boy to keep the steam up, he popped across the field and had a get-together with his friend. It was four hours later that a rescue party arrived, expecting to find a derailment or some such catastrophe, only to discover Donald

Macaskill and his friend Ewan, 'with drink taken', having a rare old time.

The scenery was astonishing. How I wished Nathalie and Grandfather were with me. The hills were white-topped from a recent snowfall and lower down, the ground glowed orange in the evening sunlight. Spring seemed close to bursting through, although the only green to be found was on the pines on the islands: tall, thin, ancient trees with deep heather beneath. There wasn't a ripple in the water. I watched keenly for a glimpse of the otters I knew lived here.

I looked away from the window, wanting to share a smile of appreciation with someone. No one was looking. They had headphones on, were reading or trying to get reception on their phones. The line was voted the most beautiful railway journey in the world and it mystified me that the only thing the passengers seemed interested in was the Harry Potter viaduct.

I'd written a list of a hundred places to visit and things to do, and the first to be ticked off was coming up: the station. My heart was pounding as the train rounded a corner. Below us was Glenshian, and unseen on the bend in the Ailort River lay the old Ardnish graveyard of Innis na Cuilce, the island of reeds. Before leaving Canada I had made the decision to go there on my last day. It would be the final stop on my pilgrimage, where I would pay my respects and attach Grandfather's precious plaque to the family gravestone.

I sighed. If only the two of us had made the trip ten years before. We would have done all this together and have picked out the scenes for me to sketch, to complete his map. I regretted my selfishness.

At last, the train pulled into the halt at Lochailort. I could envisage the faces of my great-great-grandparents waiting here excitedly for their son and his new wife returning from Gallipoli in 1916, a century ago. Only for them not to be on the train. The ramp where the cattle and sheep would have been loaded onto the freight cars was still there.

Below us was Inverailort Castle, in ruins now, with broken windows and trees growing out of the gutters. I hadn't expected that.

Then, at last, Ardnish, the hills stretching away from me to the west.

I savoured the word – *Ardnish*. The word that was held so dear to my family. I wiped tears away and swallowed hard. This place had seen a thousand years of our history.

I moved across to the other side of the carriage to see Our Lady of the Braes Church. White and glistening like new, it must have been renovated. Grandfather told me it had been semi-derelict when he was over here last. Then Lochan Dhu, where the best thatching reeds grew, black and bottomless, or so we'd been brought up to believe, with its small concrete bridge over the railway track that was once the start of the path to the various communities on the peninsula. Past the old school at Polnish, then on to the Loch nan Uamh viaduct with the evening sunshine almost blinding as it reflected off the sparkling sea. This was where I'd start my kayak trip, I'd decided. I wished I could get going right away; it had turned into such a gorgeous evening.

Big John was at the station to greet me. He pulled me towards him for a hug, his hand patting me on the back, welcoming me like a son. As we walked down the hill to his house, he told me that Amazon had been making deliveries for me all week and my room was full of brown cardboard packages. 'There'll be no room for you in the canoe,' he teased.

For the evening, Big John had organised a reunion of the Scottish contingent who'd come over to Grandfather's funeral, at the Arisaig Hotel. I brought along my maps and soon everyone began poring over them all and offering their input as to who lived where.

'That's Mullochbuie,' Ewan MacDonald said. 'That's where the postie lived.'

'And there,' Big John said, picking up a pencil and marking an 'X' on my map, 'is Sloch, where my great-uncle, the Bochan, lived. *Am Bòcan – truaghan nach do thachair riamh ris an tè cheart!*'

'See there?' Mairi Ferguson pointed. 'That's where the French frigate unloaded its gold and weapons. *Chan eil sinn a' creidsinn nach bidh ulaidh nam Frangach an seo* . . . Keep your eye open for the gold on your travels, Peter Angus. We all thought that if anyone was ever likely to find it, it would be your grandfather. It's over to you now!'

Something stirred inside me. Our grandfather had told Nathalie and me a story of buried treasure in the past – and his determination to find it. I had read a bit about it on the internet too. 'Remind me, please, Mairi,' I said. 'I'm not sure I can remember the details.'

'She's just the person to tell you,' interjected Big John. 'Mairi gave the talk to a full house at Astley Hall a few years ago.'

'Would've been about twenty years ago now,' said Mairi with a smile. 'But I think I can still remember.'

Everyone settled down for the story.

'Well, it all started with the Jacobite Rebellion back in 1745,' she began. 'Peter Angus, you will have heard of that?'

I nodded politely, but Mairi noticed my hesitation and helpfully embarked on a potted history lesson.

'Prince Charles Edward Stuart, the heir to the King of Scotland, was in exile in Rome. He had been led to believe that there was considerable support for him over here and, encouraged by Lord Lovat, MacDonald, MacLeod and other clan chiefs, and with the promise of backing from Spain and France, he and his Seven Men of Moidart landed to the north of Ardnish, at Loch nan Uamh. Clans gathered to support him at Glenfinnan, and within six months he had taken Edinburgh and was leading his army deep into England. It was at that point that things started to go wrong. The English Jacobite support that was expected didn't materialise, the French and Spanish army didn't invade England, and no funds were sent, as had been promised. The clansmen started to drift off home. The prince returned north, and on the sixteenth of April, 1746, Jacobite hopes were crushed at Culloden, ending with Bonnie Prince Charlie fleeing abroad once again.'

'You tell a grand story, Mairi,' said Big John approvingly.

Mairi turned to me. 'What did Donald Angus tell you about the Jacobite gold?'

I shook my head. 'It was always something of a fable in our house. My grandmother, Sophie, was very firm about it; she said it was a wild goose chase and closed the discussion down.'

'Well, I'm not so sure I agree with her,' Mairi said. 'From our perspective, this is where the story becomes interesting. The French gold did arrive, but not until two weeks after Culloden, when the prince was moving from cave to cave to avoid being captured by government troops. On the third of May, 1746, two French frigates sailed into Loch nan Uamh. They were called the *Bellone* and the *Mars*, I think I'm right in saying. They were believed to have 36,000 gold coins, Louis d'or, plus guns and supplies for the Jacobite army and, clearly, they had not heard of the massacre at Culloden Moor.

'Close behind them were three English naval ships, and a proper sea battle broke out, with cannon shot pounding into each other, causing a huge number of deaths and holing the *Mars* badly, below the waterline. Of course, this was tremendously exciting to everyone in the area. It's said the beach below Arisaig House and the cliffs of Ardnish were crowded with spectators – all of our ancestors amongst them.

'Anyway, the story goes that the *Mars* was beached at high tide so that emergency repairs could be made, while the *Bellone* fended off the attackers.'

Big John couldn't resist adding his contribution. 'You can imagine the scene: the ship lying on its side, carpenters hacking out the shattered planks with axes, men cutting new spars to fit, and tar being boiled to waterproof her. The men trying to splice a new mast onto the broken stump of the old one and sodden sails lying out to dry on the rocks. Above the noise of the waves the Ardnish people would have heard the cries of injured men being operated on by the ship's surgeon, having wooden splinters removed or limbs sawn off, and instructions being bellowed back and forth from the various work parties. They would be rushing to finish by the time the tide came back in. Dozens of men had been killed, their bodies washing up on the shore for weeks afterwards.'

Mairi took up the story again. 'It's widely believed that the *Mars* unloaded its cargo while it was on the shore, but history doesn't relate which beach the frigate had been repaired on, and the gold has never been found – that anyone knows about, anyway. I've heard it's buried on an island alongside Loch Arkaig or on an island in Loch Eilt – there are so many theories and rumours.'

A thought occurred to me. 'How come the locals didn't find the gold right away? Surely they would have gone straight down to the shore the moment it was safe?'

Big John shook his head. 'It's a mystery right enough,' he said. 'I know your grandfather got his hands on some diving kit when he was in the SOE during the war, and he and Gavin Maxwell tried to find it.'

I smiled, picturing the scene.

Big John paused, thinking. 'He told me that the water was deep and pitch-black; it was like looking for a needle in a haystack. He said after the war he knew where the *Mars* had been beached, but he never said *how* he knew that.'

'How much money is 36,000 Louis d'or?'

Mairi replied: 'Well, at the time I gave my talk I worked out that it was about ten million pounds.'

'About eighteen million Canadian . . . I wouldn't mind that coming into my bank account.'

'Hundreds of people have looked for it,' Mairi continued. 'My guess is that if it ever was there, it's long gone now.'

The visitors were standing up, getting ready to head home when one of them, Ewan MacDonald, a quiet man, spoke up. 'I read that a week after that sea battle, a Royal Navy ship, under command of a man called Fergussone, came sailing into Loch Ailort looking for the prince. As the boats were rowed to the shore, the young Clanranald chief gathered men about him and they fired at the attackers. The villagers fled into the hills and the thatched roofs of Peanmeanach were torched.'

'I never heard that,' said Mairi, clearly impressed. 'I thought I was the expert round here!'

Everyone shook my hand vigorously, offering to help in any way they could, and John and I stood at the door, listening to the cries of 'Good night' as they all headed down the hill.

I smiled to myself. What delightful people. Ardnish disciples all, determined to live their ancestors' memories through my expedition. None had ever lived on the peninsula, yet all had parents or close family for whom it had been home.

I was still wide awake, on Canadian time, and wondered if my host was ready for bed. 'Before you head up, I'd like to ask you something. Do you know if shinty is still a big thing over here? My grandfather always talked about it, and he was adamant that shinty on ice is how ice hockey was invented. I saw some boys in the town with sticks.'

Big John's face lit up. 'Och, I'm keen on the shinty myself,' he exclaimed, 'but it's not much played about here now. The children play more football, although there are still teams around Fort William. I remember as a boy watching a game at Roshven just after the war where your grandfather himself played. Well, it was more a battle than a game, actually. There was an Irish army unit staying at Roshven House and they wanted to have an Ireland versus Scotland game, with them playing hurley and us playing shinty.'

He paused to explain the difference between the two games and then took up the story again. 'The Irish were in the area as "the enemy" for a big training exercise with the SOE. There had been a bit of bad blood between them and the SOE, something to do with a boat being unnecessarily capsized and the Paddies having to swim for the shore, almost breaking the ice as they did so. The senior officers agreed to the game, as they thought it would be good for the men to have a day off, let off steam and to get the Irish and SOE socialising.'

He thought for a bit then added, 'Well, it didn't go to plan.'

'What happened?'

'Your grandfather himself was over at Roshven House, and he agreed to get an SOE team together. He said he would get sticks from the town . . .'

Big John was relishing the story; there was no thought of going to bed any more. 'Will you have a dram, An Gillie?' he asked, then bit his lip. 'Sorry, I hope you don't mind me calling you that. I know your grandfather did when he talked about you.'

I shook my head. 'No, go ahead. I like it, reminds me of him. And yes, I'd love a dram.'

My host poured me a glass and went on with his tale.

'The word went out about the big game, and a week later there must have been two hundred spectators at Roshven Farm, many of them soldiers from Inverailort Castle and Arisaig House. General Stewart from Kinloch Moidart was declared adjudicator. He stood up and read an amusing piece from the old rules of shinty. It went something along these lines: "There shall be no limit as to numbers, no differentiation between a stroke made with a hand, foot or caman, no minor matters such as boundaries, time-keeping or off-side; the arrival of fresh contingencies and the departure of the unsatisfied."'

I laughed.

'As I remember it, a sergeant major was given the role of team captain. There were eleven on each side and they were to play forty-five minutes each way. The Scots would play with their shirts off. Someone had come up with a couple bottles of illegal whisky, Irish potcheen or something, and it was passed around before the game began.'

I laughed at this. 'Was this usual back then?'

He nodded. 'Apparently so. I was with my mother, I remember. We stood with our backs to the sea and the graveyard. The field was on a slope; the goalkeepers probably couldn't even see each other. Anyway, it soon became apparent that this wasn't going to be a normal game. It was a grudge match,

An Gillie, blood and gore. We watched with our hands on our mouths as battle got going. The Irish tactic, once they started losing, was to take out the opposition at all costs. At half-time, the general called the team captains to him, and there were raised voices. Then the captains addressed their men and threatened to call off the game, such was the bruising and bloodshed. The Scots had two men hit on the head by sticks, one of whom was concussed and had to be carried off. Everyone had bleeding shins, and a couple sustained cracked ribs. Your grandfather got a goal, I remember. The Scots gave as good as they got, with a man throwing away his stick at one point and thumping the Irish goalkeeper. He said that he had every right, that every time the general's back was turned the goalie hit him with his stick!'

Big John's face was glowing with delight as he remembered the game. 'The Scots won 5–1, but the Irish refused to shake hands afterwards, such was the bad feeling.'

And with that, we retired to bed.

I woke up late the next morning, refreshed after a deep sleep, with the sun streaming through the window. I pulled back the curtains and marvelled at the magnificent view: yachts were dotted around the harbour and what had to be the island of Eigg glowed amber in the distance, its highest hill, the Sgùrr, visible at the southerly end. There was a delicious smell of bacon from downstairs.

After breakfast Big John and I headed down to Arisaig Hotel, where they were expecting us, to sort out the kayak rental. Tomorrow I'd have a lesson and then take a trip out into the bay. I was really looking forward to it; kayaking looked pretty easy and fun. If it had been the summer at home,

I'd have had a practice run there, but it had been minus ten when I left.

We were armed with a tape measure, as I needed to know exactly how much space there was for a sleeping bag, a waterproof bivvy bag, a foam mat, cooker and gas as well as provisions for two weeks along with my maps, notebook and other papers. I'd ordered a ridiculously expensive tent on the web; my host had laughed when he'd seen it, telling me there was no chance I'd fit it in. As it was, even squeezing in the rest seemed an impossible challenge.

I'd agreed with the hotel to rent the kayak for £200, with a further £200 deposit which would be refunded when I returned the craft intact. My instructor, Sarah Harper, would meet me at the marina tomorrow morning, then on Monday morning I'd be picked up from Big John's house and dropped off, along with the kayak and my gear, at the Loch nan Uamh viaduct. This allowed me three full days before departure for a shopping trip and sorting my gear out.

Later, Big John dropped me off at the two Ferguson sisters' home on his way to a doctor's appointment.

The women were keen to talk to me. 'Our great-uncle died in the arms of your great-great-grandfather at Gallipoli,' Mairi said. 'They were on a sniping mission that went wrong.

'Our family used to live at number two Peanmeanach, right next door to Donald John and Morag, and our great-aunt shared this very house we're sitting in, in her old age, with your great-great-grandmother and her daughter-in-law Louise after the war.'

I had to concentrate hard to follow who was who and the timeline, but they made me so welcome, and their tales of our shared history chimed with me. They were excited about a visitor who was expected any minute, a cousin of mine. I'd heard the name, but didn't know much about him. Hamish Mackenzie was my third cousin, the same age as me. We greeted one another, interested to compare notes. He was a stocky man, with black hair and a dry sense of humour, and a fiddler like myself. His great-grandfather Owen was Louise's brother. We hit if off immediately and agreed to meet at the Arisaig Hotel for a beer that evening.

'There's a ceilidh tomorrow,' he said. 'Why don't you come along? I'll lend you my fiddle and you can give us a tune? Bring Big John along – he likes a night out.'

I was happy to agree. Later, after supper, Mairi Ferguson and I went across the road to visit my distant cousins, Danny John and Mary Gillies. Big John joined us too, and I noticed they called him Iain Mhor.

Everyone was full of reminiscences. There wasn't one of them who wouldn't have come with me on my adventure if they could. Over tea and drop scones we pored over hundred-year-old photographs of formal-looking families, rather improbably dressed in smart dresses and suits, lined up on the doorstep of their Peanmeanach houses. When I asked about their attire, Mairi told me that the photographer would have provided it.

Then, using my photocopy of the centenary map, the old people slowly moved their fingers along, pointing out landmarks such as the path to Sloch, the well at Peanmeanach and where the peat was cut above Feorlindhu.

'I'm going to do some sketches,' I said, a little shyly, 'to transfer onto the map when I get back.'

They nodded their approval. 'Donald Angus would have liked that,' Big John murmured.

As we talked, the weather outside turned from sunshine and clear skies to black clouds, and soon we had torrential rain hammering against the window, which then turned to bright sun again in minutes. It didn't seem worthy of mention by my hosts. All the people I met there, apart from Big John, whose uncle lived at Sloch, were from Peanmeanach. I already knew a lot about the village but I probed for information about the folk from Mullochbuie, Lower Polnish, Glasnacardoch – where were they now? When were the crofts last lived in? I'd discovered for myself that the history of these places was sparse even now and that, when this generation had gone, they would take their knowledge with them.

'My great-aunt Mairi and your great-great-grandmother Morag became inseparable over the years,' Mairi told me. 'Always to be found together collecting shellfish, which they stored in hessian bags until the next Clyde puffer called by, or collecting crotal for dyeing the wool, or working the loom to make tweed. Mairi didn't get too involved with the animals, mind – that was Morag's job – though at clipping and lambing times everyone worked together. The people at Ardnish were very poor, except during the war, strangely enough, when they were in a relatively good position compared with some. They had peat for fuel, they grew vegetables, they had a cow and hens, and plenty fish from the lochs and the sea. The poor city folk had their ration cards and that was that.'

'Can you remember anything more about Morag?' I asked.

'She was tiny, well under five feet.' Mairi smiled. 'Her back was bent over from digging and cutting peat, her face brown and wrinkled from being out in the rain and the sun all day. Well into her eighties, she could still do a good day's work clipping sheep or even cutting the peat. She never stopped being busy – always fixing fences in the worst weather, weeding the garden or cutting reeds for the roof thatch. She was a nightmare in the house, though. She'd pace around like a cat, could never sit down and relax. Her two sons were both much taller than her, and your grandfather, Donald Angus, would tower above her like a giant. Her husband, Donald John, who lost his leg in the Boer War, would sit outside the house weaving baskets or playing his chanter while his wife would walk past him, not a word of complaint, with load after load of seaweed on her back to fertilise the potatoes.'

'What a woman.'

'She was inseparable from Broch, her collie dog' – Mairi frowned – 'but then, she and animals were as one. Even the Ferguson dog, which was renowned for its ferocity, would approach her when she came for a visit, sideways like a crab, tail wagging and smiling, before lying on its back for a tickle.'

'Once when Morag was over at Roshven in the garden,' Big John added, 'a man from Roybridge arrived by boat from the station at Lochailort with a delivery for Mr Blackburn: a young, fully trained collie. Mr Blackburn kept the dog in the house for several days, making a fuss of it, and getting it used to its new surroundings before finally letting it run around in the garden. That was the last he saw of it. It ran the forty miles back to its previous owner within a couple of days.'

'How on earth did it find its way back?' I asked. 'After being on a train and a boat?'

'Dogs are wily . . . and so are their owners,' Big John said. 'I know of a man on the island of Mull, a bit of a rogue, who sold his dog several times.'

I could sense that the old folk were tiring now, whereas I was wide awake. I took my leave and made my way down to the pub to meet Hamish. On the way, I passed a young man who looked as though he'd had a terrible accident. His left cheek had been split open, quite recently it appeared, leaving a sinister red scar like an exaggerated, lopsided smile.

My cousin was already at the bar when I arrived. Settled by the fire with our pints, I asked him about the man I'd just encountered.

'Did he get knifed?'

'Ah, that's Iain, a nephew of Big John as it happens. Quite a funny story, actually, unless you were him of course. About six weeks ago he was driving his estate car back from the Fort, over the Mhuie early in the morning. There was snow on the road and he hit a stag. The car wasn't too badly damaged and the deer was lying across the road. Not wanting to waste the meat, he dragged the stag into the back of the car, planning to gralloch and butcher it for the freezer when he got home to Arisaig. Anyway, it turned out that the stag had only been stunned and it came to in the car. Can you believe it? Iain had his collie with him and a terrible commotion broke out, with the collie barking like fury and jumping back and forth between the front seat and the back, nipping at the deer. Meanwhile, the stag's thrashing around and Iain's trying to avoid the antlers while holding the dog back and stop the car careering into the loch . . .'

By this stage Hamish and I were crying with laughter, him struggling to continue with the story.

'He gets out, rushes around to the back of the car, opens the boot and tries to pull the stag out by its hind legs but an antler got caught in the padding of the back seat or something. So he reaches forward, manages to release it, and immediately the antler whips back and catches the inside of Iain's mouth. All of a sudden he's being played like a salmon on a fly and the collie's still jumping all over them, determined to get involved.'

Both of us were laughing so hard by this stage, Hamish could hardly get his words out. 'Being a crofter,' he continued, 'he has a knife, so he manages to get it out of the sheath. He then stabs the stag in the neck, like a man possessed, and the beast finally stops moving.'

He paused to swig his drink. 'But that's not the end of it. A Rabbie's Tour minibus pulls up, the collie's still barking like mad, Iain's car is halfway across the road, the stag is lying half in, half out of the car, and your man has got a massive gash across his face, most of his front teeth missing, and the snow around him scarlet with blood. The driver gets out, then all his passengers get out, Italian tourists, to see what is going on. Some take photographs while Iain is trying to explain what happened, but he can't get the words out properly. He's sounding like a madman. So the bus driver calls the ambulance and they leave him bleeding in the snow with his mad dog.'

'A true story,' he chuckled.

'I believe you,' I gasped. 'Fancy another pint?'

Chapter 14

The next morning, a crisp one, I showed up at the marina at nine o'clock sharp. A slim, rather serious-looking woman introduced herself as Sarah Harper, looked me up and down – I was in my shorts, track shoes and lightweight waterproof jacket – and said nothing.

She had two kayaks with her and she began to talk me through the basics. 'I gather you have a big trip ahead of you,' she said, unsmiling.

I nodded.

'Have you done much of this before?'

I shook my head. 'Er, no.'

'Well . . . it looks easy, and it is easy on a day like today in a bay, but if something goes wrong, like the weather changes and you get swept out to sea, then you have a problem.'

I felt a little afraid of her no-nonsense manner. She clearly wasn't impressed with my plans.

'Okay, let's go through the basics: how to put on a spray deck, how to lower the little rudder, which end of the paddle is which . . .'

As she talked, I paid close attention and she began to ease up a bit, even smiling a little towards the end.

'It will all come with practice,' she reassured me. 'We'll start with some easy stuff in the bay then go out to sea – if you can handle it.'

We set off and had an uneventful trip in and around the numerous sandy islands in Arisaig Bay – the Skerries, she called them. I had to paddle up into gushing water between rocks as the tide came in, then kayak across the main stretch, which was more like a fast-flowing river. Then we went out into the ocean and practised riding the waves onto the shore and out again into the breakers. My heart was in my mouth a couple of times as it seemed certain I was going to capsize. But the kayak smoothly rose and fell despite what seemed to be a huge swell, and gradually I began to find an easy stroke rhythm.

'It's much easier to learn when you're not laden down with twenty pounds of kit,' Sarah warned me.

Big John was at the jetty when we got back. 'How was it?' he asked.

'I feel like I'm tackling the Tour de France with stabilisers,' I replied. 'And it was much colder than I'd anticipated.'

We all went into the café. I reached into my pocket and drew out my kit list. 'Would you mind looking this over, Sarah, and telling me what you think?'

When I returned to the table with coffee and cake for three, I could tell she was not happy.

'A few things missing here, Peter Angus,' she began. 'Dry suit, or at least a neoprene jacket, gloves, insulated hat, sunglasses, sun cream and moisturiser. The reflection of the sun at sea will burn you to a crisp, especially with your pale complexion. Spare paddle in case yours floats off? Waterproof matches and case for your mobile phone? Oh, and dry bags, one for each of the compartments and another for between your legs in the kayak. You can put a bag behind you under the net on the top of the kayak, too. Every spare inch will be needed.'

She looked up at me and must have seen my crestfallen face. 'Look, I'm being cruel to be kind. You can't go on a two-week kayaking tour at this time of year without the proper kit. The water is the same temperature as it was in February, about six degrees. You'd only last fifteen minutes at the most if you capsized in that waterproof jacket you're wearing.'

'Okay. Can I get what I need back in Fort William? I'm heading off the day after tomorrow.'

She shook her head. 'Not everything. Glasgow or Edinburgh perhaps, certainly by mail order. I'll give you a couple of website links.'

I agreed to meet her again at nine on Monday morning, and walked dejectedly with my host back to the house.

'We can go to the Arisaig Hotel and ask for another paddle,' offered Big John. 'You will take her advice, won't you?'

I nodded miserably. Sarah must have thought I was a complete idiot. I cursed my slapdash planning on the equipment front. I should have done far more technical research in those long, dark Cape Breton evenings when I was immersed in Ardnish history. I had looked up sea kayaking, and seen the pictures of people in Hawaii or wherever, laughing and splashing each other with their paddles.

I was even more miserable when I looked up the kayaking websites and totted up the cost of the items on my new shopping list. It was unaffordable. A drysuit cost £525, a neoprene jacket £275 ... And a delivery time of three to five working days to the Highlands. My whole trip would have to be delayed by a week. I had figured on spending about $1,500 on renting my kayak, buying a sleeping bag and a good gas cooker, but now, adding in all the other gear, it was turning into more than twice that. This was becoming ridiculous.

'Tea?' Big John asked.

We stood companionably in the kitchen.

'She thinks I'm mad doing this trip by myself,' I admitted, 'and stupid for not having researched it and coming properly equipped. Maybe I am an idiot? Perhaps I should just walk around the peninsula instead.'

'Nonsense, Peter Angus,' Big John snorted. 'It's Health and Safety gone mad! Just stay within a five-minute swim from the shore and you'll be fine. It's not as if you're canoeing around the Hebrides.'

I went into my bedroom and began ripping the packaging off all the deliveries I'd ordered in advance, then laid the stuff out on my bed and stood back. I could see straight away that I'd ordered far too much, including the $500 tent, and that there was no space to fit it all in. What a waste of money. I still didn't even have the packets of dried food, a pot to boil water and eat food from, not to mention all the other stuff. Sarah said I had to take at least two litres of fresh water. Well, that wasn't going to happen. I was in the Highlands after all. When had getting water been a problem here?

I resolved to do what Big John said and hug the shore. I'd ignore Sarah's advice and do without the dry suit or neoprene. Thank goodness my sister wasn't here to say her bit. I knew she'd be demanding I follow my instructor's advice.

Chapter 15

Big John was glad to see me going out for the evening and declined my invitation to come along. He told me, with a glint in his eye, that he was an early bird and I'd been keeping him up, so he'd be glad to see the back of me for the evening.

The band was going strong when I arrived at the hotel. I bought myself a beer and settled down to enjoy the music. It was a quiet and soulful tune, with people chatting happily over it. I could tell they were fine musicians, though.

After a while they took a break and Hamish came over to join me. 'You still happy to play?' he asked.

'Yes, but your guys might not know my tunes,' I replied uncertainly.

'Och, they might just, you never know. Alan on the banjo and Jack on the box there have been across to Celtic Colours and knew Buddy and Natalie MacMaster a bit. They've heard you play at the Interpretative Centre in Judique, too,' he said with a cheeky grin. 'We've been doing some research on you.'

I launched into 'The King George Medley' followed by 'David's Jig', my bow just flying. The band joined in and matched me; I couldn't shake them off. Hamish had got his hands on another fiddle and we led each other on.

The word must have got out that a fine session was taking place: by eleven that night you couldn't fit another person in the room. In my whole day in the village I'd hardly seen anyone under fifty and now the bar was packed full of young folk. Where had they all come from?

'Hamish, will the folk here have seen step dancing, do you think?' I asked.

'They'll have seen Michael Flatley on TV probably, but not the old Highland equivalent. Let's give you a go at that.'

My feet had been itching to get going since I arrived at the bar, despite wearing the wrong shoes and being soaked in sweat from cranking out the jigs on the fiddle. I wondered at the fact that the people in Arisaig, Nova Scotia, had kept so many of the Highland traditions going long after they were lost in Arisaig, Scotland.

Hamish and his team started off slowly and gathered momentum, clearly enjoying the experience. My feet flew as the audience clapped time with the tempo and I finished to a round of whoops and applause. It was exhilarating to have such an enthusiastic audience.

To my surprise, Sarah joined me at the bar afterwards. I hadn't noticed her in the crowd. 'Ah, the intrepid Canadian explorer,' she said wryly.

My face fell.

She burst out laughing. 'Oh, don't worry! You can certainly dance and play music a lot better than you kayak. I'm most impressed.'

I bought her a glass of wine, and we found a quiet corner. 'How amazing that you're related to Hamish,' she said. 'He's a rogue, but a fun rogue.'

'He is,' I agreed. 'But tell me about yourself – what brought you to Arisaig?'

'Oh, I came up for a summer job as a kayaking guide after university and found myself staying on. It's my dream job in my dream place. I work as a carer in the old folks' home in Mallaig during the winter months.'

'Good for you,' I said. 'I'd like the kayaking bit.'

'Are you planning to get a dry suit and some good gloves before you set out?' she asked.

I hesitated before replying. 'I'm afraid not, Sarah. I can't afford all the kit and I can't delay my trip for a week. I need to get going.'

She shook her head disapprovingly. 'Well . . . you'll need to be especially careful when the tide turns, and at the entrance to the rocky beach at Sloch. You'll be fine if the weather holds, of course. I hope it does, for your sake. Let's take a look.'

Our heads were bent close together as we looked at the Met Office website on her phone. 'Okay,' Sarah said. 'It's good for the first few days, with just the odd shower, then a low front coming in at the end of the week.'

'I should be at Peanmeanach by then,' I said.

'Calm seas, Peter Angus, that's the most important thing, until you get the hang of things.' She finished her drink and got to her feet. 'I'd better head off. I've to give someone a lift back home to Morar.'

We said our goodbyes and I joined the other musicians at the bar.

'How did you get on with Sarah?' Hamish asked. 'Gorgeous, isn't she?'

'She is. She's been so helpful with my trip. Took me kayaking today, out on the Skerries . . . She thinks I'm a clown, though.'

'She's got a boyfriend,' Hamish said ruefully. 'A fisherman called Tom. Works on a huge boat out of Peterhead, away for weeks at a time, down to the Falkland Islands or across to the Grand Banks. We don't see much of him over here . . . Everyone fancies Sarah . . . Hey, you were talking for an hour with her. She's only ever given me five minutes!' He laughed. 'Maybe she doesn't think you're that much of an idiot.'

The next morning, I went with Big John to Mass at St Mary's at ten o'clock. The church was enormous. Big John told me on the way that Lochaber was the only place in Britain that stayed Catholic during the Reformation, hence Cape Breton being Catholic, too.

The priest was visiting from Eriskay and the elderly congregation was delighted to have some Gaelic in the service. I noticed Sarah going up to communion with a man who must have been at least forty, but by the time I left after Mass she was gone. I was glad. I didn't want to meet her fisherman.

Later, I caught the train to the Fort for supplies, taking with me my empty backpack and an enormous list. My research had been revelatory. I discovered that a two-week supply of dried food took up a considerable amount of space and cost far more than real meals, but you only needed to add boiling water. Energy bars, Compeed for the blisters I'd be bound to get on my hands and pills to disinfect the water despite Big John striking this off the list as nonsense. Toilet roll, baby wipes, an insulated beanie, a wind-up charger for my phone so I could listen to audiobooks and music at night. My pack was bulging as I got the bus back that evening. There was no late Sunday train.

That evening, Big John and I sat in the sitting room surveying the floor. Every inch was covered.

'There's no way I'm getting all this in the kayak, is there?' I said.

'Barely half, if you're lucky,' Big John agreed. 'How about if you walk to Peanmeanach and leave your pack there? You could tuck it away in one of the ruined houses. Then you'd have something to look forward to. Clean clothes, for a start.'

I brightened considerably. 'That's an excellent plan. I'm meeting Sarah tomorrow, so I'll ask her if she'll run me along to the path in her Land Rover and delay the kayaking for a day.'

'I don't know what you'd do without us, Peter Angus, your logistics department,' Big John said with a smile.

Chapter 16

Next morning, I walked down to the shop and found Sarah already there, leaning against her blue Land Rover. Its trailer held my blue kayak.

'You okay with the change of plan, Sarah?' I asked, once I'd explained things.

'It's fine,' she replied. 'Early April isn't too busy for me. There's mobile reception on the ridge, so if you called me on your way back, I could pick you up at the end of the day. It's only fifteen minutes down the road.'

'That's really kind of you,' I said.

'If it wasn't for the fact I've promised to help a neighbour move house,' she went on, 'I would've come with you. It's a fantastic wander. My dog would love it.'

We chatted about her collie, who trotted happily at her heels, on the way. 'His name's Cranachan,' she said. 'Cranachan, meet Peter Angus.'

As I heaved the pack onto my shoulder, I began to feel really excited about exploring Ardnish. Sarah offered advice about the route as we walked. 'It's well trodden, so you can't go wrong. Just head due west for two miles towards Eigg – you can see it from the top of the ridge – then follow the track that curves left down the hill until you see the white beach and the ruins. You'll have a lovely day.'

I had the map in front of me. Out of sight over the rise was the white church of Our Lady of the Braes, which had been used by the Ardnish people. It took a good six or seven hours for the older people who lived at the end of the peninsula to walk there and back, not just for Sunday Mass but also funerals, christenings and so on. On the right was the Polnish school, now a holiday home, and five hundred metres on, out of sight down on the shore, was Upper Polnish, which comprised two ruined houses. Grandfather's map said one was once inhabited by Dhileas MacDonell, a widow, and the other by Angus and Mairi Gillies, their seven children and a servant girl. Gillies was listed as 'cottar' in the 1851 census. I'd googled the word when I was back in Port Hawkesbury: 'a farm labourer or tenant occupying a cottage in return for labour'. Dhileas may have been Mairi's mother, I remember my grandfather saying. Perhaps some of the children would have stayed with her.

As I walked, I considered the enormous amount of thought and time Grandfather had spent ensuring the map was accurate. I imagined the constant correspondence between people over here and back in Nova Scotia, getting the facts right. Throughout the map, beside each name he'd written a letter, either 'A', 'G' or 'C', which indicated whether the people had gone to Australia, Glasgow or Canada. If it was 'C' for Canada, that invariably meant near Pictou, Arisaig or Cape Breton. Grandfather had written in red the names of the inhabitants who were there at the time of the 1851 census and blue for those in the 1891 census. There had been massive emigration between the two dates, so most of the names were in red. Those poor folk, it must have been terrifying for them to board a ship and embark into the unknown.

Grandfather had also marked houses with an asterisk and barns with a hashtag on the centenary map. The very old houses would have had a fire in the floor in the middle of the room and a hole for the smoke in the roof through the reed or heather thatch. These were known as 'blackhouses'. With tiny, glassless windows, they were dark and incredibly smoky. The later houses were made with mortar and had chimneys, and it was these gable ends that were last to fall, so they were easy to identify. The barns were the same size but had neither windows nor chimneys. Grandfather had explained that the earliest ruins were just circles of stones on the ground, so it was impossible to differentiate which had been dwellings.

Walking the path high above Upper Polnish, I could make out buildings down by the shore in the distance. I didn't plan to veer off the path now and go down to the settlement; I'd be camping there tomorrow night. My walk to Peanmeanach and back with my supplies was already going to take me five hours as it was.

The track was dry at first and I made a fast pace. It felt good to stretch my legs. I hadn't been trekking for a while and certainly not with a 40-pound pack. It was warm and I soon had my jacket off. Then came quite a boggy section, where my boots immediately filled with mud, followed by a scramble up a steep hill with long stretches of quite smooth rock which sloped sideways. My great-grandfather, with only one leg, had ridden back and forth on this route for forty years. How did my ancestors manage to get ponies up here? It was so treacherous. I peered around looking for an old route but couldn't see anything and resolved to ask Big John later on.

I'm sure I'd been told that the local council had two roadmen working on the Ardnish paths a hundred years ago. Right now, it didn't seem likely – they could barely be described as paths.

I was on the ridge at last, sweating and panting. But it was the view that took my breath away. I could see for miles. I sat on a boulder and pulled out my phone. There was reception up here but nothing along the shore at all, apparently, so I knew I'd have two weeks without email, WhatsApp, anything. I had decided not to put my headphones on during the day. I wanted to hear the birds, the wind, the waves, the soundscape of nature, truly immerse myself in Ardnish.

My French-Canadian grandmother, Sophie, had been as interested as her husband in the old ways and used to tell us what the local people ate, wore and made in the villages. From what she said, I was pretty certain that in the old days the *cailleachs*, with their hessian sacks full of shopping from the Arisaig van that stopped at the track end, would have sat on this very boulder to catch their breath. They'd have caught up on gossip from the town, the hatches, matches and dispatches, and be keen to tell the others in their village the news by the fireside later. If a baby was born at night in Morar, the people at Sloch would know by the following evening. There was no need for the internet in those days. My great-grandmother Louise had been the bush telegraph of her time!

It was 10.30 a.m. I wanted to call my sister and tell her everything. At one o'clock here it would be nine in the morning with her, so I decided I'd call on the way back. I knew she would be dying to hear what it was like over here.

I set off again along the track. The hill was barren; I'd expected it to be covered in sheep. Grandfather had kept a thousand ewes on the land when he was at Laggan. He had two sheep pens, which he called fanks, one near his house and another at Mullochbuie. I'd be there in two or three days, I thought, with a thrill of anticipation. It lay just over the knoll on my right. I decided not to sneak a quick look as I didn't want to spoil everything. It would have been like peeking through the wrapping at presents under the Christmas tree.

Overhead I could hear ravens caw. They sounded close but I couldn't see them. Then, high in the sky, I caught sight of a melee. The ravens were mobbing a much larger bird – an eagle, I guessed – with a distinctive white tail. The eagle deftly twisted and turned, with the ravens constantly harassing it. Then it dropped something that looked like a fish and the ravens swooped down. Poor thing, I thought, losing his lunch.

Later, standing on a ridge, I found myself looking southwest. Peanmeanach was a mile or so in front of me but still out of sight. I marvelled at a beautiful big loch, Loch Doire a Ghearain, down on my left, which, rather oddly I thought, means 'Loch of the Horse's Hoof'. I'd heard there were small Arctic char and brown trout to be caught in there.

Sometimes Archbishop MacDonald or his brother Colonel Willie would come to visit Donald John, and they would row back and forth all day, fishing, until their bottle of Long John whisky was empty. Well, there was no sign of a boat now. It would be there somewhere, I knew, as Grandfather had told me that no one ever removes a broken boat.

I'd never fished, but suddenly felt a huge wish to do so. I wondered if Big John had some line and hooks I could trail behind my kayak. I could barbecue a fish at night. How wonderful would that be?

I searched around for the path to Sloch. It was clearly marked on Grandfather's map but not on my Ordnance Survey map. There was no trace of it at all. I sensed that there was a huge advantage in doing this journey before the bracken got going. Already the shoots were poking up. In a month, the smaller ruins and everything around them would be hidden. I hadn't considered the bracken issue before now. I'd been lucky with my timing.

The path dropped down steeply over a stream, a 'burn' Grandfather called it. The burn – I said it aloud, '*Burn!*', rolling my Rs like the Scots did – was impassable after a recent storm, so I had to skirt it and cross higher up. Then into the oak wood. The path here was pretty, cobbled almost. Bluebells were thick on the ground, young leaves were sprouting on the oak, and there was silver birch with its ridiculously bright green foliage.

At last, I could see Peanmeanach in the distance. My heart jumped and my eyes welled up with tears. It felt ridiculous, but I was coming home! I'd seen photographs of course, but nothing had prepared me for its beauty. One building stood out, intact, a green corrugated-iron roof and two chimneys. That would be the old post office, where Donald John and Morag had lived until she moved away at the end of the Second World War after his death.

However, the field was a shock. In my childhood dreams it was fenced, drained and full of haystacks and sheaves of oats. Centuries of backbreaking work by my family with the plough behind a pony and hundreds of tons of seaweed and manure from the cowshed carefully spread to get the best from the harvest had created one of the best fields in the West of Scotland, in my mind. Now, it was chest-deep in rushes, the massive drains were blocked, and the air of neglect was almost unbearable.

Mairi had described my old family house as 'the bothy'. I asked her what she meant by that and asked her if anyone could stay there. She had nodded. She felt that bothies were a good idea; landowners allowed the Mountain Bothy Association the use of them in exchange for their maintenance.

I laid my pack down in front of the bothy and looked inside. This was to be my base for two or three days, in a week from now. It was rough, but it had a big wooden platform for a bed and a fire. I'd need wood, I realised. I allowed myself just twenty minutes to look around the village, knowing there would be plenty of time later. I decided I'd leave my pack in old Mairi Ferguson's ruined house, buried in the nettles. I guessed she wouldn't mind. I counted eleven houses and checked the map. There they all were, with the names of the last inhabitants alongside.

When we were teenagers, my sister and I promised each other that we'd have a swim at the beach in front of the village the first time we visited. Well, she might have forgotten, but I couldn't phone her without telling her I'd gone in.

'OH MY GOD!' I shrieked. The water was freezing. I forced myself to keep going; even fifty metres out, it was shallow. What had possessed me to do this? I could have lied to Nathalie and she'd never have been any the wiser. I threw myself at an incoming wave and did three or four frantic breast strokes before lurching to my feet and legging it back to the beach.

Never again, I swore as I dried myself off with my sweater. A couple of hikers were standing in front of my house as I sat on the sod, hauling on my clothes. They must think me a total idiot. My teeth wouldn't stop chattering. Anyway, what were they doing in front of *my* house? I suddenly felt proprietorial and hoped nobody else would visit when I returned next week.

Half an hour later found me sitting on a rock beyond the field, five hundred feet above the village. I was delighted to find I had reception. WhatsApp clicked through, and there was Nathalie, beaming, the baby over her shoulder.

'Peter Angus! How are you? What's it like? Is everything okay?' She was so excited, the words were tumbling out. 'I'm so glad to see you. I've been wondering how you've been getting on.'

'Guess what?' I cried. 'I'm at Ardnish. Want to see the view? It's unbelievable.' I switched the camera over and did a sweep from left to right with commentary.

'Okay, so that's An Stac and Roshven, the two mountains in the sun. If I have time after my kayaking I want to climb them. Over the ridge is Grandfather's old house at Laggan. I haven't been there yet; I'll go in about ten days. Then in front is the village. Can you see the field in front, then the village, that crescent of sand and the sea beyond? Can you see it, Nat?'

'Hold the camera still,' she shouted. 'I can't see too clearly. Ah, wait, yes, just one house, with the green roof?'

'Mmm, that's as good as I can get it. To the right of the village is another bay. That's where the school is that Grandfather went to, Glasnacardoch. And in the distance you can see the islands, Muck and Eigg. Can you see them?'

'No, there's too much glare on the sea.'

I switched the camera round so she could see me. 'Next time, maybe. I went swimming, and it was colder than January in Cape Breton, for sure. And I've seen an eagle. The weather's so perfect, Nat! I can't wait to get going in the kayak tomorrow.'

'You went swimming! Well done. And does the post office still have furniture in it? Did you find Morag's high-walled garden? What about the machair and the spring flowers?'

'Jeez, Nat. I haven't paid that much attention. But I promise I'll take hundreds of pictures when I'm next here. I'll call from this same place in a week, if my battery charger works. It's a wind-up thing. I won't have any reception until then, so bye for now!'

Nathalie blew kisses at me and I hung up.

'I love my sister,' I said aloud.

I bounded up the hill, heading back. It was so good not having the pack with me. Besides, I was ridiculously excited about seeing Sarah again. It was so kind of her to come and retrieve me.

Reaching the high point, I dialled her number, feeling stupidly jittery. 'Sarah?'

'Is that the intrepid Canadian?'

'The one and only!' I grinned. 'Listen, the reception's really iffy up here, but I'll be at the lay-by by three. Is that okay?'

I thought I heard her say 'fine', but I couldn't be sure. I picked up my pace and almost skipped back towards our rendezvous point. But I was going too fast and took a heavy tumble going down the steep, rocky part, the one I'd thought would be a real challenge for ponies on the way out. I quickly scrambled to my feet, but my backside, legs, elbows, arms and hands were all thick with mud.

Sarah was there when I arrived. Her collie came leaping over the top of her as she opened the door. It rushed over to me, and I stooped to scratch it behind the ear.

Sarah was doubled over with laughter. 'Wait!' she gasped. 'I need to take a photograph of you like this. You've got mud all over you, even your face.' She showed me the photograph. I was filthy from head to toe.

'And you're not getting in my Landie like that, so you'll have to take your trousers off.' She started laughing again as I stripped off, self-consciously.

'Do you have time for a cup of tea?' I asked. 'At the marina?'

'I'd love to, but you can't go in there with no breeks on,' she said, grinning. 'People will talk if I arrive with a semi-naked man. I'm really sorry but my shift at the care home starts at five.'

I wished the drive had been longer. Sarah was full of questions. Which house had my family lived in? How come it had taken me so long to come over, if I was this interested?

I made the mistake of confessing I was quite weary.

'Tired!' she scoffed. 'After that wee stroll?'

Later, I lay in the bath and thought about her. I loved the way she teased me and made me laugh. Then, armed with a cup of tea and toast, I told Big John about the eagle and the ravens.

'A white tail, eh?' he said. 'That'll be a sea eagle. You'll see golden eagles, too, this week. They nest on An Stac and the Rum Cuillins. I often see them soaring on the thermals. There are a lot of sea eagles now. In fact they're becoming a real pest to sheep farmers, especially in the spring when they take the lambs. There was an article in the *Lochaber News* about a crofter I know in Glenuig who has those little black Soay sheep. Well, he lost almost all his lambs to sea eagles. If your grandfather were farming on Ardnish now, he'd be outside our MSP's office making a real stink about it. The conservation bodies are so powerful, it's hard being a sheep farmer.'

The next morning, Sarah came to the house to pick me up. My new friends were all there to see me off, even Hamish. I was touched. We drank coffee outside the house.

'I should be at Peanmeanach next Monday night, I reckon, six days from now,' I said.

'Great. This good weather is due to hold until then,' said Sarah.

She had written out the tides for the fortnight ahead for me on an A5 card and laminated it at work. I was so touched at her thoughtfulness.

'It makes a massive difference,' she said. 'Around here, the tide runs at four knots, which is as fast as you can run. So go with the tide; it's so much easier.'

Big John handed me fifty metres of fishing line, some brightly coloured lures all wrapped around a piece of wood so they could be tucked into the netting and his folding saw, saying, 'You'll use this more than anything else, I bet. Take it from me, Peter Angus, a good fire at night will make you happy.'

Chapter 17

We packed the kayak on the beach. I had two dry bags: one contained my sleeping bag, bivvy and blow-up mattress to go in the front compartment, the other, food and the cooker for the rear. I had a clear bag for my map, notebook and phone that I could put under the netting at the front and wore my little binoculars around my neck.

I was nervous. The heavily weighed-down kayak felt incredibly unstable as I wobbled off into the swell. Sarah and Big John waved from the foreshore as I set off, just as the Harry Potter steam train clickety-clacked across the viaduct above us.

Today, my plan was simple: get used to the kayak, head west along the north face of Ardnish, have a good look at the caves from the sea and then go to Upper Polnish, my first night's pit stop. I'd take a break after a couple of hours to rest and stretch my legs at the base of the cliff below Mullochbuie. The tide was going out in the morning and would turn at 2 p.m. I was interested in experiencing the difference of paddling with and against the tide; it couldn't really be that massive, could it?

Ard nam Buth was the first settlement on my route. I found a beautifully situated Victorian cottage, with boats and kayaks dotted along a private bay and stooping oak trees on the knoll behind. Grandfather had said that two of the daughters of the MacEachen family who lived at Mullochbuie were maids at the house in his grandfather's time. Other family members worked there too, building paths and landing stages. There were hordes of MacEachens in Mullochbuie in 1851. The people from this clachan suffered terribly from tuberculosis, I'd read. Up behind the house I wanted to have a look at the stone circles. The map said that there had been two old blackhouses here. I decided to walk back over from Upper Polnish later, knock on the door, and see if the owner would mind my looking around.

Then into Loch Beag, the 'Little Loch'. It turned out to be a narrow fjord, quite dark, with no pasture. But to my surprise I found a well-used camp: a wooden building with a green tarpaulin roof and a polytunnel behind. It could only be seen from the sea. There was a rubber dinghy and a number of wrecked boats on the rocky beach, although I couldn't see any people. The hillside was dotted with clumps of young, purple-flowered rhododendron. Big John had told me what a menace this was on the west coast; he feared the beautiful barren hillsides would be thick with it within a generation.

Then there was Upper Polnish, which seemed to have obvious ruins. I looked forward to coming back. Even with the sun out, at eleven in the morning, it was in the shade. I guessed it would be a month or more before the sun would rise high enough for the rays to reach the village.

I paddled hard, grateful for the spray deck; I would have been soaked and freezing without it. Even in a calm sea, water still splashed over the kayak now and then due to its being so heavily laden.

I was heading due west along the north shore of Ardnish, to below the old settlement of Mullochbuie ('ridge of yellow' in Gaelic). I could see caves along the base of the cliff. They were on Grandfather's map but not the Ordnance Survey one, surprisingly, as Loch nan Uamh actually means 'Loch of the

Caves'. I couldn't wait to explore them tomorrow. Looking up the cliff face, I couldn't see any attraction in living up there whatsoever. There were three houses, a sheep fank and several outbuildings at Mullochbuie. Why?

I thought I'd power myself along and see if I could get to the end of the peninsula before the tide turned, so, leaning forward, I really went for it. Within minutes, I was sweating and breathing hard, my shoulders aching, the kayak slicing through the water. I felt exhilarated. *I can definitely manage this trip*, I thought to myself.

I rounded the point into the bay at Sloch, marked *Port an t'Sluichd* on the map, thinking I'd really got the hang of this kayaking. I spotted a round, seaweed-covered rock that was submerged by the swell one minute and the next protruding twenty centimetres out of the water as the tide receded. With a couple of strong paddle strokes, I found myself precariously balanced on the stone. Then the tide lifted and I was off again. It was fun. I decided to do it again.

Of course, that didn't work out well. In the space of a second, I tipped over, my body twisting awkwardly as the weight of the kayak trapped me in. I floundered, trying to get my elbow under my body to lever myself up, as every few seconds the sea rose and covered my head. After several attempts to release myself, my eyes smarting from the salt water, I was becoming really scared, beginning to doubt whether I'd be able to release myself.

It was probably only two or three minutes, but it felt an age before the tide finally lifted the kayak just enough for me to move my body into the right position, pull the spray-deck strap and roll forward and out.

The water was only knee-deep. I waded to the shore, dragging the kayak behind me. I pulled her up onto the stones, shaking with nerves from the scare, my legs like jelly. I pulled off my sodden shirt and spread it on a boulder. Looking back at the rock, only twenty metres away, the sea was calm, just rising and falling gently. It didn't seem possible that I'd just had such a scare.

It took me a good ten minutes to stop shivering, even though the sun was warming me up. If Sarah could have seen me now, she would have thought I was an idiot. I remembered Hamish's words to me in the bar: 'Never underestimate the chance of things going wrong at sea. They always do.'

I found it hard to imagine a less inviting harbour to bring in a boat: rocky entrance, an exposed bay and a wall of seaweed cast ashore by the waves and wind. I dragged the kayak further away from the water and checked to make sure my dry bags had done their job. I perched on a rock overlooking the old village, and dug out my sandwich, Tunnock's wafer and can of Irn-Bru. 'A traditional Scottish treat,' Sarah had said as she handed them to me. As I ate, I watched a drake desperately keeping two other drakes away from his girl. As he chased one off, the other made a move, back and forth, back and forth.

I felt more settled now; my heart had stopped racing and there was warmth in the sun. I took out my sketch pad and pencils, and began to draw the hamlet. There were primroses everywhere, even a clump of daffodils by one of the ruins, in a large, grassy field, with low houses in surprisingly good condition at the far points of a triangle, each accompanied by two or three outbuildings, perhaps a steading for a cow or two, and a smaller storage building, which I'd read was sometimes called a *cleit*. The Bochan had left here in 1920, his great-nephew had told me a couple of days ago.

I lay back on the smooth rock and shut my eyes. I felt content. Only six weeks ago, in the depths of a bitterly cold

Canadian winter, I'd been miserable: Grandfather was dying and my job was unrewarding in so many ways. Pushing away the memory of my idiotic spill in the bay, I thought, *look at me now*. I could never have envisaged taking a month off, visiting Ardnish and having this adventure. Grandfather would have been so pleased.

I stood up, stretched, packed things away and headed back towards my camp for the night. It was still an hour before the tide started to come in; I'd be against it for a while. It was a different kettle of fish from this morning, with a tide of four knots, and despite paddling as hard as I could, I made slow progress. My merino undershirt was still damp from the capsize, sweat from the exertion was pouring down my chest, and spray was splashing my face and running down the inside of my jacket. It was a lot less enjoyable than on the way out.

Eventually, I found an inlet amongst the rocks and bobbed there for a while to recover and wait for the tide to turn, wishing the sun reached into this chilly, dark, north-facing corner. Then, amongst the seaweed, I spotted a movement as a small, brown flat head poked up, with ridiculously long whiskers. Then, behind the first, another – much smaller. A mother and baby otter. They looked at me from perhaps only ten feet away. I didn't dare blink for fear of scaring them off. But they decided I was no threat, and I watched, transfixed as they cavorted in the seaweed and clambered on the rocks, once appearing with a small fish that the mother let the youngster eat. I was entranced. It wasn't until they disappeared for good that I realised quite how cold I was. I should really get to Polnish and get a good fire going. All the way back, I smiled. What a treat I'd just had.

Upper Polnish faced south but it also faced the hill, meaning there was no view and no sun. I was surprised to see quite how many buildings there were, but I could only properly identify one house with windows and possibly two others. Walking round, I counted ten ruins, a couple of which would have been their *cleits* for storing food, and several obvious cattle byres. Grandfather had marked Allan Morrison, Mary MacDougall, Ranald and Sheena MacDonald and their nine children as the people living here at the time of the 1851 census. He'd also labelled a building at the bottom of the hill with the word 'smokehouse'. I guessed the fishermen must have smoked herring and other fish here.

I settled on the best house, the one furthest east, for the night and set off to find some wood for the fire. Then I pulled out my most appetising food of the week: masala curry with rice, naan bread and a sachet of real coffee. Perfect. It would be dark around eight, so after I finished my meal and washed up in the stream, I had some time for exploring.

I had decided, before travelling to Ardnish, that I wasn't going to just show up at a settlement, do my drawing and leave. I set myself a mission for each community I visited. I would try to find out where they cut their peat, where they grew their potatoes and oats, where their spring was for good water and the fank for the sheep and cattle.

Here, I saw that the peat was cut from an acre of flat ground to the south-east, perfectly square, sunk down by two feet. I could see where a trench had been cut to encourage the water to drain but had blocked up and become boggy. The lazy beds were there too – raised ridges two metres wide to allow potatoes to grow on drier ground. Grandfather had said that potatoes were the only food that people could live on entirely and the Highlanders, like the Irish, came to depend on them almost exclusively for food, which was why, when there was a blight just before 1850, there had been starvation.

I searched for a fank but found none, nor could I find a noost for a fishing boat. I clambered over the knoll and down the steep slope through the oak woods to the well-hidden, green-roofed house. I shouted, but no one appeared; no dog barked either. There were two old buildings, but I didn't want to go snooping too close to someone's home. I decided to carry on, following the railway line to the Ard nam Buth peninsula.

'Hi there!'

I turned around to see a young man emerging from the house. He introduced himself as Matt and invited me to have a beer with him. His girlfriend Hannah came out to join us and we sat on a rock overlooking the water. He was very knowledgeable and showed me the old buildings behind his house where he stored his sports equipment, including a kayak. Turned out he had kayaked everywhere around here.

'Where are you spending the night?' he asked.

'Upper Polnish,' I replied.

He frowned. 'You should stay here,' he said. 'That old village has a *buidseachd* on it – a spell.'

I asked him what he meant.

'The last witch of the west lived there. Mary Campbell. She was betrothed to a man who was from the village, but a week after the wedding he went missing, never to be seen again. His family emigrated, leaving her alone. She lived on for a further thirty years and struck fear into the area with rumours of her powers. If you crossed her, she would put a curse on you. But women would still go to her if they couldn't have a baby or if they wanted an ailment cured. People would leave money or a gift on a rock for her in payment, and if she didn't think it was enough, they would hear her shout after them as they ran away up the track.'

He paused, took a swig of his beer. 'Do you believe in ghosts?'

'Er, no, I don't think so,' I replied.

'Well, what finally happened is that she cursed a woman from Glen Mamie for some reason. That winter, the woman died, and her two sons who were away in the army during the Peninsular War came back on leave. They discovered their mother dead, having been cursed by Mary Campbell. So they decided to come and kill the witch. But as they approached, with their swords drawn, she knew what they were coming to do and called out to them as they approached, "*Ma chuireas tu làmh rium, gheibh thu bàs!*", which means "Touch me and you will perish". They set fire to the thatch, cut off her head, and sat it on the stone lintel above the door. Then the brothers returned to the army in Spain. They were killed on the same day as each other and buried out there.'

I shuddered. 'Which house was hers?'

'It's the one to the east, furthest from the beach.'

I gulped. That was where I had made my camp.

It was practically pitch-black now. I took my leave of my new friends and had to find my way back to the village, stumbling over tree stumps and boggy holes despite the torch on my phone, my mind racing with images of the tale I'd been told.

I carried my gear away from the house to a flat dry spot, two hundred metres closer to the shore, and endured the most restless night of my life. Again and again, I was woken by screeching. It sounded so human. I was pretty certain that it was owls up in the oak trees, but my mind was imagining Mary Campbell coming to get me. I gave myself a strict talking-to about not believing this nonsense and tried to drop off to sleep, but every screech had me jerking awake again, quivering in panic.

I was hugely relieved when dawn broke. I decided to have a quick look around and then head off pretty damn quickly. This place was too spooky for me. I had had every intention of staying put for a while to decide on which building would form my pencil sketch but here, instead, feeling like a cheat, I took a few photos with my phone, to draw up later.

In the house I had meant to camp by, I found the metal blade of an old peat spade. I picked it up and took it out to scrape off the moss on a flat stone lying on the ground by the door. It had initially seemed as if there was an inscription, but actually there was nothing. Disappointed, I dropped the spade to the ground and heard the distinctive clang of metal against pottery. Kneeling down, I pushed my hands into a clump of young nettles, pushing the soil away from a white bowl and using the blade of the spade to lever it up.

I leapt backwards in horror. *Oh my God!* It was a skull, the eyes full of soil, the jaw missing. I dropped it like it was red-hot. The hair at the back of my neck was bristling and I had broken into a cold sweat. I hated this place.

It can't have taken me more than three minutes to jam my gear into the kayak and start paddling, shaking like a leaf throughout. I paddled as fast as I could to a point of land opposite which lay in full sun, where I could have some breakfast, listen to some music and calm myself down.

I was muttering furiously to myself about what a hellhole this place was. First, the ignominious dunking, then the discovery of the skull. My immediate reaction was to head back to the road, leave all my stuff in a heap, and walk to Lochailort station. I could get a flight home first thing tomorrow morning. But later, after my first coffee, I thought I'd give it another couple of days. I would climb to the top of the hill to get reception, call Sarah and ask her to come and pick me up. I could spend more time with her. I sighed. I'd only just begun my trip and this was the second time I wanted to abandon it all and fly home.

And yet, an hour later, I was warm, had downed a second coffee, was full of ready-to-eat porridge and determined to stick to my itinerary. My pride wouldn't let me quit over this. How would I explain to Big John, Nathalie and Sarah that I'd been frightened into quitting by a ghost story?

I clambered back aboard my kayak and set off, pulling up later on a small, east-facing stone beach in the shadow of the Ardnish cliffs. Well hidden from above, I'd seen the caves here the day before. There were three, close together, none deep. I reckoned four people could stand in each to get out of the rain. One had a proper pond in it and another had a three-foot-high drystone wall across its face, thick with moss, looking like it had been there for ever. What on earth was that there for? I wondered.

As I dragged my kayak high up the beach, I recalled Grandfather telling me about hunting for the Jacobite gold and how he'd spent days looking for it on the north side of Ardnish. Maybe it had happened right here? Mind you, Grandmother Sophie had always said it was just a wild dream of his.

As I clambered along the base of the cliff, I saw a sudden movement. It took a moment for my eyes to adjust, but there, not far from me, stood a hind and her calf, so graceful. They stared at me for a few minutes, all three of us stock-still, apart from their twitching ears, before they slowly moved off.

I didn't get around the corner for a while and when I did, it seemed to be a dead end. There was no sign of a route up the cliff face without a rope and harness. There was a tower of rock, about twenty-five metres high, like a giant finger pointing to the sky; however, behind it, hidden, I found a twisted sliver of a grassy staircase where the most sure-footed would be able to make the ascent to flatter ground. It would be impossible to see from a boat.

I wandered back and forth along the shore and decided that this was the only route that would allow me to get up to Mullochbuie. The rocky shore was completely exposed to the weather; there would have been no chance of the people living in the crofts above having a boat here.

I gathered the two bags and struggled up the steep face. The community here must have lived the hardest life on the peninsula. There'd be no fishing, and from my earlier walk along the track to Peanmeanach, all I had seen on the hill was bog and sparse heather growing between the cracks in the rocks.

I reached the top after a hard, almost vertical climb and stood, squinting in strong sunlight after the gloom of below. The cold wind was no longer swirling around as it had been at the bottom of the cliff; here, it was more of a warm caress. I dropped my bags and set off to explore.

Mullochbuie seemed to me a glorious sanctuary, an entirely different world from down below, with a lush grass field of about ten acres. Leaning back against a fallen oak, I took out my pad and began to sketch. The most easterly ruin consisted of two chimneys made with mortar and facing each other, a length of cast-iron pipe lying on the ground and no sign of stone between the two chimneys. Had there been a prosperous family here, around 1900 perhaps, who started building a modern farmhouse and never completed it?

An impressive Scots pine stood above the far chimney, and fifty metres beyond that lay the remains of a perfectly formed blackhouse with a byre. Above, a track snaked into the hillside, as good as the day it was cut.

A pair of geese were nesting in the rushes at the far end of the field, the noise of their honking carrying across the five hundred metres that separated me from them. I wandered towards them, marvelling at everything. *This place is an idyll*, I thought, although I reminded myself that it would be less so on a stormy, wet January night. There was another ruined building, south-facing, which sat under a ten-metre-high rocky ridge with thick-trunked, short oak trees, bent over from the wind. I stood on the ridge and looked to the north, down into Loch nan Uamh. The scene of the naval battle. The locals would have had the perfect view of the action from here, all those years ago. Mairi Ferguson had described it so vividly that I could envisage the ships below under full sail, the bodies and timber in the water, and hear the boom of cannon. It was a stirring image.

Another two hundred metres on were buildings so exquisite I began to feel tears well up: two attached cottages that, apart from having no roof, were as good as the day they had been abandoned. They still had lintels above the doors and windows and beautifully constructed rounded walls. They would each have had a fire in the middle of the room even at the time of the 1891 census. Beyond these cottages, I found a byre set against a rock.

I wandered further up the hill to find the best place to capture it all on my sketch pad. Grandfather often spoke about this place. He had a fank here, and at clipping time there would have been five hundred ewes. A couple of shepherds – Gibby and Jimmy, I think he called them – used to help him gather and clip. It was lambing time now; I'd seen some from the train along Locheilside. This field would have been full of mothers and their newborn in Grandfather's time. What a sight it must have been.

I settled on a grassy hummock and began to sketch the two cottages. I knew Nathalie would love to see the drawing. She would badger me, asking if they had a garden or any old horse tack or kitchen implements still around. It seemed tragic to me that the village now lay empty and derelict, the children, sheep, cattle and horses that I would have seen here a hundred and fifty years ago long gone. I fancied that two old men would have been sitting on a wooden plank in the sun as their dogs would run towards me, barking at the stranger, and women would call to each other as they planted crops in the runrig up the hill.

The people who had lived here had been named MacEachen, MacDonald and MacVarish, according to Grandfather's map. He had noted that they spoke only Gaelic, even as late as 1891. Twenty-four people lived at Mullochbuie in 1851; forty years later, only thirteen.

The descendants of those MacEachens, MacDonalds and MacVarishes lived in cities now: Toronto, Glasgow, Melbourne. Like me, they put on their suits and went out to an office to stare at their computer screens all day long. They had two point two children and most would have forgotten their history. Only their names remained to tell of their proud ancestry.

The last thing I sketched was the fank. The first thing that caught my eye was the size of the stones in the wall. I tried to lift the end of a corner one at the entrance. Bracing my back, I bent my legs and strained. It moved not a centimetre, as if it were mortared to the one below. I reckoned it would have taken at least four strong men to lift it into place. I stood back and marvelled: were the people much stronger back then? I couldn't believe they would have a block and tackle, and how would they have shifted the rock across the field? It was astonishing. I guessed that my grandfather would have worked here;

his hands would have been on this enormous boulder a hundred times. My grandmother would have been helping in the fank, too. Maybe they sat here and had tea when they'd finished. They would have been my age, younger even, desperate to make ends meet, to eke out a living from the poor ground.

I went to fetch my belongings and set up camp. I was exhausted after my sleepless night, but unlike Polnish, this place had a good atmosphere. I wanted to make the most of the warmth of the sun before it sank down over Eigg to the west, and then enjoy my hot meal of tomato soup followed by chilli con carne with rice.

But sleep didn't come quickly. My mind kept turning over, reflecting on this new experience and my feelings about it. Aunt Maggie had recently said that I needed to be more self-aware. I'd nodded, not entirely sure she meant.

I took a long, hard look at myself. From when I was ten years old I'd become used to the fact that I would not do well at school. Since then, I'd expected to remain a poorly paid junior clerk, and I certainly didn't expect the sort of girl I was interested in to be interested in me. Why would she be? I was a loser.

But now, after absorbing the words of my grandfather's eulogies and hearing from the Scottish visitors what great people the Ardnish Gillies were, my mindset was shifting. I *was* capable of doing well at work, in fact I was good at it. People warmed to me, I could tell a story, and they wanted to listen to me. I liked Sarah – could I be good enough for her? I began to feel that perhaps, just perhaps, I could be.

Chapter 18

Twelve years earlier

'Why did you leave Ardnish, Grandfather?' Nathalie asked all of a sudden. 'You seem to love it so much.'

'Don't get him started,' I whispered, keen to get back to my computer game upstairs.

But he was off. 'Well, year after year, I'd get back from the auction mart in Fort William, having sold our entire year's work. I would be hugely disappointed by the low prices we'd got for our lambs and calves. It was September 1951 – I remember the date exactly as your grandmother was pregnant with your aunt – and I'd just returned. I looked at her across the sitting room and just shook my head. She could sense my disappointment without my having to say a word. She came over to me with tears in her eyes, put her hands on my shoulders, and said, "What's the point, Donald Angus? What's the point? We'll starve here. We can't live on dreams anymore."'

He looked at us sadly. 'She'd had enough. It had been a terribly wet summer, the hay was ruined, and she was due a child. We sat late into the night and talked. There was no doctor within a day's travel, the house needed a new roof, winter was coming, and there was no money left – not a penny. She was due to give birth around New Year and was terrified at being so cut off. Her father was a wealthy man, and he'd promised to set us up if we went to Cape Breton. I remember it as if it were yesterday. She went onto her knees and pleaded, "For me, Donald Angus, for our baby – we need to go!"'

Grandfather bent his head and rocked back and forth as he remembered. Nathalie rushed over to comfort him.

I sat, squirming uncomfortably at seeing him in that state.

'I loved her, you see, and that overruled my love for Ardnish. So I agreed to emigrate.'

'Sounds like you did the right thing,' Nathalie soothed.

'In case I changed my mind, she started packing her clothes and few treasures straight away. It only took an hour. She hardly cast a backward glance as I rowed her down the loch. Where I saw the rugged beauty of home, she saw only hardship and misery.'

'Did you not leave together?' Nathalie asked.

He shook his head. 'Your grandmother took the train down to stay in Glasgow. I was to follow in a month once everything was sorted and we would sail together. I went to see the auctioneer in the town to arrange a clearance sale, lined up four men to help, and between us, we drove the animals the full length of the peninsula from Sloch to the road. The sheep and cattle were loaded onto the train from the ramp at Lochailort. Then I had a week to kill before I was due in the city, where we were booked on the *Nova Scotia* liner. I had no intention of sitting around in Glasgow at a loose end for a week, that was for sure, so I walked around the peninsula over two days, trying to store everything in my memory. Who lived in which house, the names of the children who were at school with me at Glasnacardoch, who was buried where at the back of the big field at Peanmeanach. There is no inscription or gravestone, but I knew that Johnny Bochan was behind the massive boulder at the west end, buried with his favourite collie, which died the same day as himself. The famed fiddler Lochie MacVarish was under the oak tree ... who else but me would know these things?

'The houses at Peanmeanach were all becoming derelict by then, even my parents' house, the old post office. There were holes in the roof and a sheet of corrugated iron had come off. Mairi Ferguson's house had no thatch left at all, and the wooden beams, window frames and doors had been burned by a group of riveters laid off from the Glasgow shipyards after the war. They'd come up with rucksacks full of whisky to drown their sorrow the previous Hogmanay.'

Grandfather paused to sip some whisky. 'I do have a funny story, though, from when I was home on leave from the army ... Would you like to hear it?'

I brightened up. Grandfather's army stories were always his best.

'Well, there was a stag about five hundred yards from Peanmeanach; we could see it clearly with the glass, which is what the Lovat Scouts call a telescope. My grandfather – your great-great-grandfather – decided to lay down a challenge. "We could do with some of that venison, young Donald Angus. Could you kill him without a rifle? And I do have my old Lee Enfield, before you ask, but no bullets left." I asked if he had heard of anyone achieving a feat like that before and he said yes, but only the once. I accepted the challenge. At dawn the next day, I put on my father's old tweeds – always the best thing for concealment on the hill – smothered my face and hands in peat, and had a quick squint through the glass to see where the stag was. Once I'd spotted him, I headed along the hill so that I was downwind of him. In the heat of the summer's day, I knew he might well lie down and doze off at around three in the afternoon; it's funny how they all seem to do that.

'He was a fine fellow with eleven points on his antlers, resting in a hollow high up on the hill above the village. So, armed with my father's five-inch gralloching knife, I crawled the last twenty yards, an inch at a time, and was just gathering myself to leap on him when he suddenly jumped up and was off. He must have caught my scent. I don't know who was more startled, him or me! I cursed him, before heading home to the ribbing from my family, who had watched it all.

'My grandfather told us about the Danish man who had pulled this off just a few months before. They were keen to see if I could measure up. The man's name was Anders Lassen. He was a well-known hero in the SOE, given many prestigious missions.'

'So the stag was free and the family went hungry?' Nathalie asked.

'Tell the truth, I shot him a few days later, when I came back with some other soldiers under the pretence of fieldcraft training. Having all these men was ideal for dragging the eighteen-stone weight of him back to the village. We hung him in an unused blackhouse for my grandfather to butcher; he fed the five people of Ardnish for weeks. Nothing went to waste.'

Grandfather paused, caught up in his reminiscing. 'That reminds me of the skate story . . .'

'Tell us!' Nathalie cried, keen not to go to bed yet.

'When my grandfather was a boy, he and a friend walked along to the Singing Sands, stripped off, had a swim, and then lay on the rocks to dry. On the shore on the way back, close to home, they found a skate, full of eggs, stranded on the rocks. They wrapped their shirts around her sting and dragged her along. She must have weighed fifty pounds and was awkward to carry, but they were determined. My grandfather was so pleased; hunger was always an issue and he hadn't had skate before. And this one was huge! They had to build a fire outside, lay a sheet of metal on it, and cook it that way. My grandfather wanted to invite everyone over to share it. In the end, there were only a few of them to eat it, but that skate could have fed fifteen. It was delicious, I was told.

'Anyway, to get back to my last days on Ardnish . . . After Peanmeanach I then walked down to Sloch. That's where I got the farm tenancy when Jimmy MacDonald had a terrible accident and broke his back.'

This was new to Nathalie and me. 'How did he break his back?' I asked.

'Now, that is a story. A cow had managed to work its way along a grass ridge with a cliff both above and below her. She couldn't, or rather wouldn't, reverse, and it was too narrow for her to turn around. She had been there for two days and was becoming more and more distressed, so Jimmy made the decision to climb down to her, until he was on the ridge at her head. He tried to push her backwards, but she wasn't budging. So he worked his way alongside her, but she then moved towards the edge of the ridge. All of a sudden, her weight pushed him off, and he dropped eighty feet, landing on his back on the rocks by the water. His wife saw everything. She was elderly, though, and couldn't do much to help. But she rushed as best she could forty-five minutes along the shore to get help at Peanmeanach.'

Nathalie had her hand to her mouth, her eyes wide as Grandfather continued.

'Father Angus, the priest, my uncle, was at home and he took charge. We put the boat in the water. Then he, Aunt Mairi, my mother, grandmother, Mrs MacDonald and I rowed up the loch as fast as we could to where he lay, with the tide already lapping at his coat. He was unconscious, thank God. There was much discussion. We were worried that he had a broken back or neck and a move might kill him. The wife was in tears, and Uncle Angus said the last rites, just in case. It was then we looked up and watched that damned cow happily backing up to a place where she could turn around and get to safety all by herself.'

'No!' Nathalie's eyes were wide. 'What happened to Mr MacDonald?'

'Well, with much effort and manoeuvring, we managed to get him into the boat and lay him as carefully as we could across one of the seats and our knees. Uncle Angus rowed the two miles to the jetty near Inverailort Castle. Shepherds and stalkers came rushing down, made a stretcher, and took him up to the train to Fort William and the Belford Hospital. Sadly, it was soon clear that he would never again be fit enough to run the farm, and so, even though I was very young, the factor on the Arisaig Estate let me run the farm as a trial, with my grandmother's help for a year. He was worried that I was too young and my grandmother too old and we wouldn't manage, but as it turned out, we did just fine for a while. Grandmother was remarkably fit and strong, and I was determined to show everyone I was capable of managing. But then the war broke out and I went off to fight, leaving her to manage by herself.'

'So after the war and Granny left for Glasgow and you'd sold the animals you went to join her?' Nathalie asked. 'You went to Glasgow then?'

'Almost,' Grandfather said. 'After the Singing Sands and Sloch, I went over to Mullochbuie and climbed along the cliffs to have one last look for the French gold. I always dreamt that I would find it, buy Ardnish and build a proper house for your grandmother. I stayed there for three days, looking everywhere.'

'Do you have an idea where it is?' I asked eagerly.

'Well,' he continued, 'there are two stories: the first is that the gold is buried along the north shore of Loch Arkaig; the second is that it is on one of the islands in Loch Eilt. However, my belief is that it's still on the south shore of Loch nan Uamh, on Ardnish land.'

'Why do you think that, Grandfather?' I urged him.

Grandfather suddenly seemed to clam up. 'Just a hunch,' he said simply. 'If I knew where it was, I'd have found it by now. Ach, I was probably wrong anyhow. Your grandmother always said I should forget the whole thing, that it was all a ridiculous fantasy.'

'So, after that, you went and joined Grandmother, headed off to Cape Breton and now we're here,' said Nathalie.

'Yes, but first I went home, dug a hole in the ground, and shot the dog.'

'Oh no!' exclaimed Nathalie.

'I had to. She was old, she couldn't come on the liner, and she wouldn't have been happy without the sheep to work. It was the hardest thing I ever did.' Tears welled up. 'I put the rifle in the grave at the same time.'

We sat in silence for a while as Grandfather composed himself, then Nathalie made us some tea.

'We left all the furniture in the house, all the tools in the shed, my old grey Massey Ferguson at the fank at the back of the house. There never was a key for the door: I just shut it and walked away.'

His words chilled me.

He continued: 'I had wanted to stand on the high point over Peanmeanach and play a few tunes on the pipes, but I was too emotional.' He shook his head. 'I went over to Arisaig House to see the landowner, Miss Becher, and tell her I was off, then to the village to say farewell to my family and friends.'

'Must've been tough,' I whispered.

'I had one more stop to make, thinking I'd never be back. I got off the train at Lochailort, left my old army rucksack at the inn, and walked down to the old graveyard on the island in the Ailort. I knelt at the grave of my father, who I never knew, and that of my grandfather Donald John, and I apologised to them for being the one who left the peninsula.'

'You had no choice,' Nathalie said quietly.

'Perhaps. But, oh, that train journey to Glasgow was miserable. After a thousand years and more of our family living on Ardnish, it was me who failed, me who walked away. The last of the famous pipers of Peanmeanach.'

He turned to me. 'I've written a pipe tune, Peter Angus – "The Gillies' Last Farewell to Ardnish". Perhaps you would play it at the Antigonish Highland Games in July? And if you ever go to Ardnish, play it for me there again.'

I nodded, unable to form words.

'Grandmother was right wanting us to come to Cape Breton, though, wasn't she, Grandfather?' asked Nathalie.

Grandfather paused, then smiled at my sister. 'Yes, she was, darling, yes, she was. And now, you two, it's time for bed. Remember to say your prayers.'

Chapter 19

I woke suddenly. Where was I? Ah, yes, Scotland, Ardnish, in my sleeping bag. The stars and moonlight were so bright that I could almost have read a book. I tried to go back to sleep but couldn't. Instead, I let my mind drift back into the past, thinking about everything Grandfather had told me about this remarkable place. He had been good friends with the very last inhabitant, John MacEachen, who ran the post boat up to Smirisary via Laggan, Roshven and Glenuig, and was known as 'Post Ardnish'. Grandfather had also talked fondly of Allan J. MacEachen of Inverness, Cape Breton, who had been Deputy Prime Minister of Canada. His family had come from this humble hamlet.

I tried to imagine cattle here. The Ardnish men were famed drovers, collecting cattle from across the Highlands and driving them south. During the eighteenth and nineteenth centuries, when the Royal Navy ruled the oceans, the vast number of sailors would get their protein from salted beef. From May each year, the drovers would visit the crofts, bargaining for cattle – often only a couple at a time – since many of the communities were very poor. By July they would have a herd of hundreds of beasts, as Grandfather liked to call them, and they would be driven south to Falkirk, or even as far as London.

As I lay there, I could see shadows moving in the field. I tensed, then relaxed. Just some deer grazing. They would be hungry at this time of year, before the grass got going. A hind was only twenty metres away. Her young were dashing back and forth, playing. It was a joy to watch them.

Much later, I woke again with a start. Light clouds were scudding across the sky from the north. My first thought was the kayak: had I pulled it far enough out of the water? I got dressed quickly and made my way down to the shore. My foot caught on something, and I tripped head first down the steep bank. Luckily, the ground was dry and I didn't slide for long, but I was quite shaken.

I knew immediately that the sea was far too wild for kayaking. I'd have to stay put and explore around here for the day, so I pulled the kayak further up the shore and headed back up for breakfast. As I climbed, I looked for the object that had caught my foot. There it was: a round, shiny black rock, about the size of a field hockey ball, balanced on a ledge. I bent down to pick it up, but couldn't. Why was it immovable? I cleared the grass and turf around it, and made a discovery. It was metal and substantial. I'd need a tool to dig further.

I went up to the old village, full of curiosity. How could I get the thing out of the ground? I had all day, I told myself. There was no hurry. I boiled water to make coffee and porridge, peered around the old buildings, then went across to the old fank and found a metal fencepost to help with my task. I had a heck of a job breaking the wire that went through it, but I succeeded and was soon back at the hillside. It was precarious work. I was perched on the ledge, digging and scraping the soil away from my treasure. It soon became clear what it was: a cannon, over a metre long, with a mount of some sort that would have allowed it to swivel left to right.

'Wow!' I exclaimed. Surely this was from the *Mars* – evidence, surely, that she had beached down below! My heart was beating wildly. Perhaps the gold had been unloaded here.

As I scraped away with my rudimentary tool, I could hear my grandmother's words of warning when I was a boy: the gold was a dream, a myth, a waste of time ... Grandfather had spent many days looking for it, but had had no success. He'd certainly never mentioned a cannon.

It took me until mid-afternoon to dig it out, and when I finally succeeded, I found there was no way I could lift it. It must have taken at least two strong men to get it here, and it couldn't have been easy carrying it up this slope. I reckoned that if they'd dropped it, the weight of the thing would have broken their legs and sent them tumbling down to the rocks below. My guess was that they dumped it here, realising how dangerous it was to continue and knowing there was no use for it. It just wasn't worth the risk.

I was weary and shivering with cold, both from the sweat of my exertions and from being in the shadow of the hill. I decided to hold off going down to have a really good look around the caves and beach until tomorrow. It was quite a clamber to get down to them, and right now I just didn't have the strength.

After some tea, a change into my dry shirt and a warm-up for half an hour in the sun, I decided to look around before I got my supper going. Grandfather had marked areas near here as 'summer pastures and shielings' and 'deer butt' on his map, in the long glen that ran down towards Sloch. I decided to take a wander down that way.

My route took me up the curving path at the west of the Mullochbuie field, above the two chimneys of the surprisingly modern-looking ruin, to a point where it intersected the main Peanmeanach path. From the main route above I would never have been able to find it, but from that point it was only a couple of hundred metres to the Sloch turn-off on the right. Again, it was a difficult track to locate, but once I was on it, I was surprised at how well-formed and beautiful it was, at the beginning anyway, where it skirted a circular lochan.

As I dropped down the hill, I lost my way and found myself sweeping back and forth across the glen, trying to find the path again. I found the deer butt first. Grandfather had described it perfectly: a chest-high circle of stone with a two hundred-metre field of vision towards the narrow top of the glen. According to local lore, the Clanranald chief would stand in here with two black powder muskets loaded from the muzzle and a couple of men with two deerhounds would hide in the rocks behind. Ardnish men and women would be paid to do a wide sweep of the peninsula and the deer would come galloping up the glen, with the laird ideally positioned to take a shot or two. If a deer was injured, the deerhounds would be released and the chase would be on, often over many miles, until the stag would eventually be brought down.

Nathalie hated this story. I remember her asking Grandfather, years ago, whether the people resented being used in this way. Grandfather was pragmatic in his response. He told us that the people were paid and that money was scarce. The deer were a menace, as they'd eat the crops, and, of course, there was meat to share and plenty of it. He explained how plenty could go wrong: the gunpowder could get wet, or the laird could miss his shot. That meant no meat for anyone.

The shielings were easy to find from there, although only one was clearly visible now; the stone walls of the others must have grown over. The stones in the walls didn't have the same tight fit as those in the permanent settlements. The building was half the size. I paced out two metres by three. It would have been used as a temporary camp for a couple of months in July and August.

I understood that women and children would bring their cattle here over the summer, to fatten up so that hay and oats could be grown on the good ground down below to provide feed for the winter. I remember being told once that after the Battle of Culloden, the clansmen retreated to their shielings to hide from the English soldiers, and concealed their claymores in the roof thatch. This shieling seemed like the perfect hiding place to me. I had hoped that I could dig around and maybe find a sword or two nearby. But there was no chance of that; I'd need a metal detector.

I sat on a boulder at the entrance to the ruin and unwrapped the Penguin biscuit that Big John had given me – he'd insisted that the orange ones were the best. I tried to imagine the people here in 1800. There were four buildings on the map. There would have been cattle grazing all across the hillside, a couple of lads with sticks trying to prevent the odd one from wandering off, maybe a cow with a halter at the side of the building getting milked, and some hens and dogs – always dogs. Perhaps a goat tethered to a post, which would be slaughtered sometime soon. There would be laughter from the burn where the mothers washed clothes. Children cavorting around too, maybe stacking stones. A *cailleach* sitting outside the shieling opposite, knitting. Everyone would have had bare feet. I shivered at the thought. The men would be away, fishing, in the army, perhaps on a cattle drove; shielings were the women's domain.

As the sun faded, it was time to go back and cook some supper, then get some rest. I was cold and hungry, but it had been a good day.

The following morning, the wind had dropped somewhat. I carried all my gear down to the shore and collected the metal post to use as a tool. I knew the odds of finding further clues as to where the gold was were slim, but thought I might as well try to narrow the possibilities. I wanted to pinpoint where the boat could have been beached, a spot that would have allowed the cannon to be carried up the bank. After all, there could have been no reason why the French or indeed the locals would have put it in a smaller rowing boat and landed it further along the shore, could there?

And if there were a large number of French dead, which it seems from the historical records that there were, wouldn't there have been a large grave? I concluded that the possibilities for the treasure were: in a cave under the cliff; in amongst a mass grave on an area soft enough to dig down; under a mound of stones; or perhaps, though unlikely, it was carried up onto the plateau in full view of hundreds of the locals who would have turned out to watch.

I created a channel to drain the flooded cave and moved stones to create a metre-deep cavity. Nothing. Then, in a boggy area, I scraped out a test hole with my hands in spots I'd identified as two possible mass grave sites in the peat. By late afternoon, my arms were aching, my fingertips raw and my clothes black from the mud. I shook my head, feeling something of an idiot. I had gold fever. Of course I wasn't going to find anything.

I clambered back into the kayak and set off for Sloch. The wind had died down, but the waves were bigger than I was used to and I was heading into the tide. Before long I was wet and freezing. What a waste of a day it had been, crouched under these cold, north-facing cliffs, digging pointless holes in the ground with my useless fencepost.

When I finally arrived at Sloch, it was almost dark and I was exhausted. I forced myself to have a wash in the freezing burn, then climbed straight into my sleeping bag, too tired to eat so much as a biscuit, far less assemble my stove and cook a proper meal.

Chapter 20

I awoke the next morning, refreshed and ravenous, and set about making breakfast. Grandfather's favourite singer, Gordon Lightfoot, accompanied the cooking of freeze-dried scrambled eggs and bacon, which I devoured with some strong black coffee. I then sat on the grass and pondered my surroundings.

I had seen a photograph of a woman outside a blackhouse here in Sloch dated 1907 and I knew that there had been eighteen people living here in 1851, farmers named MacDonald, MacGillivray and MacDougall, according to the centenary map. The Bochan was here most of the time until sometime before the Second World War. He was a MacDonald, Big John's great-uncle.

It was a heavenly morning. Before me, the Inner Hebrides framed the entrance to the bay; Eigg seemed so close, bathed in the warm peach tones of the early sun. In the sea, through the middle of the bay, I could clearly see a line of boulders, presumably a jetty of some sort. In townships like this, there would always have been a wooden fishing boat, and at the highest tide the boat would come in and everyone in the township would hurry down to drag her out of the waves. In winter, it must have been a gargantuan effort to get her behind a rocky outcrop to protect her from the battering of the westerly wind. Perhaps a pony with a halter would have helped. That was what they were used for in Cape Breton, back in the day.

I read somewhere that when the numbers of strong young people in a community dropped below four, then that community was doomed. The boat couldn't be beached and chores like ploughing and peat cutting became too much. It was a sobering thought.

My clothes were thick with mud from the digging yesterday, so I took off my plaid shirt and jeans and scrubbed them on a rock in the burn, quite probably the same one that generations of women here had used for the same purpose. I laid them out over the warm rocks to dry.

I lay down again on the machair, soaking up the spring sun and wondering what Sarah would be doing. Working in the care home, probably, or maybe it was her day off. She was such a pretty girl, with her blonde hair and cute smile, and was as sharp as a pin. That she was an adventure-training instructor was really cool too. But I doubted she'd be interested in a boring insurance clerk from Cape Breton. Although, I mused, she didn't know that guy, did she? Maybe she saw me as a talented musician and an adventurer, albeit an inexperienced one, heading off on a quest to trace his roots. Who knew? I hoped to get to know her better after I'd finished my trip. She'd had a drink with me after the gig, she'd been happy to pick me up after the walk back from Peanmeanach – she needn't have done that – and she clearly loved the fact that I was honouring my grandfather in this way. I needed to find out how serious her relationship with the fisherman was . . .

I shook off the notions and got to my feet. There was another cave marked on the map, which I quickly found, though it was more like a fissure in the rock face. I worked my way into it and pushed my way along a good seventy-five metres before I couldn't go any further. I had hoped it might open up but it was a dead end. However, I knew that where there was one cave, there were usually more, and as I began to scramble around the cliffs overlooking the bay I found another, further up the hill, completely hidden from below and with no sign of other people having visited it recently. It had a breath-taking view of the area from above. I bet it had been used as a hiding place when Vikings were in the area, and probably again when the Redcoats were searching through the villages and burning the houses. If I'd been a local and had managed to get my hands on some of the Louis d'or, this was exactly the sort of place I'd hide it. I sighed. I couldn't shake off my new-found desire to follow the smell of treasure.

It was an ideal spot to finish off my drawing of the town-ship. I made myself comfortable, my back against a rock, and drew. My sketch was definitely helped by the evening sun creating a warm and romantic image of the place.

While I sat there, I remembered going to the beach with my parents, my sister and the cousins from Chéticamp. We built sandcastles and cooked sausages over a fire. One of my cousins, Jean Charles, was very excited to find an antique bottle with a message inside it, and my father spent ages trying to decipher it with a magnifying glass. Finally, he cracked it:

Dear Mother, we have been torpedoed and are sinking. To let you know that I love you and look forward to seeing you in Heaven, God willing. Your adoring son, Caspian

My father told us that it probably came from a British ship during the Second World War, judging by the sailor's name. He thought Caspian might have been just a boy, conscripted into the Royal Navy at eighteen or even younger. I distinctly remember my father telling Jean Charles that he would have been old enough to be sent off to fight in the old days, and he was only sixteen at the time. That beach picnic was one of the earliest days that I remember vividly.

When we got home, we both rushed to show our grandparents what we had found on the beach. Grandmother told us that our family had always loved beachcombing and that when Grandfather was young, his mother, Louise, was mad keen on collecting debris from the shore. She would take a turn along the beach after a southerly storm to collect driftwood and drag it up to the house. A tree, a broken oar, planks that had been washed off a ship's deck: it would all make good firewood when it was dry and Grandfather's great-grandfather, Donald John, immobile because he'd lost a leg in the Boer War, enjoyed cutting it on his saw horse around the back of the house. There was never a time Louise wouldn't return bearing a trophy that she would proudly show off to everyone at breakfast. A tin kettle without a lid, a coconut, a leather football, a little wooden dolls' house that Donald Angus left on the top of the dresser at Laggan, in case a little girl should visit.

Nathalie and I were most impressed when Grandfather told us that once a whole wooden cabin from a fishing boat got stranded on the rocks on Goat Island when his father was a young teenager. He and his friend had brought it back, plank by plank, and Donald John, who had trained as a carpenter at Roshven House across the loch, used the teak to build a beautiful kitchen area, including a wooden sink. Goat Island seemed to have been the base for so much fun and adventure.

I woke with a start, shivering. I had dozed off, but my mind was still full of dreams: my parents at the kitchen table, Nathalie and I beside each other on the bench. Father was in the heavy, black-and-white wool jumper that he wore when he was going out to sea, his red hair lit up by the early sun coming through the window.

'Archie,' said my mother, 'be careful in the boat today. The wind's picking up. The lobsters will still be there tomorrow.'

He laughed, I remember. He was always laughing. 'You always say that, darling.' She still looked concerned, and he went over and hugged her. 'Don't worry. I'll be careful, I promise,' he insisted.

It was sad how little I remembered of my parents. Did I actually remember facts or did I invent them? Was my recollection of my mother's face real or was I thinking of a photograph in a family album? I used to think I remembered her particular scent, but that had long gone. Father was more vivid to me: his handsome, rugged face, his broad shoulders from a lifetime of manual work.

I crossed myself, as I always did when I thought of them. They were bound to be together in Heaven. I felt almost glad that they'd died at the same time. I just wished it hadn't happened so soon.

I continued my exploration of Sloch. Big John told me that the Bochan had once found washed up an almost full bottle of Russian vodka and was found, completely drunk, early in the morning when he was supposed to be out gathering the sheep. I wondered which was the Bochan's house; maybe there would be a pile of bottles outside the door.

Big John also told me that there had been an illegal still here in the old days. Barley would be brought in by boat and whisky taken away on the same day. There was little chance of the excise men finding them because every local's eyes would be on any visitor to the area, and, as fast as a boy could run, word would speed the five miles along the peninsula that strangers were coming. I would love to have found the still, but after looking around every ruined building, under every cliff and in each hollow in the ground, I could tell there was nothing man-made at all, apart from the buildings themselves, the runrigs and peat cuttings. I thought there might have been some broken buckets, farm implements, perhaps a rubbish dump, but there was nothing.

While doing my online research back in Port Hawkesbury, I had imagined being able to supplement my rations with some foraging. But, on the first night of my visit, the locals put me right, telling me that the gulls wouldn't be laying eggs for a further two weeks and nettles were only just breaching the ground. I hunted for shellfish when the tide was at its lowest, but the whelks and mussels were small and sparse and the seaweed bitter. In the autumn there would be berries of all sorts and mushrooms, they'd said, but not now.

Grandfather had said there was a deer trap three hundred metres to the north-east of their house at Laggan. A high wall sloped down towards a cliff where, centuries ago, driven deer were funnelled over the edge to fall to their death. Bull seals were hunted too, trapped on the shore and driven inland. They were vicious, apparently, always putting up a fight when cornered. Many men suffered terrible bites.

April was the hardest month for the Highland farmer, according to Grandfather. All the signs were there that summer was on its way, but the new grass hadn't begun growing yet and the winter feed for the animals was often finished, just as the livestock were due to have their young. Sometimes the cattle were so weak they almost had to be carried out of the byre. I could scarcely imagine the hardship, realising, for the first time, what a cosseted life I'd led compared with my forebears.

Chapter 21

The next morning, I woke early and walked to the point overlooking Eilean nan Gobhar, Goat Island. I had been fascinated by the place ever since I had begun my research. Apparently, youngsters would row out to it to climb to the vitrified fort on the top, sleep overnight in dens, and conduct wars over ownership of the two small peaks. I had read about the goats that used to be kept there, the fantastic harvests of goose eggs and brambles, how the best fishing in the area was off its southerly point, and that no one knew why the tidal Priest Rock was so named. I considered abandoning my plan and heading straight there but eventually decided to stick to the schedule. I'd paddle past Peanmeanach and stay near my grandparents' old house at Laggan, then head back to the old village and use it as a base to explore for a couple of days. I would get to Goat Island later.

The weather was lovely again and my spirits were high as I paddled around the most westerly point of Ardnish, through a narrow gap between a small island and the peninsula. On my left was the prettiest beach, with golden sands stretching for two hundred metres and a good seventy-five metres from the water's edge to the cliffs, now the tide was out. These were the famed Singing Sands. Apparently, a picnic there was as close as my ancestors ever got to a holiday.

I paddled onto the sand, hunted around for driftwood, and soon built a roaring fire. As I sipped a mug of tea I wondered what day it was, eventually deciding it was probably Saturday. Back home, the office would be closed. I hoped they were missing me and that Julie wasn't coping in my absence. I thought of Nathalie, with baby Mairi, back at our house – except, I realised with a pang, it wasn't *our* house any more. It was *her* house.

I began to feel slightly melancholy. It would have been nice to be sharing this expedition, this wonderful beach, with someone. I waded out to a tiny islet to admire the view. With my binoculars, I scanned Goat Island, Glenuig beyond, and around that corner, I knew, lay Smirisary. My Great-aunt Sheena, long dead, had had a fiancé from there, but he had tragically drowned, leading her to become the first of the family to move to Cape Breton. Then to the south, I recognised Roshven House, an impressive stone mansion surrounded by massive trees, with its green lawn running down to a beach. Much of the carpentry had been done by my ancestors a hundred and fifty years before, when the house was built by the Blackburn family. Above, towering over the house, were An Stac and Rois-Beinn, still with snow on their peaks.

Roshven House had been where Grandfather had trained in the special forces during the Second World War. His expertise had been in demolition and explosives. The soldiers had to run up Rois-Beinn and back before breakfast in under two hours before kayaking, or canoeing as he called it, around Goat Island in forty minutes.

I had only been on the islet for half an hour, but when I looked round, I saw that what had been six inches of water was now waist-deep. I leapt to my feet, jogged ashore and arrived back on the sand just in time to drag my kayak further up the beach before it floated off.

Later, I kayaked along the shore with the tide behind me, past Glasnacardoch and Feorlindhu, trying to count the number of buildings and identify my next drawing projects. The school was obvious. It was formed of cut stone, with neat, squared-off corners, built well after the dwelling houses. Then, with just a few more strokes of my paddles, I found myself upon Peanmeanach itself. Its beauty from the sea took my breath away. The tide was well in now, the beach a sliver of golden sand, then a grassy, tight-cropped lawn sloped up to the crescent of the village itself, although the only building left fully standing was the green-roofed bothy. I knew that it had been the last home of my Great-grandmother Louise before she and the two old ladies left to live in Arisaig in 1945. The other houses were derelict, shoulder-high shells, evenly spaced, facing the water. I spotted three people sitting outside the bothy where smoke rose from the chimney. I waved and they all waved back.

'You shouldn't plan to visit the bothy over a weekend,' Big John had advised me. 'I hear people come from all over to stay there now – stag parties and all sorts. But in April, on a weekday, you should be fine.'

His advice about avoiding weekends was sound. I would have hated to share my old family home with strangers. I dawdled, letting the current take me. It was the perfect time to let out my fishing line; with luck, I'd be eating barbecued mackerel for supper. Unfastening it from its plastic bag in the net of the kayak, I tied it fast and let it trawl along behind me.

I took the channel between Eilean nam Bairneach and headed towards the knoll where locals of the area were buried. Along with the Blackburn family was the resting place of 'The Whaler', Ronald MacDonald, believed to be the last man in the area who had actually hunted whales and the father of three distinguished pipers I had heard playing at Celtic Colours in Mabou. It was also this spot where the farmers of Ardnish would swim cows across to be served by the Roshven bulls. It astonished me how much history I seemed to have absorbed from my grandfather.

I paddled gently down the middle of the loch, enjoying the last of the evening sun. There was quite a current going through the narrows; it looked like I'd have to fight to get back through. Up on the left was Theodlin, known in the family as 'The Lost Township'. Grandfather told me that it was marked on the earliest map as a settlement of three houses but never appeared on subsequent maps, and I could only see signs of the ruins of one. He had once told me that if I was ever to visit, I should go into the hills, two hundred metres to the north-east of the remaining ruin and admire the construction there.

I decided I would go tomorrow. Theodlin sounded like a Norse name, as Vikings did inhabit Ardnish at some time. It must have been terrifying when they arrived at dawn: dozens of burly men charging into the townships, capturing the women and slaying the men.

I pulled in at a small bay which lay sheltered behind an island. In front of me was a shed and a mooring, with a ruin nearby where I planned to camp before going to visit Grandfather's house in the morning. Excitedly, I pulled in my fishing line. Nothing. I was so disappointed; I'd been looking forward to eating something that I'd caught myself.

I forced down a disgusting rehydrated meal of chicken stew and climbed into my sleeping bag. Cold, lonely and a bit miserable, I contemplated my return to work. Did I actually *want* to go back? I had stood up for myself and received a pay rise and an acknowledgement that I was good at the job. But

I wasn't looking forward to reporting to Yvonne again. It had been made clear that my career progression would not be rapid. Also, my commute was a killer, especially in the winter. I realised that I was dreading going back.

Gradually, a new idea formed. Why didn't I just start my own company? I could bide my time at Canadian Equitable, do my exams, and at the same time identify the best three or four people on the island to hire. We could have two offices: one in Inverness and, later, another in Sydney. I knew that Glenora Distillery would support me, the Celtic Colours Festival might switch, and several hotels I could think of would follow me. Maybe even Cabot Links in a year or two? I had the perfect office in mind on Central Avenue in Inverness. It was a shop beside the Royal Bank of Canada, just up from the Oran, which had been empty for a while so the rent would be low. What would I call it? CB Insurance? Island Insurance? Gillies Insurance? I smiled at the thought.

I woke the next morning feeling much more cheerful, my mind still whirring at my business idea. After a quick breakfast of porridge and coffee again, I walked briskly round the corner to Laggan. I had googled 'Laggan Cottage' before leaving Canada, but it must have been different ones that came up, because when I arrived, the cottage caught me completely by surprise. I had expected a blackhouse with rounded walls, or perhaps a mortared square building with a fireplace at each end. Instead I saw a pretty, white two-storey house with two dormer windows upstairs, a porch on the front, a lean-to extension on the end and a bench outside. It was most definitely not derelict. I approached tentatively, hoping the owner would allow me to take a look around if I explained that my grandparents used to live here. But there was no one at home. It looked like a holiday cottage, still locked up for the winter.

My heart was racing with the excitement of being here. The early morning sun was fully on the house and it was warm. I could imagine Grandmother tending her fruit and vegetables here, in the small walled garden. They used to tell Nathalie and me of the amazing cabbages and raspberries that would grow thanks to the long summer days and the damp, warm climate. Grandfather would always be tinkering with a farm implement, his collie lying in the grass beside him.

I peered through the window and gasped. The fireplace looked original, maybe the dresser and table too. What if my grandmother had placed them there? It was idyllic. I could have happily lived here, I thought, feeling more than a pang of regret that my grandparents had moved away.

Eventually I went back to my gear and took advantage of the low tide to wade over to the island in front. I took my sketch pad and pencils, and my phone to take some photographs of Laggan from the distance. Nathalie would never forgive me if I didn't have a hundred good images to talk her through.

I could hear her enthusiasm now. *It's gorgeous, what a spot! It must get all the sun . . . Look at the sea . . . If only we were millionaires and could buy it back for the family . . .*

The island was called 'An Trom', which meant 'protection' – from the weather, presumably. There was a circle of stones in the water around a small bay, marked as an ancient fish trap on Grandfather's map. He once told me that during the summer he used to string a net between this island and the one beyond at low tide, and as the tide rose, he would catch the salmon as they headed up towards the river and on to Loch Eilt. His best haul was five in one go, he'd said, one of them a ten-pounder at least. He wouldn't have been impressed with my fishing of last night.

At the point of the island, 'Post Ardnish' would pass in his boat and an exchange of letters and a few necessities would take place, including the *Oban Times* on a Thursday. I could imagine Grandfather coaxing a cow into the water from this same point while Granny sat alongside him in the rowing boat, ready to encourage the beast over to the farm opposite.

They wouldn't have recognised the view now. In their day, there was no road along the shore opposite; that had been constructed much later. Only Roshven Farm and the East Lodge would have been in view. Now, there were modern houses dotted around, with electricity and broadband, whereas it was obvious to me that Laggan still didn't have any of that. It was as cut off as it was the day my grandparents left.

I walked around the ruins to the west of Laggan, then to the small fank behind the house itself where I sat on the rusted remnants of what must have been Grandfather's old tractor. He would have sat on this same wobbly metal seat the day he left, a broken man, a failure in his own mind. He had always said he'd just walked out the door and closed it behind him, leaving decades of family history, emotional attachments, hopes and dreams behind him, to head to his wife's family home with no idea how it would work out.

Reaching behind me, I found the tattered shreds of a waxed coat behind the seat. It must have been his. Surely? I held it to my face instinctively, hoping to smell something of him.

Chapter 22

I was fascinated with Theodlin. What had happened to the missing houses? Before leaving Canada, I had peered closely at satellite images as well as Roy's Military Survey of 1747 and counted the buildings. There were five marked. Sometime between then and now, a large sheep fank had been constructed several hundred metres away, up a hill and over a ridge. I guessed the work would have been done during the potato famine of the late 1840s. Grandfather had said that the laird created work for the men on the peninsula, just so that people could survive. It appeared that the houses of Theodlin had been carried, stone by stone, from the shore up the hill and over the ridge and rebuilt as a remarkably over-engineered sheep pen. It must have been quite a task: there were hundreds of tonnes of stone here, and some individual stones were really substantial.

I sketched out the construction, trying to capture the sheer scale of the largest boulders and the perfect positioning of stone upon stone, each one painstakingly placed to scarcely let a draught through. Grandfather had said he had no recollection of the fank ever having been used, certainly not since 1900. It was basically just a massive work creation scheme.

Later, I climbed further up the hill to a ruined cottage that looked down onto the bay below. Beside it stood a massive oak tree. I poked around, pacing out the dimensions of the cottage so that I could draw it, too, and came across an old grey backpack covered in moss, which I nearly stepped on, thinking it was a stone. Beside it lay a simple hazel walking stick, completely rotten. They must have lain here for years.

Intrigued, I opened up the backpack and spread the contents on the ground: an Ordnance Survey map of the land to the east of here, a Caledonian MacBrayne timetable for the ferry from Mallaig to Armadale dated 1984, a paperback edition of Gavin Maxwell's *Ring of Bright Water*, a miniature bottle of Mackinlay's whisky, three unopened, rusty tins of food, a toothbrush and razor, a shirt and a sleeping bag – all sodden. Rummaging deeper, I pulled out a sealed plastic sleeve which contained a page that had been torn from a book. The words 'Alexander Carmichael's Carmina Gadelica, 1900' were scribbled in biro at the top of the page. I sat down and read the text:

The people of the Outer Isles, like the people of the Highlands and Islands generally, are simple and law-abiding, common crime being rare and serious crime unknown among them. They are good to the poor, kind to the stranger, and courteous to all. During all the years that I lived and travelled among them, night and day, I never met with incivility, never with rudeness, never with vulgarity, never with aught but courtesy. I never entered a house without the inmates offering me food or apologising for their want of it.

I folded the paper and put it in my pocket. I had only been in Scotland for a few days, but the sentiment resonated with me as much as it obviously had done with the owner of the bag. My Grandmother, Sophie, had spent only six years in these parts, but she always said that the people were the kindest and politest she ever met; in fact, it was those very attributes that had attracted her to Donald Angus.

I wondered what had gone on here. A traveller or hill-walker had left it obviously, but why? Had something happened? I decided to look around, to see what I might find. I picked my way around the rear of the building, and there, leaning against a large boulder on the far side of the oak tree, a hundred metres away, I found him. A skeleton, head tipped forwards – luckily, as I had no wish to see empty eye sockets and a gaping jaw. He wore a tatty woollen hat, lace-up walking boots and a long tweed coat.

I closed my eyes and turned away. What on earth could I do? Eventually, I composed myself, got my phone out and took one photograph as close-up to the body as I could stomach and then another from a distance. I could tell the police exactly where he was, but the emergency services would have a hell of a job removing him. They'd need to take a launch up the loch, then put the remains into a body bag and stretcher them down to the shore. I'd be long gone, I realised, although they'd probably need me to come and show them the spot. I fervently hoped not. I knelt down and said a prayer for the lonely traveller before turning and walking back to my camp down by the Laggan boathouse.

It took me several hours to calm down. I gathered sticks and got a really good fire going, which was comforting, but still, my mind was racing. What was the traveller doing all the way over here? There were no inhabitants living here in 1984, after all. Maybe, like me, his family were from here and he'd wanted to come back. Judging by his clothing and the basic provisions he had in his backpack, I suspected he may have been a man of the road. I wondered if he'd come here in the winter and died of exposure, or perhaps had a heart attack.

Would there have been a search party for him? Quite possibly not, if he was an itinerant. I guessed that very few people must come this way – if any – each year.

It occurred to me that I should go back and check his pockets; perhaps there would be a wallet, some form of ID? Then I thought of abandoning the trip and reporting the body to the police right away. I shuddered at the prospect.

I stared into the flames. I had just settled into my adventure and was loving the solitude and the landscape. When would I ever get the chance to come back? The poor soul had been lying there, undiscovered, for over thirty years. I decided eventually that he could wait another week.

Decision made, I pulled out my phone and made a note of the GPS reference to guide the emergency services to the body later. It was eight hundred metres up the hill from the sea, then forty metres from the north-west corner of the ruined cottage at the base of the oak tree. I realised that, if the bracken grew any higher, then the search would be more difficult, so at least I was doing something helpful.

Chapter 23

I woke early the next morning after a restless night. There was a strong, cold wind from the east and light cloud; the weather seemed to be changing. I'd been lucky so far, with fine conditions the whole time. It was seven days since I'd waved farewell to Sarah and Big John at the viaduct. I missed her.

Wind and tide behind me, I headed west again. I planned to drag my kayak up at Glasnacardoch and have a look around there and Feorlindhu before coming back to the bothy at nightfall. As I passed Peanmeanach I was relieved to see that there was no sign of life around the bothy. I hoped no one would come along later in the day.

Glasnacardoch was where the 'new' school was, in a small bay of its own, with a sandy beach and a cluster of veteran oak trees hanging over the roof. It was a fine building, with a proper chimney at each gable end and large windows. Grandfather had gone to school here, and his father and grandfather before him. They took a lump of peat or an armful of wood with them each morning for the fire. Gaelic was forbidden, Grandfather told me; the children learned Latin and English. There was a large map of the world on the wall, with the British Empire coloured pink. The teacher had a two-thonged leather tawse to belt them with if they misbehaved.

I smiled as I recalled another of Grandfather's school tales. Apparently, a textile company called J. & P. Coates had donated oak bookcases to schools all over Scotland between the wars. The Glasnacardoch one had been delivered by a puffer and nearly capsized the rowing boat bringing it to the shore. It took three men to carry the thing into the school. It was such a waste of money and effort: Grandfather was the only pupil at the school at the time and it was about to get closed down. His mother had complained that money would have been far more welcome. Before the year was out, the bookcase had been burned in the stove.

Grandfather's map showed that five houses were occupied here in 1851: MacDougall, MacVarish, Gillies – maybe my ancestors? Thirty-five souls, he had written. Up the hill behind were the old peat cuttings, probably for the whole area. Despite the fact that it hadn't rained for more than a week I sank up to my ankles in the boggy ground. If it had been like this back then, there would have been no way a pony could have been used to carry the peat away; it would have sunk.

I headed along the shore, clambering over a ridge of rocks before arriving at Feorlindhu. There was only a single black-house obvious now, in a wonderful setting. Someone had hung a buoy over an oak branch, so I eagerly climbed on and, like a child, swung back and forth, finally relaxed and happy in my own company. It had taken me some time to just appreciate being on holiday. There was a pretty carpet of primroses and huge numbers of birds, singing and flying about in all directions with dried grass and moss in their beaks for their nests. I wished I knew what species they were.

Later, I spent an hour gathering a pile of driftwood from the shore; it was good and dry after all the fine weather. Big John's saw was just the thing for cutting it into handy lengths.

With sections from a fallen oak branch too, I'd have plenty to last me a couple of days, especially if the rain came in. I found a length of fisherman's rope trapped between the rocks which was ideal for tying a big bundle together.

I dragged my kayak down to the water's edge and set off for Peanmeanach. I planned to ditch my belongings there and then return on foot to fetch the firewood. I was excited about collecting my backpack, packed with clean clothes, a razor, soap and a welcome change of rations.

Chapter 24

My first reaction was serious indignation: there was smoke coming out of the chimney of the bothy. Then a dog came bounding down to the beach barking furiously at me as I approached the shore.

The door swung open and a girl emerged, waving at me – it was Sarah. My heart leapt with delight. As I paddled closer to the shore, she walked across the machair, calling out to me, her words lost in the noise of the waves and wind.

As the kayak hit the beach, I pulled off the spray deck and clambered out rather too fast, almost tipping myself into the water – an ungainly arrival.

We stood staring at one another, grinning. It seemed natural to pull her into my arms and hug her.

But I didn't.

'This is a surprise,' I said instead.

'Well, Cranachan needed a good walk,' she replied. 'I got a couple of days off work so I thought I'd make the most of the good weather and come out here. I've brought dinner, if you're interested?'

I nodded vigorously. 'You bet.'

'You can tell me all about your trip.'

We carried my two dry bags up to the bothy. Inside, the fire was lit and Sarah had set the table with a gingham cloth, a candle, cutlery and glasses. I was completely taken aback.

'Sarah! I'm touched. This looks wonderful.' I stood with my back to the fire, realising I was beaming like a lovestruck teenager. 'Thank you.'

I went off to retrieve my backpack, with Sarah's collie bouncing along beside me. I'd never had this kind of attention from a girl. She was so forthcoming, so natural. I was used to being the quiet boy, keeping my head down. This new sensation, of being with someone I liked and who I was beginning to think quite liked me too, was exhilarating – but a bit overwhelming.

My sister had once said to Aunt Maggie and me that a girl would have to come and get me, that I'd never go and get them. Was that what was happening? And what about the boyfriend Hamish had told me about?

'Ready for dinner? Are you hungry?' Sarah asked when I returned.

'Why don't we get some driftwood first – before it rains?' I looked up at the dark clouds rolling in. 'There's some on the shoreline in the next bay along.'

It was growing dark when we got back. 'I'm going to wash before we eat,' I said. I opened my pack, pulled everything out, and there, at the bottom, lay a half-bottle of Ben Nevis whisky. 'Look!' I said, showing it to Sarah, 'Big John must have planted it in here when I was packing!'

I went down to the burn where I stripped off, washed my hair, lathered my whole body with soap, then immersed myself in the icy water. My God, it was ice-cold. But I felt fantastic as I returned to the bothy; my skin was tingling, I had fresh clothes on – and a date with Sarah.

'It's steak and a salad I made at home, nothing fancy,' she said as I opened the door.

I was thrilled. 'Can't wait,' I assured her. 'It was going to be freeze-dried lasagne.'

After supper, we made ourselves comfortable in our cosy little bothy, lit by a couple of candles and the crackling fire. Cranachan dozed in front of the fire. I pulled out the maps and my sketch pad, and talked her through the trip: the story about the witch, followed by the discovery of a skull, my amazement about Mullochbuie and what an unexpectedly gorgeous spot it was, and how I'd love to buy Laggan, my grandfather's house.

I saved the most exciting till last, and showed her the photographs on my phone of the dead body slumped beside the oak tree.

'Oh God!' she exclaimed, looking horrified. 'Don't you think you should tell the police straight away, first thing tomorrow?'

I told her, laughing, that, after thirty years, a few more days probably wouldn't matter to the tramp, or the police.

'What makes you assume he was a traveller?' Sarah asked, her voice cold.

'Well, his clothes and the contents of his backpack for a start. It looked as if he could be a hobo.' I was squirming now, sensing that I may have completely screwed up.

Sarah shook her head. 'And what exactly do you know of our travelling community, Peter Angus? What makes you so sure?'

'It . . . it seemed pretty obvious . . .' I mumbled.

She glared at me. 'How can you be so callous, so thoughtless? He was someone's son, maybe a father, a husband! A woman somewhere might be praying for him, right now!'

She fell silent.

I felt like an idiot.

'Sorry, Sarah, that came out badly,' I said. 'I got this completely wrong.'

'And what about not telling the police? It must be a crime not to report a body.' She went across to the fire and put a couple of sticks on, her back to me.

My heart was in my mouth. Had I just blown it?

'You're absolutely right. It was crass. I wasn't thinking properly. I was trying to impress you, wanting you to say "wow"! Of course I'll report it,' I said lamely.

She returned to her seat and sat quietly for a minute. 'Let's forget about it,' she said eventually. 'We all say stupid things sometimes.'

Cranachan came over and licked my hand, breaking the ice. I fussed over him for a couple of minutes, allowing us to move onto safer ground. I remembered the bottle of Ben Nevis in my backpack. 'Would you have a drop of Big John's whisky, Sarah?' I asked, reaching for the bottle and holding it up. 'A peace offering?'

She looked at me and smiled. 'Seeing it was made by my family, why not?'

'Your family?' I said in astonishment. 'Really?'

'Well, not any more,' she admitted, 'but one of my family was the distiller in Fort William. He was called Long John MacDonald and Ben Nevis is distilled in the same place as it was in 1824.'

'But I thought you were English,' I said.

'Ah, never make assumptions, Peter Angus. My mother was a MacDonald from Lochaber and my father was a policeman in Arisaig. They moved to Kent in 2002; that's where I was brought up.'

We talked late into the night. There was so much I wanted

to know about her, and she was fascinated by my trip. She seemed to love the fact that I was a musician, too.

'Thanks for dinner,' I said, 'and thanks for coming to join me. It was a lovely surprise.' I leant forward and kissed her lightly on the cheek.

She smiled. 'You're welcome,' she said, rising to her feet. 'Right, time for bed.' She began to lay out her sleeping bag in the room next door.

'What are you doing?' I asked her. 'You should sleep here, in the warm room, even though Cranachan's bagged the best bit in front of the fire.'

'No way,' she replied. 'I'll be fine in here. Sleep well.' She closed the door gently.

I clambered into my own sleeping bag and lay staring into the fire. God, I'd completely mishandled the skeleton story. It wasn't even how I truly felt. I hadn't told her how I'd knelt and said a prayer for him . . . Oh God, I'd even described him as a hobo. What an idiot! Well, I consoled myself, despite this blunder we had got on well. I couldn't get over how wonderful it was that Sarah had come to be with me and how relaxed we'd been in each other's company. I'd make up for my thoughtless remarks tomorrow. I closed my eyes and slept like the dead.

I woke to the sound of the door latch on the bothy: it was Sarah letting Cranachan out. I climbed out of the sleeping bag, pulled on my clothes and hurried outside.

There, I saw Sarah swimming along, parallel to the shore, while Cranachan ran up and down the sand, barking his approval. Retreating indoors, I got the fire going and put water on to boil; she would need a hot cup of something when she got back. I was sitting on the bench as she returned, her wet hair slicked back. I couldn't help but notice how well-toned she was; she had the body of an athlete.

'Morning,' I called. 'Are you insane?'

'I think of it as bracing,' she replied. Her face was wreathed in smiles.

'How about a bacon roll?' I asked. 'I'll do it while you dry off.'

'What shall we do now?' Sarah asked, after we'd finished breakfast. 'We've got all day, but I do need to leave first thing tomorrow. I've got work.'

'I thought we could walk around the village, find out where the spring they used for the water supply was, and visit the grave at the back of the big field. I'd like to take you to Laggan, too, do some drawing, and look for the deer trap I've heard about. How does that sound?'

'Great. You know, you must tell me more about your family's connection to Ardnish.'

I was delighted to oblige. 'Well, piping's in our blood. My family were hereditary pipers to the MacDonalds of Clanranald at Castle Tioram. The Gillies family lived here in Peanmeanach for ever, as far as could be told, right here in this bothy between the wars and in the house next door before that. The men always served in the army: the Lovat Scouts in the Boer War and both World Wars, and the Cameron Highlanders before that.'

'Did you ever think about joining up yourself?' Sarah asked.

'Never,' I replied. 'Not my thing.'

'Fair enough,' she said.

'My grandfather was the last Gillies to be in the Forces. He had a brilliant career in the army and was promoted to captain. He met my grandmother, who was from Cape Breton, while she was on a suicide mission behind enemy lines in France. She survived, and he tracked her down to Canada in

1944, and then she came back to live with him here after he was badly injured at the end of the war. They lived in a house a mile away along the loch, working the land, but farming was too much of a struggle. They left in 1951 and went to Cape Breton, where he became a carpenter.'

'What a history you have! And what about your parents? You keep mentioning your grandfather, but no one else.'

'I have an older sister, Nathalie. She's married with a baby, Mairi. We're very close. My parents and grandmother died in an accident when I was young, and Grandfather brought us up,' I replied.

Sarah reached out and put her hand on my knee, 'I'm so sorry,' she said. 'That must've been tough.'

'I'll tell you about it some other time,' I said with a reassuring smile. I knew she'd be wondering whether to ask how it happened; it was what everyone wanted to know. 'Let's go for our walk, shall we?'

I turned away to put on my boots. I always had to brace myself to tell people about the accident. I remember the children at school all crowding around me in the playground, raining questions down on me. 'What happened? Did they die straight away? Will the truck driver go to jail?' I would keep my head down as tears poured down my face until a teacher rescued me. I knew even then that they meant no harm, but still, their words rang in my ears to this day.

Cranachan ran ahead of us, disappearing into the tall grass. Sarah could tell I was still hurting, and as we walked along the path through the big field, she touched my arm.

'Sorry,' she said simply.

'It's fine, really,' I replied. 'Still touches a nerve, you know?'

'Why don't you go on with the rest of the story about your family and Ardnish?' she asked.

I smiled. 'Sure. Well, my great-great-grandmother was called Morag. She made everything happen around here apparently. She begged the laird to put these drainage channels in and fence off the field to stop the deer. It became the best piece of land on the west. It's right here.' We stopped to look.

'Shocking how quickly it's deteriorated, isn't it?' I said. 'Just a boggy marsh now.'

We went across to the wood at the back of the field. 'A few people are buried here, I think . . . Yes, look over there, those upright slabs.'

We cleared away dead bracken and moss and surveyed the scene.

'That's it, I reckon . . . only seven headstones . . . and not one of them inscribed.'

'Very atmospheric, though,' Sarah said.

'My family were buried on an island in the Ailort River, five miles away. Now that I've seen the area for myself, I've no idea why. It must've been a heck of a task to get their bodies there. Grandfather told me he wanted to be buried there too, but he knew it wouldn't be allowed these days. It gets completely flooded when there's really heavy rain, apparently. In any case, he's with his wife and son in the Stella Maris graveyard back in Cape Breton now.'

'Have you been to the island graveyard yet?'

'No, but I will. Grandfather wanted to bring me over a few years ago, but I didn't want to go and made a big issue of it at the time. I was a stupid kid, and I regret it, but at least I'm here now. He engraved a plaque for one of the graves. I've got it with me.'

'Ah, you're on a sort of pilgrimage,' Sarah said softly.

'Yes, I guess I am.' I smiled gratefully at her.

I took Sarah over the hill to Laggan, where I took a selfie of the two of us in front of the family house. I couldn't wait to see Nathalie's face when she saw me with Sarah. 'Who's the girl?' she'd shriek.

I'd tease her, saying that she just happened to show up. Nathalie would be consumed with curiosity. I grinned at the thought.

We peered through the window and explored the garden, and I showed her the tractor.

'I wonder how they got about. I mean, it's so far from civilisation,' Sarah mused. 'What do you think they ate? It must have been a hard life, but it's so beautiful. Why would they ever leave?'

'One word: hardship,' I replied.

She nodded.

'I don't suppose you want to come up the hill and see where the skeleton is?' I asked nervously.

She shuddered. 'Not really, thanks. Best not disturb the scene. I'll go into the police station in Mallaig and report it tomorrow. That way, you can make the most of your last few days. They're bound to want to interview you when you get back.'

'I really appreciate it, Sarah. I'll give you the GPS info and forward the images.' I was so grateful that she didn't mention my uncaring attitude of yesterday.

'Good, that's sorted!' She took my hand and pulled me forward, grinning. 'Come on, let's get back to the bothy.'

'My turn to cook tonight,' I said. 'No argument.' My spirits soared; she'd forgiven me.

'I never asked what job you do,' Sarah said as we walked towards Peanmeanach.

Suddenly, I felt my carefree mood darken. 'I work in insurance, have done for a long time now. It's a small branch office for a big Toronto-based company. Just a regular nine-to-five thing, you know.'

God, it sounded so dull. 'But while I've been here, I've started to think about leaving and starting up my own company. I think I've found the perfect place for an office in my hometown and I'm pretty sure some of my colleagues would join me – some clients too.'

Sarah looked impressed. 'This trip's been good for you, after all! Sometimes you need a bit of distance to think about making changes in your life. Sounds like you've done your research. What will you call it? Gillies Insurance?'

I laughed. 'I haven't quite decided. I tell you, that would get them talking back home. I don't think people would expect me to launch my own business, never mind name it after myself.'

'What are you good at?' she asked. 'Are you a details man? Ideas? Or more back-office? I'm guessing you're customer-focused. You're outgoing enough.'

Her enthusiasm was encouraging. I'd always been the quiet one in the corner, working on spreadsheets, processing claims, keeping my head down – until recently. 'Well, I have become more involved in sales recently,' I replied.

'Right. So, have you done a business plan? SWOT analysis? What you can offer the clients that they don't currently get?'

'It's all swirling around my brain at the moment,' I admitted, 'but, yeah, I'm starting to think along those lines.'

'Have you some mentors you can talk your plan through with? You'll need a couple of non-executive directors to guide you. And capital to fund it all,' Sarah continued.

'How come you know so much about business?' I asked, rather on the back foot.

'I did Business Studies at uni. But I was brought up in an entrepreneurial family, too. After the police, my dad opened a pub in Kent. My parents have four now. My mum's the people person and my dad does operations and bookkeeping.'

I watched as Sarah combed the beach for cowrie shells and held up interesting stuff for me to see. She was quite something, I thought to myself: educated, savvy, sporty *and* gorgeous. Way out of my league.

Later, after I cooked our supper, we sat outside the bothy, wrapped up against the chilly wind and nursing our drams.

'What's your plan after the kayaking trip?' asked Sarah.

'I've got an open flight home. Work isn't expecting me back for a while. I'd like to spend a few more days here, then I need to see a lawyer in Fort William. Then I have a week to do some sightseeing, climb Ben Nevis and who knows what else.'

'What an amazing trip you're having.'

'Sure is. It's changed me already.' I sighed. 'I don't know. Since Grandfather died, everything's felt different. I miss him, but I feel like I'm growing up, becoming a better person, more of a man. I think he's looking after me down here.'

'Of course he is,' said Sarah.

'I've had the most fantastic visit so far. I feel Ardnish is part of my life now, and, well, I've met you.' I laughed self-consciously.

'And I've met you too,' Sarah replied, raising her glass.

'So you're leaving early tomorrow?' I asked.

'I'll be off at six. That way, I'll make it to Mallaig by eight. I've got clothes in the car and I can shower at work. I'll go to the police station when I'm on my break.'

She got to her feet, and as she did so, the page of the book that I'd taken from the backpack on the bench caught her eye. 'What's that?'

'Read it,' I replied. 'I took it from the man's backpack. It's amazing.'

Sarah froze. 'Oh, Peter Angus! You are the pits! How could you steal from a corpse? What else did you take? His watch? His wallet?'

I couldn't believe it. 'It's only a scrap of paper! Come on, Sarah, give me a break. I took it before I even found the body. I didn't know he was lying round the back . . . I'll put it back. I'm sorry.'

'I think you should do exactly that.' She shook her head. 'Okay, I'm tired. I'm heading to bed.'

'Night, Sarah. Don't leave without saying goodbye,' I said forlornly.

Chapter 25

I lay in my bunk, thinking of Sarah next door in hers. I was struggling to make headway with her: one minute it was perfect, the next I'd screw up. If she hadn't been so angry with me, I might have had the courage to tiptoe over and tap on her door.

Instead, I tossed and turned the entire night.

Sarah came through early the next morning. She was cheerful again, my misdemeanour of last night apparently forgiven. 'Morning, An Gillie!' she said, laughter in her voice. She must have picked up my nickname from Big John. 'What are you up to today?'

'I think I'll explore Goat Island. I've heard so much about it. It was the view from my family home.'

She pulled on her jacket and heaved her backpack onto her back. 'You'll love it. Remember: be careful of the weather. Wait till it calms down. Okay, time to go! Call me when you want picked up at Lochailort.' She waved and blew me a kiss from the door – or did I imagine that?

I fell blissfully back to sleep, waking late. There was no urgency today; it was only an hour's paddle to Goat Island.

Outside, I heard the muted sounds of rain and wind. But it had always been my plan to go today, whatever the weather. Everything would be fine; it was always better outside than it appeared to be from inside. Besides, I didn't have a choice if I was to get the kayak back on time.

I left my sleeping bag on my bunk, to reserve it in case anyone else came to stay in the bothy, then packed the rest of my gear in my backpack and looked at the remnants of the driftwood pile. I'd need to collect some more when I got back, even though it would be wet. Thank goodness for Big John's saw; it had proved as invaluable as he had said.

I paddled quickly along the shore past Glasnacardoch, the tide behind me. It was pelting rain now. I was relieved I had a change of clothes waiting for me in the bothy. At the Singing Sands I turned south, knowing this to be the most sheltered route across to Goat Island. I was in the lee of a small island, and then it would be only five hundred metres to the island itself.

I wasn't far across the channel when it became clear I'd made a serious mistake. The wind had picked up and was much stronger out here than I'd realised when I'd embarked. There were rollers coming from the west with proper white caps and now the tide was going against the wind, stirring up a choppy sea. My kayak was really dropping in the dips, the swell a couple of metres high. My heart was in my mouth as I fought to forge onwards. What the hell was I doing out here?

Before long I was terrified, but I had no choice. I had to keep going. If I tried to turn and head back, I was certain to be tipped over. I tried to think rationally. What would Sarah advise me to do right now? Wave after wave was soaking me, the water swooshing right over the kayak, tipping me precariously as the wave passed underneath. The biting wind in my face and spray whipping into my eyes made it almost impossible to see ahead.

I was only about halfway across. Suddenly, I realised something else that almost paralysed me with fear: there was a high chance that the tide would carry me through the channel and straight past the island out into the open sea beyond, which was a mass of raging water now. I was a beginner, caught in a real gale. Leaning forward and using every muscle in my body, I powered on. There were rocks at the end of the island; if I could get to the shelter of them, I might have a chance. I could see that when the waves hit the point of the island a spume of spray was driven high into the air and carried a hundred metres across the sea. Seagulls were soaring above me, though I didn't dare look up; I kept my eyes fixed on the water just in front of the kayak. My arms were screaming in pain and sweat was pouring into my eyes. In desperation, I started to pray out loud, crying into the air. My voice was carried away by the wind and drowned out by the roar of the waves crashing into the rocks.

Our Father who art in Heaven, please save me. Please, God, please, God . . .

There were only a hundred metres to go now. Surely I could make it to safety? But the water between here and the rocks was the worst yet. The tide was gushing around from this side of the island and the sky was thick with spray from massive waves on the other side. The word 'maelstrom' sprang into my mind, a word I'd never even thought of before. I redoubled my efforts: just another twenty strokes, fifteen maybe . . .

A gigantic wave approached, I braced myself, and then capsized.

I was upside down, my mouth and eyes full of water, desperately trying to remember what to do. *Pull the spray-deck strap and roll forward . . . Don't let go of the paddle . . . Stay with your kayak whatever happens . . .* But it was too late. I surfaced, spluttering, choking, wiping the salt water from my eyes, the kayak already beyond reach and heading out to sea. Christ, it was cold. I pulled the toggle of my life-jacket and gratefully heard the whoosh as it inflated.

I was tumbling through the channel now, carried by the ferocious tide towards Eigg as if in a river. Goat Island was only twenty-five metres to my left, and I knew my only chance was to swim like hell to get out of the current and into the sheltered water of the island. I didn't think I had the strength. But I knew with terrible certainty that if I didn't make it I'd be finished.

It was as if I wasn't moving at all as I swam, arms and feet flailing, waves crashing over me, mouth and eyes full of water. The land wasn't getting any closer and I was floundering badly now. I could just give up, surrender; I'd die of cold in fifteen minutes, slip away quite peacefully . . .

Suddenly I was in calmer water. I was beat, finished: how the hell could I keep this effort up? My arms felt limp, power-less. I screamed with rage and pain.

I'd read somewhere that a human has forty per cent more to give than they think they do. It seemed ridiculous, but then, if my grandmother could walk the length of France with two broken feet, which she had, surely I could summon enough strength to keep going now.

I pictured her in my mind. I was a little boy, and she was holding my hand as we walked through her garden. *And these are the beans, and here are the sweet peas, aren't they pretty?* I was hallucinating. It was so vivid.

I was thrown onto the rocks by a wave, smashed against the barnacles, and I scrabbled to find a grip, but then I was ripped straight back out to sea as the wave sucked me through the seaweed. The next wave picked me up and threw me against the rocks once more, but this time I was ready. I reached out and grabbed desperately, trying to find a ledge for my feet, clinging on for dear life as the waves crashed over me. I pulled my body against the cliff and hung on, then, when the waves receded, clambered up towards safety.

I needed to get over the rocks and away from the power of the storm. My arm and hands were bleeding but I could feel no pain. I was numb. Another scramble, and I was over the other side and sheltered from the wind, although every few seconds a wave crashed behind me, sending spray high into the air and drenching me anew.

I collapsed against the rocks, gulping for air, my chest heaving. It was a miracle. I'd made it.

'Thank you, God!' I gasped aloud. My arm was bleeding badly. I could see blood dripping onto my hip and legs, my shorts crimson down one side. I'd need to wrap the wound with something quickly. But first I needed to get shelter.

My heart sank as I spotted another obstacle between me and safety: a deep channel, about two metres across, between my rock and Goat Island itself. The minutes passed, my body started to shake, and I knew I had to work out how to do this.

I counted the time between the waves. *Crash!* The wave hit the rock, the channel filled, rising a good three metres, and then it went back out, a ferocious sucking. If I got caught in that, I'd be straight back in the Atlantic and ripped to shreds by the barnacles and mussels on the rocks on the way out. Okay. Think. I figured it took thirty-five seconds from the wave hitting to the channel to it settling down again. Then there was a minute of calm before the next one came through. I'd need to throw myself in the water and haul myself up the other side, but did I have the strength to pull myself out? I could see one handhold and there were small ledges – I might make it if they weren't too slippy.

I had no choice. If I stayed where I was much longer I'd be too weak. *One, two, three, go!* I leapt into the pitch-black, churning water, then bobbed straight up as my lifejacket lifted me. I clutched for the handhold, my feet scrabbling in sheer panic, fearing the noise of the wave crashing into the crevice and the swell rushing in.

But I made it. I was up and safe. I lay flat on my back, spreadeagled, the rain on my face, completely exhausted. I could feel a pulse in my injured arm. I wanted to stay there, fall asleep, but my brain was telling me to get up, keep moving, find shelter.

Chapter 26

It was odd stumbling along the sheltered west side of the island, a different world from the hell of a few minutes before. The wind was passing over the highest point; even the water was calm close in. My body was shaking hard, juddering with the cold. I found a cave of sorts, sat on a rock by the entrance, and peeled off all my clothes. I scrubbed myself roughly with dry grass and dead bracken.

It was then that I caught sight of a nasty gash on my forearm, perhaps eight centimetres long and a couple of centimetres deep. I gathered some moss. I'd read somewhere that it had been used as an antiseptic dressing during wartime. I laid a clump of it on the wound, tore a strip from my T-shirt up and tied it awkwardly, one-handed. Then I squeezed the worst of the water out of my jacket and shorts and put them back on again, including the life jacket. I hoped its fluorescent colour would be spotted by someone.

With the rain still hammering down, visibility was terrible; occasionally there would be a brief gap and I could see land in the distance. I looked at my mobile phone. Thankfully, it had stayed dry in its little bag on a string that hung down the front of my jacket. There was no reception down here, but I reckoned if I got to the top of the island, there might be. I had Big John's number saved, and I was sure he would be at home in this weather. The rest of the gear I'd brought with me was still in the kayak. My sketch pad and pencils had gone, the waterproof matches, the biscuits and apple I had planned for lunch: they'd all been in a dry bag in the front compartment. I was devastated to lose the pad.

I climbed up the hill, through the heather and bracken, my light canvas shoes slippy and useless. Halfway up, I lost my footing and crashed to the ground, twisting and landing awkwardly on my shoulder. I was met by the full force of the wind at the top and could only crawl to the summit and shelter behind a boulder while I willed my phone to make a connection.

Not even a single bar appeared on the screen. I texted my sister: *Marooned on Goat Island. Send help.* It took ages to key in because I was shivering so hard, and then didn't send.

Damn it, nothing was going right. I wrapped my arms around my body and rocked, wondering what the hell to do next. My body was shaking, my teeth were chattering with the cold and my arm was throbbing. I held it tightly with my other hand, hoping I could get the blood to clot. My white T-shirt was soaked in blood.

The sea to the west looked more dangerous than it had an hour before. Only a fool would set forth in a proper boat in these conditions, I realised, never mind a beginner in a kayak. I had hoped that a fishing boat might pass and I could wave it down, but I guessed there was no way they'd be out of the harbour. I wondered where my kayak would end up: maybe it would wash up on a beach and instigate a rescue effort. That was my £200 deposit gone, I thought ruefully.

I walked back and forth, back and forth for ages, forcing myself to swing my arms up and down despite the pain and to stamp my feet. The storm was still raging, the rain pelting down. Surely it would clear soon and the people at Roshven House, tantalisingly close, would spot me and send help.

Sarah would be at work. She'd look out to sea at the storm and know for sure that I wouldn't have left the bothy. She'd imagine the kayak pulled up extra high because of the weather, the fire going and me sitting listening to an audio book or sketching. We had both known that the weather was going to turn, hadn't we? Like an idiot, I'd just assumed everything would be fine. I tried to imagine Sarah at work. She would be in the care home, sitting in a chair with half a dozen people around her, reading from a book, a cup of tea beside her. A white uniform on, her fair hair tied up at the back. Could it be only this morning that we'd parted at the Peanmeanach bothy?

On one hand, Sarah seemed to genuinely like me; she liked that I spoke Gaelic, and loved the idea of me starting my own business. We had chatted so easily together and she seemed to really enjoy my tales of Ardnish. She had walked all the way to Peanmeanach, brought me dinner – but she must think me a total clown now. My clumsy cold-heartedness when I called the skeleton a hobo, not getting the right gear despite her advice, and now kayaking into the teeth of a storm and getting myself into this awful predicament. Nathalie would approve of Sarah, I was certain of it, and that was important to me. I could even hear Grandfather saying, 'She's a good one, that Sarah – a Cranachan eh?' But I realised I'd probably blown my chances.

The rest of the day dragged by with my thoughts drifting from Sarah to Cape Breton and my business idea, to an image of being curled up in bed at home, safe and warm. My body wanted me to crawl into the back of the dry cave and fall asleep, but I'd read that that was a classic symptom of hypothermia. I knew I had to keep moving. I braved a walk across the narrow spit of land that almost divided the two hills of Goat Island, almost bent double as the wind hurtled through the gap. But I persisted, scuffing my feet in the sand that was exposed here at low tide.

Darkness was falling. The lights of the house at Roshven were on: surely someone would be looking out at the storm through binoculars? I would have been if I were them. There was someone on the lawn in the distance with a black dog. He wouldn't see me now in the dusk, though. I waved and shouted anyway, knowing my voice was being carried out to sea in the wind.

I was completely exhausted and needed to find shelter for the night, so I crossed back to the northerly half of the island, found the little cave again, and made a bed of bracken and heather. I just had to sleep. Grandfather had told me that in the old days the cattle drovers would sleep out night after night, often soaked in desperate weather. I could do it if they could, surely?

They may have been accustomed to it, but I sure as hell wasn't, even though I had found a square of polystyrene stuck under a rock which made a decent pillow. I wasn't sure if I was unconscious or sleeping, but I woke, shivering like hell, several times and tightened the straps on the lifejacket even further to try and keep my body heat in, curling up as tight as I could before eventually drifting off again.

When my eyes next opened it was light. I was looking straight down the loch and the rain was dripping off the rock in front of me. The wind still caused ripples on the water nearby and I could see white caps further off. My injured arm throbbed, the cloth wet with new blood. I lay still for a while. I couldn't see the benefit of moving, except I knew I needed to stomp around to warm up. I was hungry now, too. I'd only had porridge and coffee this time yesterday. My throat was parched. I needed to find fresh water.

The rain had eased off a little, but was the wind too strong for me to stand on top of the hill and wave at Roshven? It was my best chance of getting noticed – I'd have to give it a try.

Hauling myself to my feet was an effort. I was weak from blood loss, hunger and my body being chilled to the bone. I scouted around for a puddle of rainwater to drink from and eventually found a steady drip off a rocky ledge beneath which I filled my cupped hands.

As I walked back and forth, I eyed the significant quantity of driftwood on the shore of the dividing stone beach. God, if only I could light it. I'd warm up and someone would see the smoke for sure. My waterproof matches were probably half-way across the Atlantic by now.

I returned to my shelter and sat there, hugging my knees. I wondered: when does a body stop shivering and just give up? Sarah was always on my mind. She was expecting me to be camping at Lower Polnish tonight. I wondered if she was thinking about me. I closed my eyes and dozed. We are back in the bothy again, hunched over Grandfather's map, the candles flickering, our shoulders touching. She's laughing at something I've said, I'm laughing, too . . . our eyes meet, our faces only inches apart. Later that night, the door latch opens, she approaches my bunk and climbs into my sleeping bag . . . *it's cold out there, let me warm you up*, she whispers. I fall asleep, my body warm against hers . . .

It was quite some time before I woke again, my entire body shivering. I got up and walked to the most southerly point of the island. There were skerries between me and Roshven, maybe a 300-metre swim – surely I could manage that? But I was so weak, my left arm was useless, and that combined with the gale and the strong tides . . . it would have to be my last resort.

Head down into the gale, I picked through the driftwood, and selected a decent-sized plank. If I draped my body over that and swam using only my legs, perhaps I'd make it when the sea was calmer. I leant forward to begin dragging it, and my legs buckled, ankles twisting amongst the stones. It was too hard. I gave up and slumped to the ground.

After a while I forced myself to go up the hill again. I couldn't just sit there; I had to be proactive. I would try to attract attention from the Roshven people and watch for a boat. Of course, the main reason why I had wanted to come to Goat Island in the first place was to climb to the summit and look at the fort. Yet every step up the steep hill was a struggle. All I wanted to do was lie down and sleep. My feet in those ridiculous canvas shoes couldn't get a grip so I constantly fell; the brambles tore at my ankles as I went but it didn't seem to matter – they were numb already. The primroses and the tiny tree shoots coming into leaf offered scant comfort.

During the balmy days of last week I had envisaged coming here, lying on the peak in the sun with my sketch pad. Now I knew that just lifting my head over the ridge would see me hit by the full force of the wind.

I'd read online of the old fort at the top of the southerly summit. It was pre-Roman in age and vitrified, which meant it was made of stones molten together with such intense heat that scientists had been baffled how it was achieved. I remembered a line: 'The temperatures required to vitrify the entire fort structure in-situ are equal to those found in an atomic bomb detonation.'

Grandfather had said that the Gillies family had been on Ardnish since God was born. Perhaps they had been on this island, fighting off attackers? If so, where was their water supply? Shelter? Surely they would not have been here all year round, throughout the winter? If this was what the weather was like in late April, I could hardly bear to imagine what it would be like to be trapped here in early February. I had been desperate to pace it all out, take photographs, do my drawing. I had absolutely no strength. I crawled the last few metres into the shelter of the fort wall and lay there, exhausted. The stones were glassy, as if they had oil on them.

After a few minutes, I rolled onto my stomach and raised my head above the parapet. I could see the walls, which stood about two feet high, disappear along the ridge and that was all. I wished I had the strength to walk around. I took the phone out of its little bag and peered at it. My text still had 'not sent' against it. I tried again. There was a long wait, during which my hopes rose, then a ping and 'not sent' appeared again. The sea beyond was raging just as yesterday and not a boat was to be seen. The Sgùrr of Eigg was visible in the distance but low cloud hid Rum behind it. I could see Muck too, from time to time. My grandfather had said that on a clear day, you could make out the island of Barra from where I was now. And to the north, the Cuillins of Skye would be clearly visible. Well, to be sure, I saw none of that today.

I thought how lovely it would have been to have come here with Sarah, to have a picnic in the sun, to lie entwined on the grass. I imagined us kissing deeply, her arms around me, holding me tight. She must have been here before. It would be on every kayaking group's itinerary, wouldn't it?

I must stand up, I told myself. I struggled to my feet and stood leaning into the bitter wind. I was hyper-aware of my body temperature dropping. I waved, pathetically, towards the big house. 'Help! Help!' I croaked, into the storm.

It was even more slippy going down. I slithered about twenty metres at one stage and banged my sore arm hard on a rock. I just sat where I stopped and started to sob. I knew I might die here. I began to shout: 'God! Hello, God, can you hear me? I'm your friend, help me! Please! God are you there?' Who was the patron saint of the lost? St Anthony, was it? I resolved to pray to him.

I inched back towards my cave and crawled inside. The next few hours passed in a blur. I woke in the early hours to find I had stopped shivering, but I knew that was a bad sign, so I forced myself up again. It had stopped raining, the moon came and went through the clouds, and everything was bright. The tide was right out. I tried stamping my feet and beating my arms pathetically around my chest. My stomach was gurgling like mad and I had a pounding headache now, too. I was desperately thirsty again and went to find the place I had found water before. There was a seal just offshore, watching me. Maybe it was a mermaid. But didn't they sit on rocks and lure sailors to their death?

I went along the rocks, picked off mussels and sucked out the flesh. Uncooked, they were disgusting. I picked out the inside of a periwinkle and ate that, too, but quickly decided I'd rather die of hunger. I noticed a bright green seaweed: sea lettuce. I'd read that locals ate it in the old days so I tried a piece. It was a mistake. I retched and retched, but there was nothing to vomit.

I checked my phone. No texts, no emails, nothing. I still had plenty of battery, though. I thought about leaving a fare-well video message to Sarah, to tell her that I knew she thought I was a stupid idiot but would she perhaps see through that to the real me? Maybe I should tell her that I was in love with her.

Finally, I saw the man with the black Labrador walk down to the beach again. I struggled to my feet, waved and tried to shout, but once again, it came out as no more than a croak. Why couldn't he see me? I despaired as I saw him turn and walk back to the house. I sat there with my back against the cliff, watching seaweed ebb and flow, listening to the gentle rumble of stones being rolled by the tide. Nothing mattered any more. Suddenly I felt at peace. I tried to remember the various stages of despair. Was the last one acceptance, once hope had been extinguished? My body slumped forward, my head hanging down.

After a while I scrolled through the photographs on my phone. I saw Nathalie in bed with Mairi the day after the birth, then earlier ones of Grandfather and Broch. There was one of my parents, on their wedding day at St Margaret's of Scotland in Judique, which had sat on the mantelpiece at home all my life. I peered closely. They must have been my age. They looked ridiculously young. I was shocked to realise that I couldn't really remember them. My mother looked shy. I kissed the screen.

If I didn't get help today, it would be too late. My body was shutting down. My parents would see me sooner rather than later.

Above me, the seagulls soared and dipped. A gannet, with its yellow neck, dropped from high like an arrow into the sea, and two oystercatchers picked amongst the stones on the shore, only a few metres from me.

I no longer fought to stay awake. I wondered if death was close. What would I miss most? Right now, it would be Sarah. We hadn't spent much time together but I knew I adored her.

I was leaning against a rock, drifting into unconsciousness. The wind dropped, and the sun came out. I could feel its warmth on my face. But I didn't have any strength left. My eyes were closed tight, my mother was kneeling beside my cot, tucking my blanket in. She put my little white teddy in my arms and leant forward to kiss me. *Good night, darling, God bless, see you tomorrow.*

I woke with a start, to the penetrating sound of a horn. With a huge effort I opened my eyes and saw a bright orange boat, very close to the shore, with two people climbing out at the front.

Then, I heard a man's voice: 'Are you all right? Wave your arm!' I didn't wave, my eyes shut again. A dream.

'Peter Angus, you're alive! Oh, thank God! We thought you were dead when we saw you through the binoculars!' Sarah's face was inches from mine, her hands cupping my face.

I managed to smile. It still didn't seem real.

Two men began peeling my wet clothes off, rubbing me with a towel and wrapping me in a blanket and silver sheet.

Sarah grasped my hands. 'You're so cold! Your hands are freezing. Hold on – a helicopter is coming.'

Shortly afterwards, the helicopter landed on the flat area of ground in the middle of the island and, with a man on each side, I was carried over, put on a stretcher and lifted on board.

'Is he your partner?' I heard one of the crew members ask Sarah.

'He is my friend,' she said firmly, climbing into the helicopter before there could be any further discussion.

Chapter 27

I was detained at the Belford Hospital in Fort William for three days. My heart rate was monitored, and I was initially given oxygen to help me breathe. There was some concern about my renal function but I soon got the all-clear, thankfully. I had been worried about hospital fees but was informed that there wouldn't be any. The doctor told me that he had never come across anyone whose body had dropped to such a low temperature. He reckoned I had been only an hour away from death. The medical notes at the end of my bed said that the coastguard helicopter had noted my temperature to be 30.5 degrees, with my skin blue and cold to the touch when they picked me up. That was seven degrees below normal, I was told: severe hypothermia. The cut on my arm had required twelve stitches, and my arm, swollen and purple, was bandaged and placed in a sling.

Sarah visited each day. I had grapes and magazines galore, and she would arrive with a fresh coffee at nine in the morning, having rearranged her shifts at the care home and kayaking lessons to be with me. We talked for hours. I couldn't get over how warm and intelligent she was, and I looked forward to her visits so much.

'What caused you to come looking for me?' I asked her on my first day in hospital.

'Well, obviously I knew the weather had been much worse than expected. I'd been watching the sea and thinking of you. I knew you wouldn't be daft enough to go kayaking out to sea – or at least, I *thought* you wouldn't – and I was pretty certain that, if you did go out, you would be just creeping along the shore to Polnish.'

I felt a glow of pleasure at her concern. 'Sarah,' I said quietly, 'it's lovely of you to visit me like this, but, well, I bet your boyfriend isn't too happy about it . . .'

'What boyfriend?'

My heart was pounding. 'Er, the fisherman from Peterhead?' I could feel myself blushing. 'I saw you at Mass with him on Sunday . . .'

'Peter Angus,' she said sternly, 'he's my mother's little brother. I stay with him and his family in Arisaig. But it's true that the guys round here think I have a boyfriend in Peterhead. I won't be putting them right, either. It saves all sorts of hassle.'

We grinned at each other. 'Okay, right . . . Sorry, I interrupted your story – please go on.' I couldn't think what else to say. My heart gave a little skip of pleasure at this news.

'Well, I decided that because of the weather you would definitely arrive at Lochailort early on Friday, so I went along there with the trailer for the kayak.

'I was quite relaxed when I arrived at the bridge at Lochailort. I sat there for half an hour with my binoculars and then I went down to the cottage at Upper Polnish to see if you might have spent the night, but there was no sign. Honestly, it still hadn't dawned on me that there might be something wrong. It didn't occur to me that you'd be daft enough to head for Goat Island.'

'I'm sorry,' I mumbled.

'I had to get back to work, so on my way back to Mallaig, I dropped in on Big John. Your sister rang while I was there. She'd had a text from you saying you were stranded on Goat Island. She couldn't get hold of you on the phone, so she rang the only person she knew–'

'That's amazing,' I interrupted her. 'Thank God! I sent a text twice, but both times it failed.'

Sarah nodded. 'I was getting really worried by then so I rang my friend Chris. He's a member of the lifeboat crew. I told him you were marooned on Goat Island . . . but obviously I didn't know you'd capsized and were hypothermic . . .'

She brushed a tear from her eye.

'Chris said we should head down there to pick you up. He told me to drive up to Mallaig and come out with him and a friend in his RIB. Chris had his lifeboat radio with him, and we heard the police talking about a blue kayak being found washed up on the beach at Back of Keppoch. That's when it became serious. The radio was going non-stop. Chris told them that he believed the kayaker was in Lochailort, probably on Eilean nan Godhar, and that he was on the way. The coastguard controller said that a helicopter was en route, too.'

I winced. 'I've caused so much fuss.'

'Well, accidents happen, Peter Angus. Don't be too hard on yourself. But we all knew that someone would only survive fifteen minutes in the sea at this time of the year. And I had to tell them that you didn't have a dry suit. Chris gave me such a hard time for letting you go without one . . . I feel so bad about that. I should have insisted.' She looked into my eyes. 'I'm sorry.'

I shook my head. 'No, no! It was my decision. You made it very clear. It's just that the weather was so perfect when we were having the lesson and I was worried about the cost . . . I'm the one who should be sorry. It was reckless.'

'I prayed for you,' she said. 'I was frantic by then.'

'I prayed endlessly too.'

'So, the wind had eased a bit by the time we went around Goat Island and it was me who saw you first through the binoculars. You were lying with your back against a rock. You were so still . . . God, it was horrible. I thought you were dead. Chris was shouting at you while they lowered the anchor and he gave a couple of blasts on the horn. That's when you moved your head.'

'I don't really remember,' I admitted.

'I honestly thought you were dead – we all did.' She bowed her head.

Instinctively, I leaned forward and hugged her. 'Thank you,' I whispered. 'I don't have the words . . .'

It was at that moment that Big John popped his head round the ward door and caught us in each other's arms. I pulled away clumsily, feeling my cheeks flare.

'Someone's feeling better.' He smiled.

'It's so good to see you, John.'

'I have some good news for you. The kayak was picked up at the campsite at Back of Keppoch. I collected the dry bag from the hotel, and here it is.'

'That's amazing,' I gasped, taking the package. 'Thanks.'

It was all there and, luckily, dry. The maps, my wallet and, most importantly, my sketch pad.

The evening before I was due to be discharged, the arrival of two police officers at my bedside caused quite a stir on the ward. Sarah had reported the discovery of the skeleton at the police station in Mallaig and they were due to visit the site tomorrow. I was cautioned and everything logged. I showed them the photographs and GPS location on my phone, and they put up a satellite map on an iPad so I could identify the exact spot, for good measure. They told me they would be in touch after they had been to recover the body and, meanwhile, I was not to leave the country.

The following morning, Sarah came in on the train to carry my bag and take me back to Arisaig. I'd made an appointment to see Katie MacPhee, the lawyer, and asked the nurse where the office was.

'Just across the road, on the other side of the supermarket,' she replied, 'and the *Oban Times* wants a word too. A reporter came by and left a number.'

'I can meet you afterwards at the coffee shop.' Sarah said.

'No, no, you come along too,' I insisted. 'It will just be family papers.'

First, we called into the *Oban Times* office in the High Street. They had heard all about my escapade on Goat Island, but I assumed they knew about the skeleton from someone at the hospital so I started telling them about that. The prospect of a story about a dead body on a remote peninsula was far more appealing to them than one about my near-death experience, it seemed. The journalist told me that they would check their missing persons' files from the 1980s and promised to have someone follow it up. I told him I had no reason to believe that anything untoward had happened to the man. Before I left, the journalist took some photographs, read back my quotes to me, and reassured me that they would do some research and speak to the police. She hoped the story would run this coming Thursday.

Katie MacPhee came down to the reception to meet me. She checked my ID and asked me to sign a release form.

'Did you ever meet my grandfather, Katie?' I asked.

She shook her head. 'I'm afraid I didn't. This box has been in storage for decades. At Christmas, I received a letter instructing us to hand it over to Peter Angus Gillies, but I was only to do so face to face; on no account was I to post it out to you.'

'You must have found that strange.'

'Nothing surprises me anymore,' she replied with a smile, before shaking our hands and showing us out.

And that was it: family papers. There was an envelope with my name on it and a small cardboard box containing a file and a couple of antiquarian leather-bound books, handwritten, in Gaelic.

I sighed. This was my legacy.

Sarah and I caught the 12.12 train back to Arisaig, and as it moved off, I read the letter from Grandfather.

Dear Peter Angus,

I am leaving you the family papers – perhaps you will find something interesting in them.

Your loving Grandfather.

Nothing personal, no clue. My heart sank. I felt bitterly disappointed. I guess my hopes had been raised because Nathalie had been left the house; I'd wondered if Grandfather might have left me some property – anything to even up the inheritance he'd left my sister.

'You look miserable,' Sarah said.

'Well, I am disappointed,' I replied. 'It's just some old manuscripts saved from the fire. My sister was left a house worth three hundred and fifty thousand dollars and I was left five thousand in cash. I hoped that this package would balance things out somehow.'

'What are the books?' Sarah asked.

'They're the books of the bard Ronald MacDonald. I'm a direct descendant of his.'

'Really?' She opened one. 'Ah, they're in Gaelic.'

'So what?' I replied, slumping back in my seat, frowning.

Sarah closed the book and rounded on me. 'You're acting like a spoilt brat!' She thumped me on the leg. 'You should think yourself lucky. These books look wonderful. I wouldn't be surprised if they were really important. Why on earth should you expect something for nothing, anyhow?'

We continued the journey in silence. At Arisaig, we climbed into her Land Rover at the station. Sarah drove me to Big John's but stayed in the car as I got out.

I leant through the window and apologised.

She stared straight ahead. 'Forget it,' she replied, and drove off before I could get another word out.

No hug, no farewell, no plan to meet again. I didn't even have a chance to thank her properly for saving me, for coming to the hospital. I stood on the pavement, head down. My mind was spinning with everything that was going on: my trip around Ardnish, my ordeal on the island and the box of trash I'd just retrieved. And all of it was mixed up with my complete failure to get anywhere with Sarah. I felt as though I'd reached an ending. I was once more thinking I should just go and place the plaque on the gravestone and fly home early.

Chapter 28

Next morning, I sat in Big John's sitting room, gazing out over the beautiful Arisaig Bay, now as flat as a millpond. Big John had given me a cup of tea with too much sugar, put a rug over my legs and another over my shoulders, and turned up the heating.

'You need to sweat it out, Peter Angus,' he told me solemnly. 'It'll help you recover. By the way, I've been speaking to your sister on the phone, and she wants to have a chat with you when you feel up to it.'

I was more settled this morning. I'd slept well, glad not to have the night-time bleeps and bustle of the hospital ward, and I'd resolved to not give up on Sarah. As soon as I could I'd meet her again and give her a huge bunch of flowers to say thank you.

I picked up the box from the floor. With a sigh, I began leafing through the contents. The file contained the tenancy agreement between Arisaig Estate and Donald Angus Gillies, dated 17 October 1945, a stack of bills and a notebook itemising the number of lambs sold and prices fetched from the Fort William mart. He'd got seventeen pounds and four shillings for two hundred and eight 'Top Blackface Lambs' in August 1951. There was a quote for re-roofing Laggan in Ballachulish slate from McLaggan Builders in Fort William dated July that year, at twenty-five pounds. No wonder they left.

I opened the books next. I skipped through pages of verse and song, but then, thoroughly bored, just as I was about to toss them aside and make myself a sandwich, tucked inside the back cover of the larger volume, I discovered a very old, faded letter, written in French and dated May 1746. On a separate sheet, in my grandmother's handwriting, was a translation in English, dated 28 January 1946.

Sir,

Thank you for rescuing me and tending my wounds, though I fear I am weak now and will not survive. To repay your kindness, this letter will lead you to the place where the Louis d'or have been left. Be quick to find it – a messenger has been sent to le Jeune Chevalier telling of its whereabouts.

I was aboard the frigate Bellone. *We lay offshore protecting the* Mars, *which was badly damaged and had been beached while repairs were made. Beyond us at the entrance to the loch sat two English frigates; we expected a further attack at any time.*

With my looking-glass I spied the Mars. *The sailors were sent up the ridge to protect the men working to repair the ship below. Many bundles of muskets and other supplies were stored in a cave. There, too, is the gold sent to your King to support his army – the Louis d'or.*

It lies in the cave to the left, 200 toise east of the village on the north side.

The Mars *was pulled off the beach at high tide, and as she set sail, she fired a salute.*

Once again, thank you for helping me.

Good luck, my friend!
Lt Henri Giraudeau

'Oh my God!' I cried.

Big John came running through. 'Are you all right?'

'Have a look at this,' I said, thrusting the letter into his hands.

He sat down beside me and read the letter, before rubbing his forehead and looking at me. 'Well, people from around here have been looking for that gold ever since the sea battle. That's some clue you've been given.'

'But why didn't Grandfather find the treasure? It doesn't make sense.' I thought hard. 'I'm sure I once heard that there was a letter in French given to my ancestor Donald John by your ancestor Johnny Bochan from Sloch, but Grandmother had been quite dismissive of it.'

Big John smiled. 'Well, he did spend a lot of time looking for it – more than he would let on. You'll remember how your grandmother got fed up hearing about it and banned the subject. "That bloody gold", she used to say.'

'I'll head over there tomorrow and have a look,' I said.

'Well, laddie, not so fast. You aren't strong enough yet. Your arm needs time to heal, and we don't have a car to get you around.'

'Maybe Hamish would come?' I suggested. 'Not sure he has wheels, though.'

'Or Sarah?' said John. 'She'd have more chance of getting off work.'

I'd confessed to Big John last night that I'd put my foot in it with her – yet again. 'She probably won't even take my call,' I said.

'Give it a try,' he advised.

I really didn't want to make that call, and kept putting it off. Big John came through to tell me to offer Sarah a bowl of his special pasta tonight – how that would definitely do the trick – so I finally plucked up the courage.

'Sarah, it's me.'

'Hi, Peter Angus,' she replied.

The rest tumbled out. 'Listen, you were so kind to me, coming to find me, caring for me in the hospital, everything. I messed up. I didn't thank you properly. I may still have been in shock or whatever, but really, truly, I am so grateful for everything you've done for me.'

There was a silence at the other end of the line, then: 'No worries. I'm glad you are okay.'

Her tone was softer. I began to feel a little better. 'Sarah, there is an extraordinary letter we really need to show you. Big John thinks you'd be really interested, and he wants you to come to supper tonight. He's doing his special pasta. I'd like you to come, too. The letter . . . it's a big thing,' I added encouragingly. 'Will you come? Please?'

She arrived at seven on the dot. I opened the door and found myself at a loss for words. Her hair was tied up, she wore a gold necklace with a Celtic cross on it, like the one I'd drawn for Nathalie after Grandfather's funeral, and she was dressed in white jeans. She looked beautiful.

After what seemed like ages, we both smiled and moved forward to hug.

'Come in,' I said at last. 'Big John tells me his pasta is world-class.'

After dinner we sat around the fire, nursing our host's carefully poured whisky. I was bursting to tell Sarah everything.

'So,' I began, 'John and I want to let you in on a secret, but you have to promise not to say a word, okay?'

'Is it to do with your family papers?' she asked.

'Yes.'

She was smiling. I wasn't sure she was taking it seriously.

'Right . . . well, it's to do with Bonnie Prince Charlie's gold. Have you heard of it?'

'Of course I have,' she replied. 'Anyone who's lived in the area for a while has heard about it. It's every kid's dream to find it. But isn't it all a myth?'

I shrugged. 'I don't know for sure. In fact, John, why don't you tell us some of the rumours, before we concentrate on what we actually know?'

'There are several theories,' Big John began. 'There was some research done by a university student, which was widely reported in the newspapers and had treasure hunters swarming all over the area back in about 2003, I think. They reported that a local man called Neill Iain Ruairi, on his deathbed, had told his family that he had been passing along the lochside as the gold was being buried. He hid in the trees until the men had completed the task and then he returned later and helped himself to a bag of Louis d'or. He told his family that there was a bag of gold coins buried near Arisaig, under a black stone with a tree root springing from it.

'And there was another theory that the treasure was in fact 1.2 million Spanish livres in a number of chests. One was taken by MacDonald of Barrisdale; the rest were hidden on Loch Arkaig side and the location entrusted to Locheil, the chief of the Cameron clan, and then later to Cluny Macpherson, the Macpherson chief. Macpherson was hiding in a cave for eight years, and Prince Charles, when he was back in France, accused him of stealing the hoard. Locheil's brother also came back from France to look for it but he was caught by the

English and hanged. But Clan Cameron records do describe some gold coins being found in the woods in 1850.

'And the last, and most romantic, rumour, is that it's buried on one of the islands in Loch Eilt, but every inch of those islands has been scoured by people with metal detectors over the years. Worth a shot, I'd say – back in 2003 the papers said it was worth about ten million pounds.'

'Okay, enough with the myths and legends,' Sarah said. 'What's going on?'

'According to family lore,' I began, 'on the clifftops on the north side of the Ardnish peninsula and along the shore at Borrodale, there were hundreds of locals watching the sea battle as it took place. Our family wouldn't have wanted to miss a thing, Grandfather said. The *Bellone* and *Mars* had intended to unload French and Spanish soldiers off to join the Jacobites, as well as muskets and, of course, the gold, to pay for the uprising. Then the French were told that Prince Charlie's army had been routed at Culloden just two weeks before, but the gold was still needed to help him and others to escape.

'Two English frigates had followed the French ships up the coast and the next day they came and trapped the French in Loch nan Uamh. The *Mars* was badly damaged by English cannon and had to be beached to avoid sinking. But nobody knew where or, indeed, if, anything at all was unloaded.' I reached across to the coffee table and picked up the letter. 'Until this!' I brandished it proudly.

Sarah's eyes widened. 'What does it say?'

I read it aloud, then replaced it on the table. 'I think it has to be under the cliffs below Mullochbuie. When I was kayak-ing along there, I took a particular interest in the shore. There are a few caves and an east-facing stone beach. I wonder if that was where the *Mars* was repaired. I looked up "toise" online, and it's roughly a metre, so the distance on the Ordnance Survey map from the ruins to that beach might be about right, although neither the caves nor the stone beach are marked, oddly, even though Loch nan Uamh means "Loch of the Caves".

'It really looks like the perfect place for the *Mars* to be patched up and the gold to be hidden. The locals couldn't have seen onto the beach from above and the English frigates would have had to be hard against the cliffs to see into it too.'

Sarah sat forward. 'Okay, so this is what we know that no one else does – at least no one else alive.' She gave me a sympathetic look. 'We know it's Louis d'or and not Spanish gold, as one of the stories suggested. We know it was definitely taken off the ship and didn't go back to France and that it was put in a cave, about two hundred metres east of a village, on the north side.' She paused. 'That means below Mullochbuie, right?'

'There are caves at Sloch,' I added, 'which is where the Bochan's family who had the letter hailed from, but I think that's just where Henri wrote the letter. The place is so open; the gold would have been taken by the locals before the French ships had even set sail. I'm sure he means below Mullochbuie.'

I paused, suddenly realising that I hadn't mentioned the cannon. 'Wait, wait . . . I'm being an idiot. I *know* the *Mars* was beached at Mullochbuie. When I was coming down the steep slope towards the shore I caught my foot and went flying. I thought it was a rock, but it felt odd, so I dug it out. It turned out to be a massive cannon that had been sitting on a ledge and grown over.'

'Well, that's that sorted,' said Big John, laughing and coming to my rescue. 'We have the correct place.'

'We can split the money between us,' I said. 'After all, the French sailor's letter was written thanking your family for rescuing him, Iain Mhor, wasn't it?'

'Och, nonsense! I'll not take a centime. What would I use it for at my age?' replied the old man firmly, getting to his feet. 'Right, you youngsters, I'm off to bed. Let me know your plan in the morning.'

We wished him goodnight as he disappeared upstairs, leaving Sarah and me alone.

'Well, what do you think? Should I go hunt for the treasure? Or can you hear my grandmother reminding me it's just a wild goose chase?'

'You should definitely go,' she replied. 'There's your discovery of the cannon and the letter gives information that only your grandparents knew, so you have far more facts to go on than all the other people who have been looking. It would be mad not to go to Mullochbuie while you're here and still have the time. You would always regret it if you didn't.'

'Would you come with me?' I asked. 'It's just that this arm of mine will take a while before it's strong again.' I was going for the sympathy vote here.

Sarah paused and bit her lip.

'Could you get some time off work? It would be fun! Please . . . come.'

'Well . . .'

I moved over to the sofa and sat beside her. 'I know I say stupid things, but it's because I'm trying too hard to impress you. If we spent more time together, maybe you'd come to like me as much as I do you?'

'You are sweet,' she said quietly. 'And I do like you. That's why you see so much of me.'

'So you'll do it?' I held my breath.

She took her phone from her bag and scrolled through her calendar. 'I have a zero-hours contract at the care home, so that'd work . . . and I heard on Nevis Radio that there's terrible weather coming in, non-stop rain, so there won't be any kayak courses for a while . . . so, yup, I'm up for it.'

'Oh, and by the way, I'll not take a centime either,' she said. 'No discussion, okay?'

I took her hand. 'I'm so pleased we're going together, really I am.'

I leant forward and kissed her lightly on the lips.

She smiled, then stood up, straightening her clothes. 'Okay. I'd better go – Cranachan needs a walk, then bed. How about I pop around tomorrow morning when John's around and we can come up with a plan?'

Chapter 29

As planned, Sarah returned the next morning. She was greeted by Big John, who poured her a coffee from the pot on the stove. We settled down for a blether, as he called it.

'So, you're a Cranachan?' Big John asked Sarah.

'I am, through my mother's side.'

'Well, you two have a strong connection there,' Big John remarked. 'Your two families have been linked for at least six generations. Peter Angus's family were very close friends of Archbishop and Colonel Willie MacDonald, both Cranachans, in the first half of the last century. Three generations who served in the Lovat Scouts together from the Boer War in 1900 through until the end of the Second World War. And, Peter Angus, it was your Great-great-aunt Sheena who went out to Cape Breton and met the Miramichi MacDonalds, who are Cranachans too.'

I looked at him in alarm. 'Sarah and I aren't related, are we?'

He chuckled. 'Not at all. It's just generations of friendship, no more than that. At your grandfather's funeral I met Louise MacIsaac and Joanne MacDonald, cousins of yours, Sarah. Do you know who I'm talking about, Peter Angus?'

'I do indeed, great friends of our family,' I replied. 'But I've never quite understood why they are referred to as the "Cranachans".'

'I can help you there,' Sarah said. 'Cranachan is a farm, a good mile from the nearest road, four miles up into Glen Roy. The house is big, stone-built, with five bedrooms and steadings for horses. Huge Scots pines tower over the place. They would have farmed cattle and then sheep there, had a few pigs and a couple of fields of crops. The family who lived there, our MacDonald ancestors, took the name of the place and became known as the Cranachans.'

'Ah, I've got it now,' I said.

'In the old days of clan warfare round these parts it was important to be as big and strong as possible, to do battle with the huge Lochaber axes and to work the farm. Feats of strength were an everyday spectacle, and every village inn would have a stone that the young men would compete to throw over a branch of a tree. And prizes for feats of strength and endurance were given out at local games.'

'How far back can you go?' I asked.

'Well, my mum's told me all about this, and as far as I can remember, the first we know of the Cranachans was Allisdair Mhor, or Big Allisdair, from Bohuntin above Roy Bridge. He was said to be the tallest man in Scotland, red-haired, and celebrated for his cattle-thieving centuries ago. He was captured and expelled overseas. The six Cranachan brothers, and me, too, are descended from him. They were born in the early part of the nineteenth century and were tenant farmers. At least three of them were noted for their strength; they won the shot-putting, hammer and even the hill races at every Games. In 1849, they were invited to a Scottish Society Games in London, which Queen Victoria and Prince Albert attended. Colin won the hammer, Archibald came third, and Colin then won the foot race. Mum told me he was described in *The Times* as arriving at the finish "like a stag from his native hills". He was presented with a gold medal as the competitor who won the largest number of prizes at the "fête", as they called it.

'Mum's convinced my Cranachan blood is where my athleticism comes from,' she added, with a smile. 'Anyway, their older brother John didn't enter the games as he was too old, but he was apparently the best athlete of them all. It's him who was reported in the *Dundee Courier* as rescuing his crippled brother when a bull made for him. He broke the beast's neck – aged eighty!'

Big John chimed in: 'Yes, and it was Long John, a first cousin of the six brothers, again perhaps the tallest man in Scotland at the time, who founded what became the biggest distilling company in Scotland in Fort William. And of his grandsons, Andrew became the Archbishop and his brother was Colonel Willie.'

'There was a great female Cranachan, too – an Australian cousin named Mother Mary MacKillop. She set up an order of nuns to educate the rural poor and became Australia's first saint.'

I recognised the name. 'Yes, I remember people from Stella Maris at home going to Rome for her canonisation.'

We all sat in silence for a few minutes.

'We're all very proud of being Cranachans,' Sarah said, 'even my dog.'

We all burst out laughing.

'We should probably start planning our trip,' I said.

'Well, I'm going to Inverness tomorrow. Give me a list and I'll pick up anything you need. I've got my brother's Land Rover so there's plenty of room.'

'Okay,' I said. 'I think we'll need to stay at Mullochbuie for a couple of days, maybe three, so we'll need my tent and some food. And a pickaxe, shovel and metal detector, plus fifty metres of rope to help us get up and down the cliff.'

'I could borrow a shovel and pickaxe from my boyfriend – sorry, my uncle,' Sarah said, giving me a wink. 'And I've got a climbing rope and a couple of harnesses, so I can easily belay you down. If we're going to be totally secretive about this, I'll need to come up with an alibi about where we're off to. I couldn't leave the Land Rover in the lay-by at the start of the Ardnish walk for several days; people would ask what I was up to. But there is a hidden quarry nearby. I could park there. Problem solved.'

She kissed me on the forehead. 'Right. Got to go. I've got a minibus full of teenagers needing lessons before they set off on their Duke of Edinburgh trip. I hope they pay more attention than you.'

I followed her out to her car. 'Sarah?' I said, lightly catching her hand.

'Yes, Peter Angus?'

'Would you let me take you to dinner tomorrow, at Arisaig House? I've heard it's good.'

She smiled. 'Yes, please. That would be lovely.'

That night, I lay in bed thinking of her. She was completely up for our big adventure – and we had a date too. Things were turning around.

Then my thoughts turned to Grandfather. He would be so pleased if I found the gold, he really would. I wondered if the real reason why he hadn't found the treasure himself was simply that they didn't have metal detectors back then. He would have been able to take a rope and get down the cliff for a look, probably, but nothing more.

I'd done some research online on metal detector stockists that morning, and had given MacGregor's a call, doing my damnedest to sound like an eighty-something Scotsman.

'No, we don't stock them. Have you tried HIS?' offered the woman. I rang them next, explained that I was in Inverness on Friday, I was elderly, and would really appreciate it if they would try and find me one; I'd heard from someone in my local history group that an Altai Treasure Seeker 5 would suit my purpose.

She'd put me on hold, returning a few minutes later to confirm that they could have one ready for Saturday morning and it would cost £195.

Big John had nodded and given me the thumbs up, whispering that he would stay with his friend for an extra night.

The rest of the day had been spent compiling a list of what kit we needed. I had about $1,100 left from Grandfather's will, and I would get the £200 kayak deposit back from the hotel.

The adventure was becoming real.

Chapter 30

The next day found me alone in the house. Big John had gone off for his medical appointment, the shopping list was done, and I was scanning through the Gaelic books Grandfather had left me, trying to decipher the bard's handwriting. I was still not quite back to full strength and had been told to keep warm and stay indoors for a while, but I planned to have a wander along the shore later.

Earlier, I had found a chanter in the house and was trying to learn a tune that had lain amongst the family papers I'd collected from MacPhees. It was a pibroch called '*Thaing Me Righ Air Tir Am Muideart*' – meaning 'My King Has Landed in Moidart' – and had been written to commemorate Bonnie Prince Charlie arriving in 1745.

My mind wasn't on it, though. I couldn't help glancing at the kitchen clock every few minutes as I waited for the sound of the Land Rover coming up the hill.

Relax, I kept telling myself. You're having the most exciting holiday imaginable, you're about to go on a date with the girl of your dreams, and you have a letter which may lead you to the most sought-after treasure in Scotland.

I decided to Facetime Nathalie.

I was dying to tell her all my news as soon as we connected, although I could hear Aunt Maggie's voice in my head, telling me that it was polite to ask after others first. 'How is wee Mairi?' I asked.

'Oh, she is just perfect,' Nathalie cooed, showing me the baby in her cot, fast asleep. 'Look, the family's red hair is really showing now. She slept through the night last night – she's a little star.'

It was only three weeks since I had left. It seemed a lifetime.

'Have you got over your little accident, eh?' she asked.

I had played down the tale of the capsizing and getting stuck on the island so as not to worry her. She was obviously so wrapped up with Mairi she had not fully absorbed how close I had been to dying.

'I have, and I'm going on a date tonight.'

'Really?' squealed Nathalie. 'A date! That's far more interesting. So, tell all – who is she? Do you have a photo? Tell me everything!'

'Where to start?' I grinned. 'Well, her name's Sarah and she's beautiful.'

'Go on.'

'She works as an outdoor adventure instructor in the summer and in a care home in the winter. She has a collie dog called Cranachan and she's a cousin of the Miramachi MacDonalds in Judique. Will that do?'

'Nice work!' Nathalie beamed. 'Send me a photo.'

I knew she would be flipping through the *Mabou Pioneers* book to see if she could make the connection the minute we hung up.

'Where are you going on this date? It better be somewhere good.'

'Arisaig House,' I replied. 'We're having dinner there tonight.'

'You better scrub up, bro, and shave – promise me you'll shave?'

'No time,' I said, 'she's due any second. Sorry.' She was doing a good job of being my mother. 'Oh, and I picked up the papers from the lawyer in Fort William,' I added casually, knowing how interested Nathalie would be.

'Wow, I'd forgotten all about that. What was in them?'

I kept my voice deadpan and matter-of-fact. 'Some books, and a two-hundred-and-seventy-year-old letter that our grandmother had translated from French, giving some excellent directions to the Jacobite gold.'

'No way!' Nathalie cried.

'I actually kayaked past the very spot a couple of weeks ago. Sarah and I are heading across for a proper look next week.'

'Hmm. She's probably only interested in you because of the gold.' She forced a laugh after she spoke, but I could tell she half meant it.

'I don't think so,' I replied. 'Oh, that's her car now.'

'Stay on the line! I need to meet her!'

'Not a chance.' I smiled. 'Bye, Nat, love you. Give Mairi a big kiss from Uncle Pete!'

Arisaig House wasn't a house, really; it was a castle. We were seated at a table by the window, with flowers and flickering candles, from where we could see Ardnish, in fact the very shoreline we would be exploring next week.

Sarah looked stunning. Her hair was pinned up, and her gold earrings and jewellery gleamed against her fair hair and skin. She wore a stylish white shirt and her mouth had a hint of red lipstick – very different from Sarah the kayaking instructor, in her green Montane jacket and leggings.

She ordered monkfish on a bed of samphire with a herb salad from the garden, while I went for local venison with a burgundy sauce, mustard mash, baby carrots and roast parsnips.

'I'm going for the good stuff while I can,' I whispered. 'Next week, we'll be eating freeze-dried curry, outside, in the rain.'

I poured some wine and felt myself relax. 'Why don't you tell me about your family,' I urged.

'Well, my parents met at Lochaber Athletics Club. Dad had been posted to the police station at Arisaig and Mum was a teacher at Lochaber High. They moved down south and into the pub business when I was ten. I'm an only child – spoilt rotten.'

'I don't see any evidence of it,' I said. 'You did business at uni, didn't you? So where did you learn to teach kayaking?'

'I took a course at Loch Eil Outward Bound during a uni break. I loved every minute. That's enough about my life – oh, apart from my dog. I adore him.'

'He's lovely,' I agreed. 'Did you get him as a puppy?'

She shook her head. 'He was given to me by a friend who'd decided that having a dog in an Edinburgh flat didn't work after all.'

There was a pause. This should have been the moment when she would ask about my family, but I knew she wouldn't.

I took a deep breath . . . 'My parents and my grandmother were killed in a car crash. My grandfather brought us up, from when I was ten and Nathalie fourteen.'

She reached across and covered my hand with hers. 'Peter Angus, if it's too painful . . .'

I shook my head. 'I'd like you to know. Perhaps it explains . . . what sort of person I am . . . or used to be.' I paused, before going on. 'The three of them were heading off to Halifax early one morning – to a funeral, ironically. They had just crossed the Canso Causeway and were on the highway. The road was pretty much empty, but then a truck pulled out from the Tim Hortons car park, right in front of them. They were all killed outright . . . Turned out the driver was four times over the limit.'

Sarah's face was wreathed with concern. 'I'm so sorry.'

'Thanks.' I took a sip of water and continued. 'Nat and I had just arrived at school. Grandfather had gone off to the scene of the accident straight after, with a friend of his. Our teachers must have heard the news at lunchtime, but it had been decided that we weren't to be told there. I remember thinking it was odd that a friend of my mother had come to collect us, as we'd been making our own way home for years. She chatted away at us, non-stop, and it felt a little weird. Then, when we got home, Grandfather sat us down in the kitchen – I remember he'd made us hot chocolate, our favourite. We could tell something had happened . . . and then he told us.'

Sarah shook her head in disbelief, tightening her grip on my hand.

'Nat was in a terrible state immediately, but it took until after the funeral for it to sink in for me. The worst thing was hearing Grandfather cry that first night. He was downstairs with a whisky bottle and we were in my sister's bed, holding each other tightly. My God, we said more than a few prayers that night. Aunt Maggie arrived from Ontario the next afternoon and began organising everything.'

'There was a discussion about whether we should go to live with her in Ontario, but we didn't want to. In retrospect, I think it was better for Grandfather that we stayed. He had us to live for.'

I was grateful how Sarah showed sympathy but didn't

overdo it or press me for more details. I didn't cry as I spoke, either, as I would have done a year ago.

'What happened to the truck driver?' she asked.

'He was breathalysed at the scene. It turned out he'd been drinking heavily the previous night and was still heavily intoxicated. He went down for manslaughter for sixteen years. And then he showed up at Grandfather's funeral.'

'What?' Sarah cried. 'That's appalling!'

'I'd hated the man for sixteen years, I had a newspaper article with his photograph on it in my chest of drawers, and I stuck a fork into his face so many times you could hardly recognise him. At the funeral I lost my temper and attacked him. I don't know what came over me; I'm normally a pretty mild person. Apparently he'd come to apologise.'

'What, he waited sixteen years to apologise?' Sarah said indignantly.

'Well, he was in prison for most of that time. Maybe he had a tragedy of his own? I know his mother died while he was inside. Perhaps his guilt overcame him . . . who knows?'

'The accident must have really scarred you and Nathalie.'

I nodded. 'You know, I'm glad I confronted him. I guess I needed to vent all that pent-up anger. But now, I feel I've almost come to accept the deaths, you know? I'm ready to move on.'

Sarah nodded. 'So your grandfather raised you himself?'

'He did. He blamed himself for not pushing me to go to university,' I continued. 'He told me a few times that I wasn't making the most of my talents.'

'What did you think?' Sarah asked.

I shrugged. 'I don't know. Maybe I was too scared, too comfortable in my home environment, with just the three of us. Anyhow, in his will, he left our house to my sister, his money to Aunt Maggie and a letter for me – telling me to man up.'

'Ouch.'

'He reminded me that I was from a distinguished family, that I should stand tall, be confident and earn respect. He was disappointed that I was so introverted, that I wasn't determined to get out there and make things happen. Anyhow, he did leave me the money that's allowed me to come here.' I looked at her. 'I don't want you to have a low opinion of me.'

'I don't,' she said simply. 'I appreciate your honesty.'

I smiled and squeezed her hand. 'Can we move on to safer things now? Change the subject? Tell me, what's your favourite film?'

'Oh, that's easy,' she said, '*The Angels' Share*, Ken Loach. It's about whisky.'

'I guessed from the title,' I replied. 'My grandfather worked for the Cape Breton Whisky Company; I think he must have told me the expression.'

'You haven't seen the film? Oh, you must! I'll make sure of it.'

We settled down to enjoy the food, passing our forks across to each other to taste and chatting away happily, until we had finished the bottle of wine and everyone had left the restaurant.

'We're splitting the bill,' Sarah said, reaching for her bag.

'We are not,' I insisted. 'Aunt Maggie told me that a girl would never forget if a man let her pay on a first date.'

'I like the sound of Aunt Maggie,' Sarah laughed.

'I'm not taking the risk! You might not come out with me again,' I said.

'I will, Peter Angus. I will. And thank you for such a wonderful evening.'

We stood outside by the Land Rover. I pulled her gently towards me and kissed her. She held me tightly, her hands in my hair, caressing my neck, and I realised I had been waiting for this moment ever since we had met.

The lights went out in the building behind us, and slowly we drew apart.

'Let's go,' she said, shivering slightly. 'We'll catch our death out here.'

As we drove the short distance to the village I was in a state of excited anticipation, sure that Sarah felt the same.

She pulled up on the main street. 'I'm going to say goodnight here,' she said.

She must have seen my face fall in the street light. 'Oh, right. It's just that Big John is away and . . .'

'Then you'll get a good night's sleep,' she said with a smile, pushing me gently from the car.

Chapter 31

I woke early, washed my clothes, prepared a shopping list, read a bit more of the bard's book, then ventured out for a short walk. I planned to go down to the shop and buy some lunch, then along to the church. I needed to thank God for coming to my rescue on Goat Island.

As I queued in the Spar, I glimpsed the woman in front of me passing over her newspaper to be scanned. I gasped. There was a large photograph of me, on the front of the *Oban Times*. I read the headline: TWO SHOCKS FOR CANADIAN VISITOR. I grabbed a copy for myself then found a bench on the sea front. The story took up the whole front page and was continued on page five. There was a photograph of Sarah, looking gorgeous and windswept, and an aerial shot of Peanmeanach. My near-death experience and the discovery of the mysterious skeleton were given equal billing.

There was a separate section about the walker. He was believed to have been a retired soldier, Charles MacVarish from Edinburgh, who had been exploring the old settlements from Fort William and up into Skye in 1988. He had left a wife and two young sons at home. His wife had believed he was on his way to Meoble along Loch Beoraid from Glenfinnan and that was where the mountain rescue had focused their search back then.

I grimaced. Sarah was right to have given me grief about the man having a family and my description of him as a hobo.

Somehow, reading the press account made the events seem far more dramatic. I went back to the shop and bought two more copies, one for Sarah and a second one to keep. I took photos of the articles and sent them to Nathalie, who would be bound to pass them on to the *Oran* in Inverness. It was a perfect story for them. I was thrilled to think that everyone on the island would know what I'd been up to over here. I wanted my generation at home to have a changed image of me. What an adventure I was having! No one knew of the hunt for the Jacobite gold, either – if we found that, then that really would be a front-page story everywhere.

It was my first bit of exercise in almost a week, and even though I was well wrapped up and it was a warm day, I felt weak and shivery on entering the church. As I knelt there, with my small votive candle flickering in front of the Blessed Mary, it occurred to me that I had a long list of thank-yous to be said. I thanked St Anthony for the rescue. God, for introducing Sarah into my life. Big John, for his kindness. And Grandfather, for looking after me from up above; I felt sure he must be behind all my good luck. St Mary MacKillop had said never to ask for anything. 'God would know,' she had declared, 'just pray.' Before I rose to my feet, I couldn't help myself; I bowed my head once more and whispered, 'Please, dear Lord, help us find the gold.'

I hadn't been back at the house for a minute before Nathalie rang. I held the phone away from my ear as she berated me for not telling her the full story, while I tried to explain that the newspaper had made much more of it than it was.

'It's a miracle you were rescued! And a skeleton! What's going on over there?' We talked for a good half-hour as I gave her a full and honest account of my ordeal, before I heard Mairi's cries in the background and Nathalie finally let me go.

I was making coffee when there was a knock on the door. I opened it and my heart leapt. It was Sarah, a huge smile on her face.

'I wasn't expecting to see you today!' I beamed, pulling her towards me for a hug.

'I know,' she replied, 'but I need to check you out. Can't be setting off on our big expedition if you're not up to it. Come on, we're off on a trip. Get in the car.'

'Have you seen the newspaper?' I asked. 'Look, front page!'

'Wow,' she said, after reading it avidly. 'Makes it all seem so exciting.'

'Read this bit,' I said, pointing out the section about the army man. 'You were right, again – I'm so sorry.'

She smiled. 'His widow will be so pleased that he's finally been found, no doubt.'

We took the Rhu road, a tiny track, coming to a stop every minute or two for the sheep and new-born lambs that were everywhere.

'Blackface,' Sarah said. 'It's the breed your grandfather would have had. Their lambs are the cutest. This is why we've come here first. We get my three favourite things: lambs, daffodils and sunshine all at once.'

'They're delicious, too, I'm told,' I ventured.

'Shh,' she said, putting a finger to her lips, 'they might hear.'

Once we had parked, Sarah took out a small backpack, which she wouldn't let me carry. I had Cranachan on a lead, and we walked, slowly, for half an hour until we arrived at the most picturesque, sandy horseshoe beach. The sea was an emerald green, as I imagined the Caribbean would be, and a little island sat in the middle of the bay. The tightly cropped grass along the shore was dotted with masses of tiny flowers, and black cows watched us intently from the hill above. We paused to marvel at the perfection of the place.

'This is my favourite spot in the whole world,' Sarah said. 'I wanted to bring you here.'

'I can see why,' I replied. 'It's beautiful.'

'Come with me,' she said, taking me by the hand. 'Let's look for cowrie shells.'

Barefoot, we walked along the sand, bent double, searching. Sarah had five shells in her hand before I found my first. 'Men are rubbish at finding them,' she teased.

Inside her pack was a tartan rug, a flask of coffee and some flapjacks.

I was speechless at how charming it all was, so unexpected, so romantic.

We lay on the machair, comfortable in each other's company and chatting happily.

After a while I began to shiver, so we drove down to the Lochailort fish farm and parked near Glenshian.

'I've always thought Glenshian is a lovely name,' she said.

'It means "Glen of the Fairies", doesn't it?'

Sarah nodded and pointed up the river. 'Your ancestors' grave is over there somewhere. Shall we wade across?'

'Yes, good idea – it'll be a reconnaissance. We can come back with the plaque later.'

I was mystified as to why the graveyard was here. It was such a long way from Our Lady of the Braes and even further from Ardnish itself.

We walked along the river, peered at the map and waded over.

'It's called "Island of the Reeds" in Gaelic,' I said.

There wasn't a reed to be seen.

Eventually, we found the site on a raised area, about seventy-five metres square, a sea of brambles and bracken. Clearly visible was one cast-iron crucifix and perhaps fifteen uncut, flat stones to commemorate the dozens, maybe hundreds, of people buried here.

'Grandfather told me that his parents and grandparents were buried at the furthest south-west of all the upright stones, and that's where he wanted the plaque attached,' I said.

We walked round in silence. Not one stone had an inscription engraved on it.

'This must be the one,' I said as we reached the southernmost stone. 'I'm sure of it. It's squint, though. Do you think we should straighten it?'

'No, I'd leave it. I think it's quite fitting as it is,' Sarah replied.

I knelt down and brushed away the moss and bracken. 'I wonder how many of my ancestors are here. I'm going to say a prayer for them, for Grandfather, too. He would have liked to have been buried here.'

Sarah knelt beside me, and took my hand.

We fished out stones from the river and built a small cairn behind the gravestone. 'I want to leave a mark, so I can tell my children and grandchildren how to find it,' I told Sarah. 'Grandfather so wanted to come here with me about ten years ago. He was desperate for us to visit his parents' and grandparents' gravesite, but I was too selfish and refused to come, so he didn't, either.'

Sarah took my hand. 'I know, but you were just a boy, Peter Angus – don't blame yourself.'

'This was my real mission: to come here, on his behalf. I'm so pleased to be here. Now that I've been to Ardnish I can really feel the history of my family and the peninsula in my bones. I'll be proud to call myself an Ardnish Gillies for the rest of my life.'

'So it's mission accomplished, isn't it? You've had an adventure that you can tell those children and grandchildren all about, plus you're off to hunt for gold . . . and you've found me!' Sarah laughed.

We drove to Fort William to pick up some provisions, Sarah intent on demonstrating that we could do better than the freeze-dried food I'd survived on during my kayaking trip. She sent me off to buy beer and wine and do other errands in the distant corners of the store.

'Let's go up Glen Roy,' suggested Sarah. 'I can show you where my family comes from and we can show Cranachan his spiritual home.'

I was feeling tired after the morning's exertions but there was no way I was going to refuse.

As she drove, Sarah pointed out St Margaret's Church in Roybridge. 'There were two archbishops in Scotland in the 1940s; one was a relation of mine, Archbishop Andrew MacDonald of Edinburgh, and the other was Donald Campbell of Glasgow. Both of them came from this village, strangely.'

We turned up the single-track road that ran up the glen. 'We don't have roads like this at home,' I told her.

'You get used to them,' she said, swerving into lay-bys when the locals came hurtling down the narrow road. I was clinging to the dashboard, with one arm across Cranachan to stop him being thrown through the windscreen as Sarah repeatedly jammed on the brakes.

Eventually, we came to a ravine, with a steep drop and a sharp turn onto a bridge. 'This is the bridge the Ghost of the Grey Lady frequents,' she said. 'She was called *Ban Tighearna Beag*. She was Irish, the Earl of Antrim's niece, married to the Keppoch chief around 1500.'

'Who was she? And why here?' I asked.

'Her husband was carrying her on his back across the River Roy when it was ice-bound; she was urging him on, saying, "That is but a trotting stream compared with the rivers of Ireland!" Anyway, she fell off and drowned, and it's said that she can be heard shouting for help at night. Even to this day. But she's meant to be harmless.'

'Spooky!'

'Apparently, horses refuse to go down into the ravine – they sense her ghostly presence.'

She was gesturing left and right as we journeyed up the glen. 'There on the left is Bohuntin, a crofting township, and that's Bohenie over there. And this field is where one of the Cranachan brothers saved his crippled brother from a bull. Remember I told you the story?'

We pulled into a lay-by, high above the river, and got out of the car.

'That's Cranachan over there,' Sarah said, pointing at a settlement a mile away across the glen.

We stood in silence. It was such a beautiful spot. The house was quite substantial, built of stone, with farm buildings around it and Scots pines skirting one side. 'It's revered amongst my family, just as Ardnish is in yours. Have a look at that stone – what can you see?'

She pointed to a large square boulder beside the road. A chalice was carved on one side.

'What's that all about?' I asked.

'It's a Mass stone. When Catholicism was banned three hundred years ago, a priest would come here, the word would go out, and the people would gather illegally for a service. There would have been a lot of people, because the population was huge back then and the area was completely Catholic. Apparently, there were enough men in this glen alone to raise a company of soldiers.'

'So, about a hundred men?'

'Yes. They all went off to war and never came back, emigrated to Canada, to Australia, to Glasgow for work. Now, there can't be more than four youngish men here. The glens are empty.' She sighed.

We took a path which wound downhill to the river. 'Do you see these hazel-tree shoots? These are what shepherds make their sticks from,' Sarah said.

'Ah, Grandfather had a stick from Ardnish!' I exclaimed. 'He took a ram's horn and made the handle himself. I'd love to do that.'

'Your grandfather probably called it a *cromach*,' Sarah said, correcting me with a smile, 'and a ram's actually called a tup over here.'

I searched around for a few minutes to find the ideal stick. I broke it off and swished it at the bracken as we made our way along the path.

Sarah was gazing off down the river. 'There used to be a bridge down there. My mum used to be taken across it and up to the house when she was a child. The farmer had a Land Rover with a broken handbrake and he did three-point turns on each of the corners. She's never forgotten – she says it's why her hair went white so young!

'I was speaking to her on the phone and she suggested I bring you up here. She told me to tell you that a Canadian bishop, Sandy MacDonald, who was bought up in your Inverness, came to re-consecrate the old church of Cillie Choirill in the thirties. His family were from this glen originally, and, as a child, his grandmother told him where their croft had been. She said the place would be identified by three white stones in a certain riverbed. He found them.'

'Incredible,' I said. 'You must thank her for me.'

'Mum would do anything to move back up here to Lochaber. Maybe one day . . .'

Sarah showed me the pool where her ancestors used to swim and land the odd illegal salmon or two. We tested the water; it was freezing. Cranachan was the only one of us brave enough to go in for a proper dip.

'Come on. Let's go up to the Cranachan itself. I want to do a sketch and take some photographs for the Miramichi MacDonalds back home,' I said.

We went up and looked around the old house. From there, you could see for twenty kilometres down the glen towards Fort William. We peered through the windows. The property was uninhabited, with no road leading to it, but there were some ramshackle pieces of furniture still inside. We guessed what the various outbuildings were for: a small byre for a couple of milk cows, a stall for a horse, a piggery and a coop for the hens. Perhaps a goat or two. We sat on the hill by the sheep fank, a couple of hundred metres up the hill, and I pulled out my pad.

As the afternoon turned into evening, we lay in the heather, Sarah's head on my chest, our fingers entwined. I didn't want the day to end, but it was a ninety-minute drive home, so I suggested we head back.

'Not so fast, Gillies. I've got a surprise for you.' She opened her backpack and rummaged around. I could see a bag of rice and other packets of food.

'What's all this?' I asked.

She fished out a key and dangled it in front of me. 'Don't forget that John, the owner, is a cousin of mine. Let's go and have a look inside.' She was grinning from ear to ear with delight.

'Are you up for sleeping over? You didn't notice me buying extra supplies in Fort William, did you? Why don't we make camp, you get a fire going, and I'll cook some supper. Then we can cuddle up with a good movie.' She indicated her iPad. 'I've downloaded *The Angels' Share* . . .'

I was speechless. I pulled her towards me for a hug, thrilled that she had been so thoughtful. 'You are amazing,' I said.

When we checked the place out, we discovered a few beds upstairs with blankets and pillows.

'Just think, Peter Angus! My great-great-great-grandparents probably slept in this room. I can't believe we're actually staying here. Mum will be beside herself with jealousy!' Sarah looked up at me, her face glowing with pleasure.

Downstairs was a spacious sitting room with a huge fireplace, a sagging old sofa and two comfy armchairs.

'I'll go and find some wood and make the place cosy,' I said.

The film was fantastic, the food excellent and Sarah was such fun to be with. I couldn't believe my good fortune. Later, as we watched the dying embers of the fire, nursing the last of our wine, Sarah glanced over and noticed me shiver.

She leaned towards me and we kissed, more deeply than ever before. When she eventually drew back, I was desperate for her.

'Sarah . . .'

'I know. Come on, let's go upstairs.'

Chapter 32

We left Cranachan early and walked down towards the river hand in hand. Spiders' webs glistened between the branches of the hazelnut trees and the sun illuminated the hill facing us. Everything was fresh and sparkling after an overnight shower. I felt happier than I had ever been in my life as we headed home.

When Big John returned from the hospital, he found us in the sitting room, amidst piles of supplies and kit. 'Where have you two been?' he asked.

'I took him to stay at Cranachan, to see where my ancestors lived. Peter Angus is taking me to Ardnish, so I thought I'd show him my spiritual home, too,' Sarah said, looking him straight in the eye.

He paused, decided against making a comment, and turned away with a knowing smile.

'How was the big smoke?' I asked. 'The appointment?'

'Well,' he said, 'I'd been worried about a lump, but the doctor told me it wasn't anything to worry about.'

'That's great!' Sarah and I chorused.

'And I caught up with a few folk I hadn't seen for a while, so we had a rare old blether.'

After a bacon roll and a mug of coffee, Big John went to

the back door and returned with the gleaming metal detector, unwrapped, batteries in and ready to go.

'I've been dying to try it out in the garden,' he said. 'My brother dropped his car key ages ago – maybe I could find it! Mind you, the car's long gone, so maybe not.'

Sarah's climbing rope, two harnesses, shovel, pickaxe and two large supermarket bags of food took up an entire wall of the sitting room. On top of this, we would need dog food, our tent, sleeping bags, a gas cooker and all the other stuff I'd used for my trip.

'How the heck will we get all this stuff to Mullochbuie tomorrow?' I groaned. 'It'll take at least two trips, and if anyone sees us carrying the metal detector and pickaxe, then everything will be out in the open . . .

'How about I load up the Land Rover while it's still dark? Say, four in the morning? That way, no one will spot us. We could leave at seven. We could do the hour's walk in from the road first thing, with the detector, rope, axe and so on, then return for the backpacks and shopping. They won't look suspicious. When we get to Mullochbuie, we'll be safe: it looks like nothing from the track, so I can't see anyone going down the steep bank. It's not until you're there that you actually see what a wonderful spot it is.'

'Have you seen the weather forecast?' asked Big John. 'Not looking good.'

Sarah checked her phone. 'Well, it's terrible tomorrow and Monday, rain all day and strong winds, five centimetres tomorrow and the same on Tuesday, with fifty-mile-an-hour gales. But it looks nice later on Tuesday.'

Our faces fell.

'You could always delay your trip until the back end of the week,' suggested Big John.

'I can't, I'm afraid. I've got some clients for a kayak trip on Wednesday. They've been booked for ages,' said Sarah.

'Right. We have to stick to the plan. Do either of you know where we can get a big tarpaulin?' I asked. 'We can stretch it over the top of one of the ruins and put a pole up the middle. That way we can get some shelter and have somewhere to get a fire going.'

'Good thinking. I'll get one from my cousin,' Sarah replied. 'I'm sure he's got one in the byre at the back of the croft. I need to go to Kinloid, anyway. John, can we pinch your washing pole?'

I scanned the mass of equipment. 'Okay, what else, Sarah? I don't think we'll have to use the rope and harnesses. Although the grassy runner up the cliffs might be pretty treacherous in the wet and it's a mega fall onto the rocks below.'

Sarah rolled her eyes. 'Leave that to me. I trained for two years, remember.'

We were all like excited schoolchildren, anticipating the thrill of the adventure ahead. I prepared some toasted sandwiches and a big pot of tea, and we sat happily round the kitchen table, talking.

'You were in the Lovat Scouts with my grandfather during the war, weren't you, John?' I asked. 'What did you get up to?'

'Well, let me see now . . . Italy in forty-four and forty-five was where we really came into our own. At the time, it was a Lochaber man who was our commanding officer: Lochiel, the chief of the Cameron Clan,' he explained. 'Your grandfather was in the SOE on secondment, but he was sent back to run a mine-clearance course for us towards the end of the campaign. We were having a terrible time with mines then. There were the S-mines, the 'Bouncing Betties' as we called them, the

Schu-mine 42 and the Teller – the Germans were laying them everywhere as they retreated. One night alone, four Lovat Scouts were killed and twenty-two injured.

'The Scouts were accepted as pretty irregular and got away with all sorts of things that other units wouldn't have. We even had two captured Russian soldiers who were excellent cooks and became a treasured asset; they were very popular amongst the men. One was taught a few words of Gaelic and given a paybook with the name "Nicholas MacBean" in it, so if he was stopped by the Military Police he could pretend he was from the Hebrides.'

Sarah and I exchanged glances; we could tell Big John was on his favourite subject.

He continued: 'At dawn one day, Donald Angus and I were lying at an observation post with our telescopes and saw a pigeon flying away from a farmhouse in a bit of a panic, so we called on the artillery to lay a few rounds on the place. It turned out that the Krauts had a Spandau machine gun in there and would have decimated our men as they advanced the next day. Another time, at a great distance, we saw soldiers going into a small building and tucking their shirts into their trousers as they came out. Your grandfather called for an airstrike and we watched with glee as a Spitfire attacked and the men came running out with their trousers around their ankles.'

'Sounds like you had some amazing experiences together,' I said. 'I'm amazed Grandfather never told me those stories. I thought I knew all his tales.'

Later, after Big John had gone for a lie-down and Sarah had left for her cousin's, a thought occurred to me: if we found any treasure, did we have to report it?

I opened my iPad and began to research the question. I quickly found that at home the finder was allowed to keep ninety per cent of the value of the treasure and the province got the remaining ten, but there seemed to be an enormous amount of confusion, because it depended upon who owned the land it was found on and whether the treasure was lost, missing or mislaid. I searched on. In Scotland, I began to discover, it was even less clear, but basically, it seemed to belong to the Crown. The find had to be turned over to the local museum and a non-defined amount of money would eventually, after a year possibly, be made over to the person who discovered it. There were stories of the finder getting fifty per cent, but others, where the landowner's permission hadn't been received, getting nothing at all. Then there was the definition of what was treasure – a huge topic in itself.

I was unsure whether to say anything when Sarah returned, but she knew immediately that I was preoccupied. 'What's up?' she asked. 'You're looking a bit down in the mouth.'

I sighed. 'I've been looking up the law on treasure. I kind of wish I hadn't. Basically, if we find it, then we won't get to keep it. We don't have permission to be looking for treasure from the landowner and the Queen gets the lot in any case.'

Sarah's face fell. 'Of course! It didn't even occur to me.' She slumped into a chair and looked up at me.

'You aren't thinking of pulling out, are you?' she asked.

I shook my head. 'No. I'm pretty sure we would get at least ten per cent and maybe up to twenty-five. It's still worth having.'

It occurred to me that I kept saying 'we' rather than 'I', but I don't think she noticed. If we did find something, I'd share it with Sarah and Big John, that was for sure.

'What would you do with the money if we did find something?'

I reflected. 'I hadn't given that much thought . . . Well, there is something, actually. There's a wonderful piece of land not far from where I grew up on Harbour Heights Road, with Inverness Harbour on one side and the ocean on the other. I'd love to buy a lot there and build a house. It would cost two hundred thousand bucks, maybe more, then twice that to build it.' I grinned, imagining the scene. 'I'd be able to walk to my new office, Gillies Insurance Agents, in twenty minutes. I'd have a conservatory on the front of the house so I could sit and watch the lobster boats going in and out, and I could take my family on holidays – we never had them when I was growing up.'

'What about buying Laggan? You mentioned that before,' Sarah said wistfully.

'I doubt the landowner would sell the place to us, especially after we'd stolen his gold.'

We laughed, realising at the same moment that I had used the word 'us' instead of 'me'.

For the remainder of the afternoon we busied ourselves checking the equipment. I read the instructions for the metal detector. Big John had taken the car back to his brother in Mallaig and would get the train home, telling us he would be back at half past six. We played The Proclaimers at full blast and danced around the room.

'It would make much more sense for you to stay the night, Sarah,' Big John said later that evening, to my delight.

We all played cards after supper, but our minds were on the expedition. We had to get an early night, what with us being up and out before sunrise.

'Och, that'll be my bed summoning me,' said the old man as he wrestled himself to his feet. 'Perhaps I'll not see you in the morning, but the best of luck to you.'

Sarah unzipped her sleeping bag and began making up a bed for herself on the couch.

'You can share my bed if you like,' I whispered, pulling her close.

She giggled and pushed me gently away. 'Not tonight, Peter Angus – there'll be none of that under Big John's roof! Off you go to bed. We need to be fresh for the morning. And don't you think about sneaking down. Cranachan will bark and wake Big John. Won't you, Cranachan?'

Chapter 33

What can be more miserable than waking to your alarm in the pitch-black with the rain hammering against the windows and knowing you have to go outside?

I had told Sarah that I would pack the Land Rover and she could sleep on; I'd go back to bed for an hour and a half afterwards. I crept downstairs and entered the sitting room. Cranachan wagged his tail, but to my surprise didn't make a sound. Sarah just rolled away to face the cushion. I hadn't expected her to take me at my word.

With her head torch on, I went back and forth in the rain, getting soaked and all the while wondering what on earth the neighbours would think if they peeked out of their windows and saw my highly suspicious activity. Probably that Big John Ferguson was getting burgled by his Canadian guest. I fully expected a light to go on, or a police car to appear around the corner. Before long the Land Rover was full. This is ridiculous, I thought, as I dried myself off and fell back into bed. How could we possibly need all this gear?

At seven, there was a knock on the door. 'Wake up, lazy bones! Bacon and eggs, ready in five minutes! Make sure you shave, though,' she said with a wink.

I smiled. She didn't like kissing my stubbly face.

Despite his farewells of the previous night, John was up too, pouring coffee. 'I can't wait to hear your news when you get back. My fingers are crossed for you. That patron saint of yours, the one who looks after lost things, what was he called?'

'St Anthony,' Sarah and I said simultaneously.

'Yes, him. Get him onside again.' He grinned.

It was only ten minutes' drive through deep puddles to the start of the path. Sarah parked in the old quarry she had mentioned, out of sight of the road. We loaded up with the tent, a plastic bag with the tarp in it, the wooden pole from Big John's garden and the metal detector over my shoulder, and set off. Even Cranachan was subdued as the rain came down in sheets. We had mud up to our ankles and water was gushing down the path as if it was a river bed.

'What the hell are we doing?' I said to Sarah. 'I feel a complete idiot. We should still be in bed, not hunting for fool's gold.'

'Hope our tent doesn't blow away,' Sarah replied through gritted teeth.

We trudged along, heads down, with not another word spoken. After an hour of misery, I pointed down the hill. The low stone buildings were just visible through the mist and rain. 'There we are – Mullochbuie. Honey, we're home!'

'I've been along this path several times and never spotted them before,' Sarah said. 'I see what you mean when you said they look uninviting from the path. Desolate's more appropriate.'

We scrambled down the steep bank and arrived at the buildings.

'They're quite cute, aren't they?' said Sarah. 'The tarp should fit nicely over the top, weighed down with stones. We can have the tent at one end and the fire at the other – perfect. How about I set it up and you go back for another load?'

I was happy to agree, but it took me ages. I must have looked like a Nepalese Sherpa, with Sarah's enormous backpack and bright blue climbing rope over my shoulder and a dry bag in each hand.

I staggered back and collapsed against the wall. 'My God, I'm exhausted. Can't we just climb into our sleeping bags and forget the whole thing?' I was only half joking.

Sarah had set up an excellent base camp. 'The floor of the old house is pretty well-drained, and the tarp's a fantastic addition. Good call, Peter Angus,' she said as she proudly showed it off. My spirits had lifted considerably by the time we got the gas burner on and had our coffee in a huddle in the shelter.

'They really positioned the houses well to get shelter from the wind,' I said.

'Yup, but they never got the view of the sea as a result,' Sarah pointed out.

We discussed the plan. We needed to find a tree or something to set up a belay for the rope, or perhaps just a handline to hang on to. The steep, grassy runner would be treacherous after all this rain. It wouldn't be easy to get down with the metal detector, spade and all the other equipment.

An hour later, we were looking down the cliffs, agreeing that the top third of the slope wasn't too bad. Then, looking down to where the cannon was, what had been just a careful scramble for me two weeks ago now looked pretty dangerous.

Sarah could see I was uncomfortable. 'I'll go down, see what is down below, then we can discuss the best plan,' she said bravely.

She lifted the rope off her shoulder, dumped it, and before I could get a word out, she was off. I guessed that her adventure-training experience had given her a lot of confidence and she definitely had a lot more expertise than me. She had good climbing boots on whereas I just had my Blundstones, which weren't ideal. I sat and watched, holding Cranachan by his collar. The dog was staring down the hillside, straining and whining.

Just then there was a cry from below. I gasped as I saw Sarah begin to tumble, over and over, until she disappeared from view over a ridge. I jumped up, and Cranachan pulled away from me and bounded down the slope.

'Sarah! Are you all right?' I shouted. 'Sarah!' My voice was carried away by the wind. I cupped my ear to listen. I shouted her name again, then again.

My heart was racing as I grabbed the rope, tied it round the tree, and began to ease myself cautiously down the hill.

I reached the spot where she had fallen. Another few metres and I'd be at the end of the rope. I got to the rise, looked down, and saw the dog. I knew that Sarah wouldn't be far away.

'Sarah! Sarah!' I shouted.

She called back weakly, 'Down here! I'm hanging onto a tree! Quick, please, I can't hold on . . .'

I let go of the end of the rope and, kicking my heels hard into the turf, went down as quickly as I could.

There she was, close by, off to one side in the trees. She was looking up at me, wide-eyed, petrified, both hands clutching a spindly silver birch, her body hanging over the edge, and the rocky beach far below. The sea was churning, waves pounding on the rocks and spray being blown against the cliffs below.

'I'm coming! Hold on! Cranachan, you stupid dog, get out of the way.' I pushed him aside.

'I can't pull myself up – the tree's too slippy,' she screamed. 'Help me!' Her eyes looked beseechingly into mine, wet hair plastered to her face.

I dug my feet into the moss, leant forward, and managed to grip the back of her jacket.

'Be careful,' she whispered. 'We'll both go over.'

Frantically, I looked below her. 'I can see a ledge below your feet and a bit off to your left – you can drop onto it,' I shouted.

It felt like an eternity. Her fingers were losing their grip, and I knew I wouldn't be able to hold her full weight from my awkward position. I only had seconds. 'Sarah,' I said, forcing my voice to stay calm, 'you're going to have to let go of the tree and swing to your left.'

'I can't!'

'Yes, you can. At the same time as you drop, you'll be able to grab the tree beyond – can you see it?'

I indicated with my head towards a silver birch. God, I prayed it would hold.

'Yes . . . no . . . Oh God, I'm too scared!' she sobbed.

'I've got you. Don't worry,' I lied. If she went, we both would. 'Okay, do you understand what you need to do? Sarah, you need to trust me.'

I looked into her eyes. 'I love you, Sarah. Trust me.'

She nodded once, almost imperceptibly.

'Ready? One . . . two . . . three . . . go!'

With a shriek, she suddenly dropped. I could feel myself lurching forward for a second, one foot losing its grip, perilously close to toppling over.

'I've got it!' she gasped, her voice high-pitched with relief.

But I saw with horror that the sapling was bending over at an alarming angle. I moved a metre to my right, still looking down on her, then wrapped my legs around a tree trunk and lay on my stomach, seizing the back of her jacket again. 'Grab my jacket, climb up, using me, until you get to the tree behind me. I've got a good grip. Come on! You can do this . . .'

'I need a minute,' she gasped, 'to settle down.'

'You don't have a minute, Sarah. Come on!' I cried desperately.

Hearing the urgency in my voice, she climbed up, using me as a ladder, her boots scraping down my back as she scrabbled for a grip, apologising as she went. She made it, collapsing on the soaking wet grass. I struggled back up the bank to join her.

'Jesus,' she panted, 'I thought I was a goner . . . both of us.'

I slumped onto my backside, feeling a cold sweat sweep over me. I giggled with nervous relief, wiping sweat and rainwater from my eyes. My legs were trembling with fear. We crawled up to the ledge where the cannon was and lay against each other.

'You saved my life!' Crying now, she held my hand, leant over and kissed me. 'Thank you.'

'This is the exact spot I had a tumble,' I told her, 'when my foot caught the top of the cannon. The grass was bone-dry then, and it's not as steep as further up so it wasn't a problem.'

Sarah was gradually coming to her senses, though she was still clearly in shock. I took her hand and held it to my chest. 'Can you feel my heart? It's working at double speed.'

She nodded. 'So is mine.'

I looked at her. 'You know what? I think we should head home. This is ridiculous. If we don't fall to our deaths, we'll die of pneumonia. Besides, you've had a hell of a scare. You probably need to rest up.'

There was a pause and then Sarah started to laugh. I looked at her in amazement, then within seconds I was laughing, too. Cranachan cocked his head and looked at us in puzzlement.

'We'll discover the gold and be hugely rich for a couple of days before we die of cold,' I stammered, gasping for breath and clutching my stomach.

After a couple of minutes we recovered and lay still. Sarah moved back to the edge and looked down at the cannon. 'How on earth did they manage to get it up this far?' she said. 'No wonder they didn't drag it up the steep bit. It would've been impossible.' She turned to me. 'We might as well go down, just for a look.'

'Sure?' I asked.

'It's like falling off a horse, you need to get right back on. Come on!'

'Okay. If we go to the left then I think it should be quite a safe route,' I said. 'Will you be okay?'

She nodded. 'Yup, I'll be fine.'

We scrambled downward and reached the bottom of the slope without further mishap. Then we looked up to where Sarah had been dangling.

'It would have been a thirty-metre drop and broken legs at the very least,' I said quietly.

Sarah put her arms around my neck and laid her forehead on mine. 'You risked your life, Peter Angus. I wouldn't have trusted anyone else not to just let go – you know that, don't you?' She kissed me again and again.

'Well, I said I loved you, and I meant it,' I replied, hugging her tightly.

Chapter 34

We searched around the bottom of the cliffs along the shore. It was obvious where I had been scrambling around in the peaty areas.

'I got covered in mud and God knows what in there,' I told Sarah. 'I had to take off my clothes and scrub them when I got to Sloch.'

Cranachan was up to his chest in the black goo; he'd need to have a swim before he was allowed back in our den.

We went further along and peered into the caves. 'I'm surprised how small they are,' Sarah said. 'And why has the middle one got a sort of half wall across the entrance?'

I shrugged. 'No idea . . . So, since I was here last, we now know that the cave on the left is most likely where the treasure is. That makes it pretty easy, doesn't it?'

Sarah, looking doubtful, stood in the centre, arms held out. 'I can touch each side. I don't think it's big enough to take a stash of guns and a number of chests of gold.'

'I know. I hope you're wrong, though. The metal detector should alert us pretty quickly.'

Water was dripping down the outside of the cave, but inside, there was room for the two of us to sit side by side in the dry.

'Look at all the mussel shells on the floor. Birds, maybe otters, must bring them in here to open them,' Sarah said, lifting a handful and letting them fall, one by one.

We clambered outside and looked back up the cliff. 'We'd better get back up to base camp and get the detector and tools,' I said.

It wasn't an appealing proposition. I really didn't want to tackle the climb again; the thought made me distinctly queasy.

Sarah sensed my mood and rubbed my arm reassuringly. 'We've come this far,' she said, 'let's keep at it. In any case, going up is always easier than coming down.'

We stood in silence for a few moments more. We were completely sodden, with not a scrap of dry material between us and the steep hillside above us running in water.

'We're crazy,' I said.

Sarah's expression grew sombre. 'Peter Angus,' she said quietly, 'what happened up there . . . I was a bit slapdash . . . I was showing off . . . I'm sorry I put you through all that.'

I pulled her into a hug. 'It's okay. We're fine, and that's all that matters. I must say I was very impressed, though, when you shot off down that slope without a worry about your own safety!'

She laughed and shook her head. 'Come on. Let's have a cup of tea and warm up. We'd better wear the harnesses when we come back down, though. Thank goodness we brought them! I'll sort out a good place to tie the rope off.'

Sarah was right. Going up seemed safer and was definitely easier than coming down, but this time we made a point of kicking good steps in the sodden ground, like stairs.

I put some water on to boil and we towelled our hair.

'I can't bear not putting dry clothes on,' Sarah said, 'but we should keep them for the end of the day, I suppose. We won't be long down there, will we?'

We stamped our feet and slapped our bodies to keep warm while nursing our tea. Sarah looked fondly at her dog. 'Poor Cranachan, he looks miserable, doesn't he? I'll feed him now, I think, cheer him up. Be careful about leaving the flap of the tent open, Peter Angus, otherwise he'll soak everything.'

The climb back down, an hour later, was much safer than before, despite the continuous rain turning the hillside into something resembling a river. Sarah had set up an abseil system, which was reassuring. She came down behind me with the detector and shovel over her shoulder, feeding the rope through the aluminium figure-of-eight at her waist.

Once we were safely down and unroped, I got the detector going. We were still about fifty metres from the cave, but almost immediately, it started indicating that there was metal beneath its search head.

'This is going to annoy me if it keeps sending out alerts like this,' I said. 'Just a pile of rocks here.'

'Let's have a look anyway,' she replied, 'and we can see what's what.'

After a few minutes, Sarah reached into a fissure and picked something up. 'Bone . . . I wonder if it's human. Doesn't look like sheep, that's for sure.'

I caught up with her and examined the bone. 'Wow, that could be human. The burial ground? Perhaps the gold is in the same hole? Let's have a good look round here.'

An hour later, we had fished out a pile of bones, some pieces of leather, a belt buckle and the barrel of a pistol. We stood side by side, gazing solemnly at our find.

'A great many French sailors on the *Mars* died around here,' I said. 'This will have been the burial pit, no doubt about it. Our family folklore was that bodies washed up for weeks after the sea battle, from both ships.'

'Poor souls. I'll bet some hadn't even heard of Scotland before they set sail,' said Sarah.

As we dragged more and more stones away, I wondered how many women would have enthusiastically pulled bones from a possible mass grave while wondering which part of the body they were from. She suggested that I take some photos, saying, 'We'll have to report this, that's for sure. You'll certainly be seen as a suspect now, with all these bodies you keep finding.'

We had been digging for a couple of hours and had reached bedrock. We were both exhausted as well as shivering with the cold.

'We need to get out of here,' I said. 'I'm bushed.'

'Me too,' said Sarah. 'Let's put the bones back and pile rocks over them first. We can get a couple of bits of wood and make a crucifix; it'll last until the next storm at least.'

We decided to leave things as they were, put the tools in the cave and return the next morning.

'I can't wait to wash my hands,' Sarah said. She headed across to the sea, then thought better of it. 'I've got some soap up top – we can do it properly there.'

'It's more than our hands that need washing; we're black with peat,' I pointed out. 'What a shame we didn't find anything. I was so sure we'd discover the gold today, after all we've been through.'

Back at the camp, we shed our soaking clothes and scrubbed ourselves in a burn. After zipping our sleeping bags together, we were soon cuddled up, congratulating ourselves on the comfort of our camp. Cranachan had been forbidden entry into the already cramped tent. He wasn't happy about being excluded and paced back and forth outside for a while, whining to make his dissatisfaction known.

We had agreed, coming up the hill, that dinner would be an energy bar and can of Coke. We were too tired and cold to do anything other than go to bed.

'A pretty memorable day,' said Sarah as the rain battered down on the tarpaulin and the wind howled through the oak trees. 'A long walk in with heavy loads, then you saved my life, then we rummaged through the two-hundred-and-seventy-year-old grave of dozens of Frenchmen – and all in a horrendous storm.'

We lay in silence, holding each other tight, gradually warming up.

After a few minutes of silence, I said, 'Penny for your thoughts?'

Sarah sighed. 'I was just thinking of the people who used to live here. This sort of weather would be a regular occurrence in the winter. They wouldn't be able to dry their clothes, would they? No wonder they suffered from pneumonia; I'm sure their thatched roofs would have leaked terribly. It must have been miserable.'

'Yes . . . but then summer would come, the lambs and calves would be running about, the hills purple with heather, sunshine for sixteen hours a day and the best scenery in the world. I know my grandfather had to be dragged away from here, despite the hardship. His wife once said he'd prefer a wet day in the Scottish Highlands to a sunny day anywhere else. Absence makes the heart grow fonder and all that.'

I thought about it some more. 'Grandfather had been in the French and Italian Alps during the Second World War, and in the Rockies and Cape Breton, too. He knew how wonderful other places in the world were, but it was Ardnish that was home. Even after he left, his heart was always here.'

Sarah smiled. 'My mum feels the same. She has a terrible yearning to be back in the Highlands. She knows all the

Highland poems and listens to BBC Scotland online when she's working in her kitchen in Kent. During the winter, when their pubs are quiet, they rent a cottage overlooking the bay in Arisaig for a month and walk for hours each day, regardless of the weather. She's always looking to see what properties in the area are coming up for sale. She loves that I'm living up here.'

'I love that you're here, too,' I said, kissing her.

Sarah laughed. 'She's always quizzing me about men and disappointed I don't have a boyfriend. As soon as I tell her that I was hanging onto a sapling, about to fall over a cliff, and you saved me, she'll love you from the off. And then when I tell her you're a piper, fiddler and Gaelic speaker from Cape Breton, she'll be over the moon. And my dad will be really impressed that you're starting your own business. He really respects people who do that.'

I'd had a pretty low impression of myself over the years, but listening to Sarah describe me like this made my heart soar. Grandfather, in his letter, had told me to 'stand tall' and, finally, I felt I was.

The next morning, we rose bright and early, excited about the day ahead. I made double helpings of porridge and coffee for breakfast.

We grimaced as we pulled on our filthy, wet clothes from yesterday, but it didn't dampen our spirits.

'We will remember this as discovery day,' Sarah said brightly. 'The day when a young couple discovered Scotland's biggest treasure trove. We'll be all over the news!'

'Ever the optimist!' I laughed.

I was eager to get back down the cliff and start digging. I still went gingerly down the hill, despite being roped up. Sarah had clearly forgotten all about her fall. She was talking cheerfully about the hinds being about to calf and her hope that we'd see deer from our tent tonight, then asking me to admire the lichen on the trees, when all I wanted to do was watch where my feet were going.

Later that day, after hours of backbreaking work, we had lowered the floor of the most easterly cave by about three feet after chucking out tonnes of stones, but the detector wasn't picking up anything at all. We tried the machine in the other two caves just in case, but nothing.

Eventually, we sat, dejected and exhausted, in the rain. 'The cannon is here, we found the grave, the letter makes it quite clear that this is where the *Mars* was beached, and the treasure must have been deposited here, at least for a while,' I said. 'I guess it's long gone.' I felt ready to give up. 'Let's head home.'

But Sarah was looking intently at the hillside. 'Look,' she said, walking across to fallen rocks to the east of the cave we had been searching. 'See there? Those big indentations up in the cliff face? The Frenchman's letter said the *Mars* fired its cannon, didn't it?'

'Yep,' I replied, not understanding.

Her eyes were shining. 'Maybe they were *deliberately* causing a rockfall, to conceal another cave.'

I stared at her. 'Oh my God, of course! You are brilliant. The French captain would have wanted to hide the stash somehow.'

I carried the detector across to where she stood. 'There's no chance of picking up a signal through all this stone, but I'll give it a try.'

Sarah was pressing her ear against the stones.

'What on earth are you doing?'

'Shh.' I watched her as she listened. 'I can hear gurgling. Every time a wave comes along, water seems to be getting in behind the rocks – I'm sure there's another cave behind here. Come and listen.'

We tried to move the rocks, but they were too big and heavy for the two of us. 'We need a crowbar,' I said, 'or a couple of strong men to help.'

'I'm going to dive down and see if there's an entrance from underneath; the water's definitely getting in somehow.' Sarah began stripping down to her underwear.

'Be careful. That water's freezing ... I know from experience ...'

She jumped in and disappeared below the surface.

Almost a minute passed. I was beginning to get worried, peering anxiously down into the inky-black water, when finally she emerged, spluttering, sweeping her hair away from her face.

I leant down and pulled her up. Her teeth were chattering as she pulled her soaking clothes back on.

'It *is* a cave!' she said, excitedly. 'I found an entrance but I didn't want to risk going in. It's definitely worth exploring, though.'

I was full of admiration, but I could see she was frozen to the bone. 'Come on, let's go. We need to get you in the sleeping bag with a cup of tea to warm you up.'

'We need to get my wetsuit and diving gear, and I need a proper underwater torch,' she said. 'I've a friend at the Underwater Centre in Fort William. Perhaps we can borrow one. And it'll be easy to find a crowbar. Big John probably has one. One way or another, Peter Angus, we're going in.'

'Just as well I have you on my team,' I said. 'I'd have given up an hour ago when we didn't find anything in that first cave.'

After we reached the top, I busied myself making supper while Sarah watched from the sleeping bag. It had finally stopped raining. The wind had dropped, and the clouds had cleared. We watched the evening sun setting over Eigg, casting its warm rays on Ardnish as we ate chicken stew from the packet and shared a bottle of beer. We decided we'd walk out tomorrow morning and Sarah would work Wednesday and Thursday as planned. We'd take the risk of leaving all our kit here and come back at the end of the week.

Chapter 35

Big John was at the door when we arrived the next morning. He read our faces. 'Nothing?'

'Not yet,' I replied.

After our badly needed baths, Sarah borrowed some shorts and a T-shirt from me and we sat in the conservatory and told him everything.

I loved her candour as she spoke. 'Okay, I admit it,' she said. 'I was showing off to Peter Angus so he could see what a mountain goat I was, but then my feet shot from under me on the wet grass. I started to fall, but by some miracle I managed to grab hold of a tree.'

Big John's jaw dropped. 'Bloody hell,' he said under his breath.

'Peter Angus was a star – without him I'd have fallen onto the rocks.' She grinned across at me, then told Big John every detail about the rescue.

I felt she exaggerated the role I'd played, but when she finished, Big John leant across and patted me on my back. 'Well done, An Gillie.'

We told him about the mass grave, the empty caves, Cranachan's indignation at being banned from the tent and the apocalyptic rain, our host enjoying every minute of the account.

'So at least you know it's the right place,' he said. 'Very clever of you to think of their being a cave under the rockfall, Sarah. You're closer to discovering the Jacobite gold than anyone else, mark my words.'

Sarah had to head home to prepare for work the next day. Before she went, we made a plan. She would leave her Land Rover, with Cranachan in it, at the car park at the marina. The keys would be on the front left tyre. She'd text me with details about how to get a dive light in the Fort. Grandfather had always said that the best meat in the world was Blackface lamb and I shouldn't leave Scotland without having eaten it, so I'd collect a leg of lamb from the butcher in Caol for dinner tomorrow night, plus provisions for the weekend. After that, Cranachan and I would go up Ben Nevis. It was a must-do while I was in Scotland, they both agreed, and the forecast was fine. All in all, there was the promise of a good day ahead.

That evening, Big John and I sat up late. A generous whisky was put by my side – he had what my grandfather would have described as a 'heavy hand'.

We spoke long into the night about all sorts of things. About how I intended to sort out my career back home, what a fine husband Iain Bec made Nathalie and, no, I didn't think Aunt Maggie would ever move back to Cape Breton, sadly.

'You've got yourself a fine girl there with Sarah,' Big John said. 'I think she's as besotted as you are.'

I beamed, feeling my face colouring. 'She's grand – we couldn't be getting on better. I told her I loved her, but she hasn't said the same to me. I just can't figure out how our relationship will be able to continue when I go back home.'

I poured out all my thoughts and fears, with my host just listening and nodding. I couldn't believe how frank I was with

Big John; I'm not sure I would have said all of this even to my sister. It was the whisky talking, I guess.

After a good while, Big John spoke. 'When I came over for Donald Angus's funeral, I had a long conversation with your Aunt Maggie. She said that you were likely to come over to visit Arisaig and asked if I'd look after you. She explained that you were shy and introverted and hadn't made much of yourself. She felt your parents' death still weighed heavily on you and that you needed to get away. I'm going to write to her, Peter Angus, and tell her that I don't recognise the person she described. I'll write what a fine young man you are. How you've managed to land the most wonderful girl and how you intend to get your own business going. I'll tell her what a credit to the Gillies of Ardnish lineage you are.'

I was prouder than I have ever been in my life to hear him say these words. My eyes welled up with tears.

The next morning, nursing a thumping head after the night before, I met Sarah's friend Finlay at the Dive Centre and borrowed the dive light, did the rest of 'my messages', as Big John called them, then drove to the Ben Nevis Inn, where I parked and headed off up the track with a very excited dog.

As I set off, I recalled Grandfather telling me that my great-great-uncle, Father Angus the priest, had, as a young man, come second in the first ever Ben Nevis hill race, over a century ago.

What a rocky, scree-covered mountain it turned out to be. There was quite a number of other people heading up, too, taking advantage of the better weather. I whistled up as fast as I could manage, the dog roaming in front. There were stunning views. It seemed I could see as far as the curvature of the earth. At the summit, an elderly man with a map pointed out the sights to me: Schiehallion, Ben Lawers, Cruachan, the hill on the island of Barra, the Cairngorms ... the Highlands at their most glorious lay all around me. I so wanted to share the feeling with Sarah, or Nathalie. Taking out my phone, I sighed. No reception.

I turned over in my mind what Big John had said last night. I saw that this trip had become a turning point in my life. I imagined my parents and grandparents looking down on me from Heaven. I cringed at the thought of my behaviour only a year or two ago. It didn't feel good to be pitied.

Cranachan and I were exhausted by the time we got back to Big John's house. I was absolutely delighted that he was intending to tackle the food while I soaked in the bath.

He prepared the most delicious dinner: lamb with fresh rosemary, mint sauce and roast potatoes. Sarah arrived at eight sharp, and Big John sat and listened while the two of us made our plans for the next day.

I tried to stifle a yawn. 'Sorry, you two. Ben Nevis is more than a hill – it's a proper mountain. It's killed me. I'm going to have to go to bed. I can't keep my eyes open.'

Sarah and I headed off at six the next morning. We had to be just as careful this time about meeting people, what with our bulging backpacks, an oxygen tank and a crowbar. Big John's neighbours must have been wondering what was going on, with these pre-dawn departures.

We reached the quarry and were sorting out our loads, Cranachan running around excitedly at the idea of a walk, when Sarah suddenly froze.

'Listen,' she said, a sense of urgency in her voice.

I looked around nervously.

'A cuckoo! Can you hear it? The first I've heard this year. Its arrival heralds in spring, apparently.'

'Lovely. I've never heard one before.'

'They're rare in England these days,' she said as we hoisted our loads onto our backs and set off. 'We never heard them in

Kent, but up here they seem pretty common. They lay their eggs in the nests of other birds, who are fooled into raising the infant cuckoo as one of their own.'

When we arrived at Mullochbuie, Sarah loaded the dive gear into her backpack and the bottle into mine, while I prepared a quick breakfast.

We trod carefully going down the slope, but it was far safer now that it was dry underfoot. I hurled the crowbar ahead of me and then went down the rope towards it, then did it again. By nine in the morning we were at the water's edge and ready to go. The sun was out, but here, under the north-facing cliffs, there was no such comfort. It was a cold, forbidding spot.

I sat on a rock with Cranachan beside me and watched Sarah preparing herself for the dive. No flippers, no rope, just a wetsuit, mask, tank and the large flashlight. What a girl, I thought yet again. She was so brave, heading down into the dark. She looked gorgeous, too.

'Be careful, darling,' I said, hugging her tight. 'You're more precious than any amount of gold.'

She kissed me hard on the lips, lowered her mask, and stepped into the water.

I sat there with the dog, seemingly forever. Occasionally, I would go across to the rock slide, press my ear against the stones, and see if I could hear anything. Then I paced back and forth along the shore, tried to lever mussels off the rock, threw skipping stones along the water . . . anything to pass the time. She had told me that if she wasn't out within forty-five minutes I should start to worry.

'Christ! Not another crisis!' I yelled in fury. I began shouting her name at the top of my voice through gaps in the rocks, my mind whirring about how to handle things. Perhaps she was stuck in the cave, the flashlight dead, the oxygen finished.

Perhaps she was stuck and couldn't get out. Maybe the air was toxic? I wondered whether to race off and get help, though that would take several hours.

I could hear Grandfather's voice in my head. 'Calm down, Peter Angus.' I stared grimly at the water, willing her to come out. I really loved this girl; I couldn't bear it if anything happened to her. I clasped my hands and started to murmur the Lord's Prayer: '*Ar n-Athair a tha air neamh, Gu naomhaichear d'ainm . . .*'

It was more than an hour later before she finally emerged. I rushed across, helped her out of the water, and embraced her. I whispered my thanks to God. Cranachan was jumping up and down frantically, seeking her attention, almost as relieved as I was.

At first, Sarah couldn't understand what all the fuss was about. 'I took the tank off in the cave, so I knew I had plenty of air,' she explained.

'But I didn't know that, did I?' I remonstrated, simultaneously furious and full of relief. 'I was worried half to death!'

She stripped off, and I dried her down with a towel; she had goosepimples all over. She laughed. 'Nice to know how much you care!'

When she was dressed and warmed up, she told me what she had found. 'It's a bigger cave than the other three, maybe twice the size. It's dry inside, but the floor is concave. I chucked out some stones from the middle to the edge and made a dip a couple of feet deep . . .' She looked at me. 'I hate to say it, Peter Angus, but if your gold was ever in there, I think it's long gone.'

My face fell.

'You need to see for yourself, though, Peter Angus, otherwise you'll always wonder. Who knows? Maybe I'm not telling the truth and in later years you'll discover I bought Ardnish, built myself a castle and married my fisherman?' We both burst out laughing. 'There was some daylight coming in from the top of the rock fall,' she continued. 'I had a look from below. I think we could move some rocks then lower ourselves in using my rope.'

'Do you want to go up to the camp, grab some tea to warm you up, then we can see if we can get down there after lunch?' I asked.

'Nope, I'm fine, thanks. Let's just keep at it.'

We set to with the crowbar and, finally, with much effort, managed to make a hole big enough to climb down. I peered in and saw a four-metre drop onto the rocks below.

It was just as Sarah had said: a massive bowl. It could easily have hidden several chests of Jacobite gold and hundreds of muskets. We swept the metal detector back and forth: not a squeak.

'Damn it!' I exclaimed. 'You were right. Someone probably took the treasure away hundreds of years ago and put the rocks back where they found them. So much for the money to build my house and fund Gillies Insurance,' I added ruefully. I looked up at Sarah. 'Come on, let's get back up.'

We were adjusting the rope and preparing to haul ourselves back up, when a last sweep with the flashlight picked up something glistening at the water's edge. I bent down to pick it up and caught my breath.

'It's a coin!' I called out excitedly. 'Look!'

Sarah whooped and hurried to join me. 'It's quite large, isn't it?' she exclaimed. 'Look – that's definitely the word "*deux*" engraved along the edge . . .'

'It's a Louis d'or coin.' My heart skipped a beat. 'There's the date – 1744.'

I grabbed the detector and began swinging it carefully back and forth, over and over again. The two of us scrambled around amongst the stones at our feet, chucking them into the water for a good hour, until the battery of the flashlight began fading.

Nothing.

We sat back against the rock edge. 'The robbers must have dropped this one on their way out.' I sighed. 'I wonder who took it? Amazing they managed to keep it a secret.'

'Never mind,' said Sarah. 'It's a wonderful discovery for us all the same.'

'Yes, I suppose so.' But I was less sure. 'Do you think we should take the search a lot more seriously? It's potentially a ten-million-pound treasure trove, and it looks like we're walking away with only a minuscule part of it.'

Sarah shrugged. 'Personally, I don't believe it's here, Peter Angus. We dug down quite a long way, used the metal detector . . . but it's your call.' She looked intently at me.

Eventually, I nodded. 'I agree. Let's go. We don't need to tell anyone where we've been. Hey, we can maybe come back one day – with a bulldozer!'

By dusk, we had hauled everything back up the hill: two trips each. We were exhausted. Sarah had climbed into her sleeping bag for a rest. I found a dead tree, dragged some branches over, and got a good bonfire going at a spot overlooking the Hebrides, making the most of the evening sun. I sat there soaking in the last of the warmth and reflecting on the day's events. I was disappointed, but deep down, I knew I shouldn't have been. It had always been an unlikely prospect – and it wasn't the reason I'd come to Ardnish. I turned the coin over in my hands, considering its value, and an idea took shape.

Chapter 36

I woke early, lying against Sarah. She was still fast asleep. I could feel her heartbeat. I felt I might be the happiest man alive. It had been less than a month since we'd met. Over the past three weeks, we'd seen each other almost every day and experienced so much together. There was absolutely no doubt about it, I had fallen deeply in love.

I didn't want to move, for this moment of bliss to end. But my mind was whirring. I had so much to do. My sabbatical was almost over and I needed to get back to Cape Breton if I was to get my business up and running by the end of the summer. I was desperately sad at the prospect of leaving Sarah.

I'd booked a flight home for two days' time, but first, I needed to go back to Innis na Cuilce and attach the plaque to the family gravestone.

Beside me, Sarah stirred and opened her eyes. 'Morning,' she murmured. 'Sleep well?'

We lay in each other's arms and talked about the day. We'd need to make lots of trips back and forth to the Land Rover with all the gear, for a start.

'I'm looking forward to getting back to the graveyard, to carry out Grandfather's wishes,' I said.

She smiled. 'I'd love to come with you, if that's okay. Can you wait till after work tomorrow?'

I was delighted. 'Of course. I'll try to meet Hamish before then – I wonder if he can get his hands on a set of bagpipes? I want to play a tune by the grave, one my grandfather wrote, called "The Gillies' Last Farewell to Ardnish". It always made him sentimental.'

'That would be lovely,' Sarah murmured.

We slogged back and forth; even Cranachan was flagging towards the end. Walkers gave us strange looks as we passed, what with the spade, crowbar and metal detector. 'Archaeology dig,' Sarah explained with her disarming smile.

The next morning was my last but one. Sarah had gone off to meet her guests and I needed to go down to the hotel to see if I could get the deposit back for the kayak and meet Hamish for lunch. Big John was in high spirits, declaring that the last few weeks had been hugely exciting and he wouldn't have missed a minute of it.

Before I set off, he took me aside. 'Do you know, Peter Angus, I'm almost pleased that you haven't found the gold.'

'Really?' I said, surprised.

He nodded. 'It might have ruined you. Sudden riches have done for many a good man. But you've found Sarah and you'll never find better than her.' He gripped me tightly by my arm and looked me in the eye. 'She's a keeper.'

'I know, I know, Iain Mhor. I won't let her go,' I replied, nodding vigorously.

Sarah met me at the Spar at five, and within half an hour, we had pushed our way through thick rhododendrons and holding our boots in our hands waded across to the island, soaked to above our knees, with the river much higher than before. Occasional showers came through, interspersed with startlingly bright sunshine.

Big John's electric screwdriver made easy work of attaching the plaque. Sarah had picked a bunch of daffodils as we walked down from the Lochailort Inn where we'd left the vehicle.

I think both of us knew that this moment marked the culmination of my great adventure. Carrying out the last wishes of an old man, Sarah far more than a holiday romance to me, and a whole new future ahead. I stood, facing west towards Ardnish, and began to play Grandfather's tune. I played on. 'Flowers of the Forest', 'The Dark Isle' and the old Lovat Scout tune 'Morair Sim'. A squall came through, with the wind carrying my music downstream and the rain causing droplets to drip off my nose. The brooding dark mountain of An Stac watched over the grave, clouds scudding past. These sorrowful laments were for my ancestors, my tribute to the old days. Sarah sat on the riverbank, looking away from me, still clutching the flowers. I could tell she was holding back tears.

At the end, the rain had passed through and a shaft of sunlight lit the island. I stood in silence and prayed, with only the peaceful sound of the river in the background.

Sarah came over and took my hand.

We waded the river and walked slowly and silently back up the hill, both immersed in our own thoughts. I was dreading the morning train to Glasgow tomorrow.

We arrived at the inn. 'My great-grandmother arrived at this hotel, at the end of the First World War, all alone. She wasn't expected by her in-laws and had never been to Scotland before. She was pregnant, too. Can you imagine how she felt?' I said as I held the door open.

A welcome fire was roaring in the hearth and we sat as close as possible to dry our damp clothes. I went to the bar and ordered drinks and venison stew for both of us, before returning to the fireside with a heavy sigh.

'I can't bear to be leaving you,' I said, kissing her gently on her forehead.

'I'm dreading it, too,' she murmured, kissing me back.

'Sarah?' I said, tentatively.

'Yes?'

'Do you think you could get some time off and come over? The flight to Halifax is only five hours and it's pretty cheap. There's so much I'd love to show you . . .'

She threw her arms around my neck, eyes shining. 'I'd love to!'

My heart leapt as I hugged her back. 'That's wonderful! Maybe you could come over at the start of July, get a job for a month or two? There's a company called MacIntyre Kayak Tours based in Mabou, just along the road from me. I could sound them out if you want?'

She nodded enthusiastically. 'Perfect. I'm freelance, so all I'd need to do is give a few weeks' notice.' She paused. 'And Cranachan can stay with my uncle – they love each other.'

As we spoke, I was spinning the Louis d'or coin on the table. She put her hand out to catch it.

'Your treasure,' she said.

'Well, technically, it's not treasure,' I replied. 'I did some checking. The definition of treasure is two or more coins, so there's no need for our find to be reported. In any case, half of it's yours.'

Sarah was shaking her head gently.

'Okay, I'll take it home with me,' I went on. 'There's a jeweller in Port Hawkesbury. I'll ask her what she can make with it that we can share – I've got something very special in mind.'

She leant over and embraced me.

I had never felt so content.

'The first of July,' she whispered. 'It's a date.'